To Mum and Dad

BEST SERVED COLD

DAVID J. GATWARD

WEIRDSTONE PUBLISHING

Best Served Cold
By
David J. Gatward

Copyright © 2020 by David J. Gatward
All rights reserved.

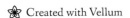

Grimm: nickname for a dour and forbidding individual, from Old High German grim [meaning] 'stern', 'severe'. From a Germanic personal name, Grima, [meaning] 'mask'.
(*www.ancestory.co.uk*)

CHAPTER ONE

JOHN 'BEEF' CAPSTICK HAD THE TEMPER OF A BULL with a sore head, and the build and face to match. He was the kind of farmer all the others avoided, and who took pride in the fact that they did.

Living out beyond Gayle at the upper end of Wensleydale, deep in the shadow of Dodd Fell, John ran the farm which had been left to him by his less than dear old dad over a decade ago. Drowning in debt, and yet somehow managing to stay just outside the clutches of the bank, John hated his life but knew nothing else. The farm's tumbledown house, and its surrounding outbuildings, stood dark and grey, as though forever damp and dejected, crumbling slowly into the earth, dying a slow death born not only of neglect but good, honest meanness. They reflected John's life daily and he'd long ago decided to do nothing to change it.

None of this was John's fault though, or at least that's what he told himself, and anyone within earshot, piling the blame onto his father, shouting at the ghost of a man he'd grown up hating, and yet never been brave or courageous enough to stand up to or just simply move away from. But this was the dales, so where the hell was he supposed to have moved away to anyway? He'd grown up on the farm, knew nothing else but farming, and his blood was in the soil in more ways than most, spilt not just from thorn and nail and angry hoof, but the hard slap of a calloused hand across the face, a leather belt across the back of his legs, a thrown rock or branch.

The wounds on the outside healed, but the ones inside festered, and John grew up to be a moody child, an angry teenager, and finally a rage-filled adult. He never wondered what his mum would've thought of the man her baby had become, because he'd never known her, and that was the one thing his dad had reminded him of daily.

'You killed her, lad, you hear? Took her from me the day you were born! And nowt good's come about from having you instead of her, that's for sure. Should've been you, not her, you hear? Not her!'

Lad was about as close to calling him by a name as his dad ever got, though usually, he went with something more coarse, spitting the words at him like bullets as he ordered his son out onto the farm to work in all weathers, one hand cracking him hard across the back of the head, the other holding the bottle he loved more than his own flesh and blood. And the worse the weather was, the harder his father had driven him, hoofing John out into the thickest snow and the hardest rain, never caring as to whether his only son was actually kitted out well enough to not come back half-drowned or frozen to death or, on the sunnier days, burned to the bone.

John had ended up being called Beef at school, not just because everyone had a nickname, nor indeed because of how he'd seemed to grow at twice the rate of his peers, but because that was usually all he'd ever had for lunch. But it was never the good stuff, just a few slabs of corned beef from a tin, dropped in a Tupperware box, with a couple of slices of bread. He had to prepare it himself after all, and if he took anything else, his dad would get angry, call him a thief, belt him one.

Unable to take his frustrations out on his dad, a man whose arms were corded with thick twists of muscle, and whom he'd once seen punch a cow in the head just to get it to move out of the way, John looked to easier targets.

The dogs chained in the yard soon realised that the boy from the house had sharper toes than the man and they would avoid him, baring their teeth and more than willing to sink them into him if he got too close. But sheep and their lambs, the few cattle in the lower field, the chickens, they got the brunt of it. And so did the kids at school.

Bullying had come to John as naturally as breathing. But then he'd had the best teacher he could have ever asked for—his father. John was bigger than most, and they all teased him because of his clothes, and the stink that followed him from the farm to the classroom. He wasn't the only farmer's kid by any stretch, but he was the only one who'd reeked to high heaven of it. And kids were cruel, but he was crueller, to protect themselves some had lined up behind him, if only to be out of the way of his fists.

If happy days had ever truly existed for John, then those days at school had been as close to such as he could ever imagine, prowling the playground with his little gang of warriors, picking on anyone and everyone, taunting people and teasing them. Making sure they were always scared. And they were, because he had tales to tell of the things he had done on his farm, terrible things that would churn the stomach of anyone unfortunate enough to be close enough to listen. Some of the stories were true, others not so much, but the effect was the same, and John relished the power it gave him. Horror stories were his currency, and he was generous.

Then school came to an end, people grew up, and what John gave out came back tenfold. Because those kids in the playground pushed too far often grow into adults who just won't put up with it anymore. Not that John cared, because out on the farm he was still the biggest and the meanest, and he had enough targets on which to take out his frustrations. And those who had hidden behind him, they continued to do so, keeping their own little under-ground economy going, never concerning themselves with what folk thought, happy to screw over another if it meant easy money, cheap booze, and a laugh at someone else's expense.

And now, years later, the fact that it was the weekend meant nothing to John; it was not a thing to celebrate. The heat from the July sun was just something else to swear at, days off were a luxury he'd never known, and the only respite would be the homebrew he drank most evenings while watching television. It wasn't the best of lives, but it was his life and the only one he knew how to live.

John was up early, like every other day regardless of how hungover he felt. Kicking open the backdoor to stare at the yard in front of him gave him no sense of worth, just a dead-ness deep inside which sunk deeper by the day, a lead weight out of view stretching down and down into the darkness of himself.

The yard itself was a mess and a faint mist hung in the air stinking of rot and decay. It was a rich smell, and sweet, and it reached into John's throat and made him cough. So he spat it out, dark green phlegm spattering in the mud.

Against the wall of one of the outbuildings, a coil of barbed wire had somehow managed to spring itself open and now sat in a pile of shit-covered straw John hadn't bothered to clean up for months.

A tractor rusted in the corner, a couple of sorry-looking hens roosting on it, staring their tiny, cold black eyes at him with a meanness John had always suspected hens harboured deep down in their souls. They were evil birds, he was sure of it, and he hated them.

Pulling on his worn and tired Wellington boots, which were covered in a painful rash of patches usually used on bike inner tubes, John kicked a stone up and out from the muck in front of him, grabbed it, and hurled it at the birds. They'd already moved by the time it arrived to clatter against the tractor, and John swore, wishing he'd hit one, but glad that he hadn't, because buying more hens was something he could be doing without. Unless of course La'll—little—Nick had managed to nab a few from down the dale. He was good at that was La'll Nick, being a sneaky little bastard with the build of a starved pixie. And down dale too many town-houses with a couple of chickens in their gardens had lost birds to his deft hands.

John chuckled to himself, the act of it causing him to cough. He'd bumped into Nick the day before during a trip into Hawes. Nick had managed to pass on to John a few crates of beer he'd nabbed from a delivery truck he'd seen outside a pub a few weeks ago. He'd waited for the usual noise about it to die down, then called John and said he had some going spare. Good stuff, too, and John had enjoyed far too many of them the previous night. But free booze was there to be enjoyed, wasn't it? And he couldn't help but enjoy it more knowing that someone else had paid for it.

The rest of the yard was a confused mess of half-empty fertiliser bags, orange baler twine, farming implements, and broken fencing. But John didn't see any of it because it had never looked any different and it was all that he had ever known. So he strode out from the house and into the day, wiping his nose on the back of his left hand still grubby from the day before, remembering halfway across the yard that the task he'd set for himself was to take the one working tractor on the farm, hitch a trailer to it, then drive up into the steep fields on the fell behind the house and bring in the hay bales he'd done the week before. There had been rain since, so they were probably ruined, but John didn't really care. The animals would eat the hay or starve.

Turning back to the house, John quickly grabbed himself a half-eaten pie from the fridge, filled a grubby old lemonade bottle with water, then headed back outside. Which was when an arm hooked itself around his neck, a kick to the back of his knees took his legs out from under him, and John found himself suspended in the air just enough to start choking. He struggled against the vice-like grip under his chin, his hands clawing uselessly at the arm which held him. Violent swearing and curses, threaded with saliva, caught in his throat, then his vision grew fuzzy, his head started to swim, and a few seconds later his world fell into a thick darkness.

When John came to, he was on his back and staring up at a blurry sky. He tried to move but seemed to be stuck hard under something. As his vision cleared, he discovered then that he was lying on grass, his body jammed under the wheel of his own double-axle trailer. Then the pain hit him, and he realised that not only was he jammed, but that his right arm, which was stuck fully under the wheel of the trailer, was clearly broken.

What the hell had happened? Why couldn't he remember driving up into the field? After all, that had been his plan, but he had no recollection of it, just the farmyard, a tightness round his throat, a suffocating darkness . . .

A hot stab of pain from his arm shot through John's body and he roared, swore, and tried to free himself, but it was no good. His arm was stuck fast and, by the look of it, crushed flat.

John looked to his left and saw the rear of his old tractor, a David Brown with little if any of its original white paint showing thanks to years of rust.

He had to do something, get out from under the trailer, get to the doctors. Farm accidents were more common than most people realised, and he'd been pretty lucky down the years, unlike a fair few folk in the dales. Tragic tales all of them, with families mourning for years after.

A shadow revealed itself from behind the rear wheels of the tractor.

John stared up at it, brow furrowed as a field ploughed deep, confusion ripping a bloody tear through his mind.

'What the bloody hell . . .?'

John's words caught in his throat not because of what was in front of him now, but *who* was in front of him. Well, it just didn't make any sense. And there was something odd about this shadow's face, like there was paint on it, but perhaps that was just the early morning sun pricking his eyes.

The shadow said nothing, just stared down at John from behind narrow, mean eyes set in a face laced with beads of sweat, which rolled earthward like spilled diamonds.

John continued to stare, unable to find the words he needed. And when he eventually did, his voice was a thing cracked with panic.

'Well don't just stand there doin' nowt!' John spat, tugging at his arm, trying to roll away. 'Get me out of here! Come on! Help me! Do something!'

The shadow cocked its head to one side, stared just a little longer at John as his swearing grew louder and more panic-fuelled, then turned back to the tractor and disappeared from view.

'Hey! I was talking to you!' John called out. 'My bloody arm's broken! Get me out of here!'

A creaking, ratcheting sound clanked from the tractor and John's voice snapped in two. He recognised it all too well: a hand-brake being released.

For a moment nothing happened. John lay in the grass, his arm in agony, his body trapped. The tractor sat motionless, the trailer waiting expectantly behind it. The sun burned down and the air, John noticed, was rich and sweet with the scent of cut grass, the aroma of summer burning its way to a still-distant autumn. Sheep called to each other on the fells around him. It was, in many ways, a beautiful dales day, the kind that at points in his life had almost made John feel that being alive wasn't too bad after all.

When gravity took hold of the tractor, John's scream tore through the air, scattering a flock of pigeons resting in a tree sat in the middle of the field. The first trailer wheel rolled painfully slowly over his arm and then onto his chest, crushing the life out of him as shattered ribs burst through his lungs, blood spraying out of his mouth, his nose. The second trailer wheel, thanks to the tractor veering to the right just a little, came at John's head. Not that he saw it, or perhaps he did, not that anyone would ever know. It eased itself over his skull, just above his jaw, flattening bone and brain, and sending the dying memories of a troubled, broken, mean-spirited man to bleed into the soil for one final time.

Far off, the sheep continued to call, as a killer carried out one final task before heading home in the sunshine.

CHAPTER TWO

DCI Harry Grimm, having been in the dales for just over three weeks now, was, quite to his own amazement —and his body's very apparent, noisy and painful disapproval—out on a run. And on a Monday of all days. What the hell was wrong with him?

There were better ways to start the week Harry was sure, but here he was, out in the cool early morning air, blowing like a dying steam train, the heat already burning up his face from the exertion.

Harry could count numerous reasons for him being out to pound the lanes, from needing to wake up after a bad night's sleep, to giving himself something else to focus on beyond being a police officer. But the main reason, the one which really pushed his sagging, wobbly arse out of his bed and into the day, was that he was pretty sure he was on his way to being a bit of a fat bastard.

After waking early that morning, and having decided a couple of weeks back that if he was going to be in the dales for a while, then he was going to make the most of it, he'd hit the road. He'd also been enthusiastically pushed into getting back into shape by Detective Constable Jenny Blades, a young woman who was as fit as a mountain goat. She'd even helped him pick out a new pair of trainers. And every time he'd worn them since, Harry had felt rather like an ageing pensioner in a new sportscar; they were too bright, too shiny, and promised speed he was pretty damned sure he would never achieve, and if he did, well it would be horrendously dangerous and undoubtedly end in calamity, blood, and broken bones.

The morning was gun-metal grey, and despite the promise of sun later in the day, the early hours were working well to give an entirely different impression. The air was cool and moist and stung a little against the back of Harry's throat as he sucked it down into his lungs. Graceful his running style was not, of that he was very sure, but he was out and moving and that meant he was, at the very least, going further than if he was just sat on his bed back in the hotel eating biscuits for no reason other than the fact that they were there.

Back in his twenties, Harry had been fit, particularly when he'd been in the Parachute Regiment. But then it was impossible not to be if you were a member of that particular branch of the armed forces. Harry had fond memories of his P Company training, not so much because it was fun, but more so because it had been a relentless attack on everything he'd ever thought he was capable of, and he'd survived it. Though memories of what he'd been like back then weren't exactly helping in the here and now. He was an out of shape, middle-aged man, and he was pretty sure that the sight of him flapping his massive feet against the ground, as his belly wobbled out in front, was something a law should quickly be rushed through parliament to prevent.

Huffing and puffing, Harry did his best to push on, and all the time his mind kept reminding him of what he'd once been, sadistically intent on motivating him by constantly reminding him of just how hideously unfit he truly was.

And to think you used to weigh eleven stone, it whispered. *Now look at you! It's enough to make someone's eyes bleed. You're a bloody embarrassment! Give up now. Go on, just give up and eat some doughnuts, a nice piece of cake. Embrace the real you. The fat you.*

Harry wasn't sure what it said about who he was that his own mind was trying to fat-shame him into moving more. It was working though, and he swore through gritted teeth and pushed on.

To get himself motivated and moving, Harry had initially started with an app on his phone which had promised to get him from a couch to five kilometres in twelve weeks. But he didn't like running with a phone, not just because people kept calling him on it, but also because the app had a horrendous, chirpy American voiceover, which Harry had ended up arguing with.

'That's one kilometre done.'

'Shut it . . .'

'You've got this!'

'Like balls I have . . .'

'Remember, never ever, ever, *ever* give up!'

'That's too many evers . . .'

'You're awesome!'

'Oh just piss off will you!'

So that hadn't lasted much longer than a few days.

Instead, Harry had managed to come up with a little three and a half mile route around the picturesque lanes of Hawes and Gayle, the two almost conjoined villages-cum-small-county-towns which sat together at the top end of Wensleydale, and was working slowly up from a mix of running, jogging, swearing, and walking, to eventually —*hopefully*—being able to do the whole thing in one go, although the swearing would probably stay. If he was honest, that was the only bit he really enjoyed, and some days his creative use of expletives surprised even him. Three and a half miles didn't sound far, but this was the dales and wherever Harry looked, wherever he walked, there were hills.

Starting from the hotel, Harry's route had taken him through Hawes marketplace then out of the town and past the garage, with a left up Tufty Hill, which was a lovely, cute name, Harry had thought, for something that made him feel like he was going to cough up a lung.

The hill was a main road but not exactly busy early in the morning and, after just over a mile of huffing and puffing, Harry took another left onto Cam Road. This turned his view from staring up the dale, to instead gaze on towards the wonderfully named Snaizeholme Fell, which rose slowly in front of him, a wide swathe of greens and browns, the fields and distant moors quietly contained inside the ancient network of drystone walls, the sheep inside them like a splattering of little dots of white paint from an artist's brush.

Harry did his best to focus on the countryside, to distract himself from the pain of moving through it at speed, but it didn't work. *Hills are bastards,* Harry thought, and pounded onwards even harder in a hopeless attempt to flatten them.

Back in his hometown of Bristol, Harry had tried and failed numerous times to get back into running. He'd always managed it enough to make sure he could pass the regular police fitness test, but keeping it going had always been a problem. Running the streets, dodging traffic, trying to avoid commuters and shoppers and then just smashing into them, just wasn't his idea of a good time. But up in the dales, Harry could already sense that running was altogether different. He wasn't any less knackered or unfit, but he was certainly getting a lot more out of it. *Enjoying was perhaps too strong a word, but it was definitely more rewarding,* he thought, as he stumbled forwards for the next mile or so, which was now all on single-track lanes, the kind that even Google hadn't bothered to send its cameras down.

From there, the route brought him into the top end of Gayle, down Harker Hill, and eventually past the Methodist Chapel, then right and over the bridge, which rose over the bubbling laughter of the clear water of Gayle Beck, and left down Old Gayle Lane. At the end of this, it was then just a left turn and back into Hawes, past the auction mart and down till the road became cobbles and the Herriot Hotel came thankfully, and at last, into view.

The last hundred metres or so Harry dug as deep as he could, upped his speed, and attempted to sprint. It wasn't graceful, and the sound of his massive feet hammering against the road was considerably louder than Harry would have preferred, but he kept going, eventually pulling himself up to a breathless stop outside the Herriot.

Dizziness at the exertion sent Harry's world a little too fuzzy round the edges and, after walking it off for a minute or so, he leaned against a wall, dropping his head forward, half wondering if he was about to throw up. But he didn't, and that was something. Not an achievement as such, but definitely a relief.

Back in his hotel room, Harry stripped and showered, undecided as to whether it was better to stand under hot water, which was more pleasant but could easily make him pass out, or cold, which would cool him down and wake him up, but was ultimately little more than pure torture. A part of him rather fancied going for a swim in a nice cold river or lake. He'd done exactly that just a few weeks ago, in Lake Semerwater. And it was something he kept meaning to get around to doing again, his swimming gear kept in his car just in case, but time had raced ahead and he hadn't since ventured back out into the cold embrace of the silvery water. In the end, he did a bit of both, finishing the shower with a cold blast that sent him dancing out of the cubicle to slam the big toe of his right foot into the leg of his bed.

'Ah, you bastard!' Harry hissed, dropping himself down onto the mattress to hug his foot, glad that today would see him move out of the hotel room and into something a little more accommodating, a small flat overlooking Hawes marketplace. Living in a hotel was nice for a while, but Harry had soon grown weary of it. And with no actual end in sight quite yet as to how long he was going to be up north, he'd pushed for better digs and they'd been provided.

Half an hour later, Harry had his bags packed, and was down in the hotel restaurant for breakfast. And sitting in front of him on the table was another reason he absolutely had to get out: a full English breakfast, with tea and toast.

Wensleydale, Harry had quickly realised, was a place populated by people who placed food at the centre of just about everything. Breakfast was not something to be had in a rush, but a meal to be enjoyed. You couldn't have a mug of tea or coffee on its own; it had to be served with cake. And cake, it seemed, if it was of the rich, moist, fruity kind, had to be accompanied by cheese, no matter what time of day it was. And that was generally a slab of crumbly Wensleydale, made in the creamery just up the road between Hawes and Gayle. Teatime was dinnertime, or was it the other way round? Harry couldn't remember, but what he did know was, that if he had either meal out at one of the local pubs, then the food was cooked well and piled high, and positively demanded a pint or two of ale as an accompaniment.

With a shrug, Harry picked up his knife and fork and tucked into the feast in front of him. It even came with a slice of fried bread, and he took great delight in shoving a piece of it into the yolk of his egg before stuffing it into his face.

This would be his last fried breakfast, Harry promised himself. He'd put on weight since driving north, and it was now time to reverse that before he didn't so much walk as roll.

With breakfast finished and his mug of tea drained, Harry left the hotel and headed off into the day. He wasn't really sure what lay before him and having had to deal with a murder in his first week, he'd been more than a little relieved that the following couple of weeks had been considerably more mundane. He'd made good use of them, getting to know the area, and was even on spoken good-morning terms with some of the locals as he walked up into the marketplace and across to the community office, which was also the home of the local police at this, the top end of the dale. The actual police station had closed over twenty years ago and with it had gone the provision of a local lock-up. If anyone needed to be taken into custody, then it was an hour-long drive to Harrogate.

Having crossed the main road running through the centre of Hawes, Harry's phone trilled into his day and it was up against his ear before he'd even had a chance to check the number buzzing in.

'Grimm,' Harry said.

Down the line, Harry heard crying.

CHAPTER THREE

'Ben?'

Even though the voice hadn't said a word, Harry recognised it immediately. The world around him dissolved and he was back down south, sitting across a table in a prison visitors' room, staring at the sunken figure of his younger brother. Even though they were miles apart, he could see him clearly in his mind: a man broken by life, drowning in memories steeped in darkness. And all because of one man, their bastard of a father.

'Harry,' Ben said, his voice breaking as he spoke. 'I . . . I . .'

Instinct took over. Harry shoved his hands into his pockets, checked for his car keys. 'Whatever it is, I'm on my way.'

Harry had no idea what he would tell the rest of the team, but right then he didn't care. Family came first, it was as simple as that.

For a moment, Harry heard nothing but stuttered breathing. He wanted to be there, to be with his brother, sorting him out, protecting him.

'It's Dad,' Ben said then, breaking the silence. 'He . . .'

Harry's breath caught in his throat and the sliver of ice that pierced him turned his skin to goose flesh. 'He what, Ben?'

No reply came, just the sound of more crying.

'He what? Speak to me!'

Harry's voice was hard as an axe.

'He contacted me,' Ben said. 'Yesterday.'

Harry was so stunned by Ben's words that he stumbled backwards a little. He shook his head in disbelief, squeezed his eyes shut so tightly that he saw sparks fly in the darkness, his hand covering them, feeling the scars on his face, a topography of pain he wore proudly.

'How? He can't have done! He's not allowed to! He doesn't even know where you are!'

Ben was quiet again, just his breathing on the other end of the call, slow and shallow.

Harry's mind was in sixth gear and still accelerating, crashing through possibilities, reasons, anything that he could think of which would have allowed their father to somehow reach out to Ben.

The last time Harry had seen the man was over twenty years ago. Ben had been ten years old. Harry had come back from another tour to find a broken front door, and in the house beyond, splintered furniture, blood on the walls, a family ruined. He should have been there to protect them, to keep his mother, his brother, safe. But he hadn't been, and it still haunted him. It always would. Professional counsellors and therapists had told him that he needed to move on. Harry, however, refused. Moving on meant the bastard had gotten away with it. And Harry would never allow that.

'Listen, Ben,' Harry said, his voice all menace, 'whoever's

responsible, they're going to regret it, you hear me? I'll call my boss, we'll get you safe, I promise.'

'You can't,' Ben said, cutting in before Harry had even finished speaking. 'He said so. He warned me! He warned me . . . to warn you.'

Harry could feel his rage building, his hand gripping his phone so tight he half wondered if it would just give up under the pressure, the shattered screen slicing into his palm.

'Warn me? Ben, what the hell are you talking about? Warn me of what? Did he call you? I need to know if he called you, Ben. We need to find out how this happened, what went wrong, and who the hell is responsible!'

'It was one of the other lads in here,' Ben said. 'Told me he had a message.'

Harry said nothing, just listened. His brother was talking now and an interruption might put a halt to it, one neither of them could afford.

'He said that dad told him to talk to me so that I would talk to you, right? And that if I told anyone other than you, he would know. He said he'd been watching me for years, keeping an eye on me. On you, too, Harry.'

'On me?' Harry said.

'Said he knew all about why you'd been sent up north. That you'd roughed up a couple of blokes, chucked them in the back of a van.'

Harry swallowed hard. He'd never told Ben anything about any of his cases, period. So how the hell had this information got to him?

'What else did he say, Ben?' Harry asked, concerned that his brother's crackling voice could give up at any moment, while in the darker part of his own mind, his thoughts were already threading together what he would do to whoever was responsible for this.

'He . . . He said he was sorry for what happened. To Mum, to me. He said you had to let it go, to stop going after him.'

'Bollocks to that,' Harry spat. 'After what he did? No chance, Ben, and you know it.'

'He said he could get to us if he really wanted to. Get to me.'

Ben's voice broke on his words and Harry patiently listened to his kid brother as he tried to pull himself together just enough to keep talking.

'He said . . . He said that he would come for me first, Harry. Not you, me. He said that was very important for you to know. That he would come for me. Get me. In prison.'

Harry clenched his jaws so tightly that a jolt of pain shot through his skull like a drill bit chewing through bone. The notion that their supposed father was swaddling an apology for what he had done in the mean cloth of a threat sent him cold.

'Ben,' Harry said, but Ben cut him off, his voice rising in pitch, his words tumbling and crashing into each other.

'He can get to me, Harry! He can get to me! I need to get out! I can't take this! I can't take it anymore! I need to get out, to get out now! I need to get out!'

'Ben!'

Harry's voice was the roar of a soldier's battle cry and Ben shut down, his voice dropping to a pathetic whimper.

'You need to listen to me,' Harry said, his voice quieter now, but no less dangerous.

No response, just a sniff.

'I'm going to sort this out right now. When we end this

conversation you are to speak to a prison officer immediately. Tell them you are in danger and need immediate isolation and protection. I will talk to everyone I need to and I promise you nothing will happen to you. Do you understand?'

Still no response.

'Ben? Do you understand?'

'I can't, Harry,' Ben said, his voice quiet and weak, the whisper of a ghost. 'I can't.'

'Yes, you can,' Harry said. 'You have to.'

'He'll know,' Ben said. 'He'll know and then he'll send people to get me. He'll know.'

'You need to do what I've said,' Harry said, working hard to keep his voice calm and measured. 'You have to.'

'I . . . I can't.'

'Ben . . .'

The line went dead.

Harry stood for what seemed like an eternity, his phone still clamped to his ear, hand gripping it hard. He was staring off into nothing, rage flooding through him like fire through a tinder-dry forest.

'Harry?'

The voice registered somewhere in Harry's mind, but he couldn't quite place it, his mind unable to break itself free from what Ben had told him.

'Harry!'

Someone was shaking him. Harry didn't like being shaken.

'What!'

The word came out, not as a question but a threat, as he turned to face whoever was trying to butt into his day.

'Matt?'

'You alright, Boss?'

'I'm not your boss.'

The man standing in front of Harry was Detective Sergeant Matt Dinsdale. He was around the same age as Harry, at least that's what Harry assumed, because Matt's age seemed to be a mystery to everyone. Matt also had the habit of being always just a little bit too cheerful. Not in an annoying way, more that it was just a part of who and what he was. He was the kind of man, Harry had realised over the past few weeks, who didn't so much see life as a glass half-full, but one filled right to the top. He'd only recently qualified as a detective, which was pretty late in his career, Harry had thought, not that Matt seemed to care about such a thing.

Matt shoved his hands into the pockets of his trousers and stepped back. 'Anything I can do?'

'No,' Harry said. 'Look, I need to make another phone call, okay? I'll see you inside.'

Matt raised an eyebrow then gave a nod. 'I'll get the kettle on. If you're sure, that is, that I can't help?'

'I am,' Harry said, seeing that Matt was being absolutely genuine, but then that was a trait he'd noticed in nearly everyone he'd met since coming north. They were who they were, no disguises. 'You do that and I'll be over in a bit.'

'I think we're good for biscuits but if we're not I'll nip out and get some,' Matt said. 'And cake. Can never have too much.'

Matt made to head off to the community office but turned back one last time. 'And you're that sure you're okay?'

Harry relaxed his face, gave a nod.

'See you in a bit, then.'

With Matt gone, Harry opened the contacts folder on his phone and punched in a number. His call was answered in just over three rings.

'DCI Grimm,' the voice said.

'Ma'am,' Harry said.

On the other end of the call, Detective Superintendent Alice Firbank, who was responsible for sending Harry north in the first place, fell quiet, her silence enough of a request for Harry to explain why he had interrupted her day so early.

'Ben called me,' Harry said.

'I'm glad to hear that he's communicating,' the DSup said. 'A very good sign indeed.'

'That's not what I mean,' Harry said. 'He's in danger. You need to get him out of there. Now.'

The DSup coughed the smallest of disbelieving laughs. 'Well, of course, Harry,' she said. 'I can do that now. We have so many free beds in prisons, as I'm sure you know, so it shouldn't be a problem to move him at all.'

'I'm serious!' Harry snapped back. 'It's my dad. He contacted Ben. Threatened him.'

Further silence.

'Are you sure?'

'I'm sorry, what?'

'Are you certain that's what happened? Ben is in prison, Harry. There is no way your father can even know where he is, never mind contact him.'

Harry breathed deep, an attempt at working to keep his voice calm and measured despite the storm raging inside.

'He said that it came through one of the other prisoners, the message from my dad, I mean.'

'Message?'

'A warning,' Harry said. 'For me to back off.'

Harry was pretty sure he heard the DSup shake her head.

'This sounds to me like a call for help, Harry. One that

you absolutely can't answer.'

'He wasn't lying. He wasn't making it up. He's terrified, Ma'am.'

'You've no proof,' the DSup said. 'Just the word of your brother. And he's in prison!'

'He knew about why you sent me up here,' Harry said then. 'The two blokes in the van. Confidential information. The case isn't even at court yet!'

'Shit . . .'

'Yeah,' Harry said. 'That.'

For a moment, neither Harry nor his DSup spoke.

'Leave this with me,' Firbank said. 'I'm on it now.'

'I'm on my way,' Harry replied. 'I'll let you know when I'm back.'

'You'll do nothing of the sort!'

The DSup's voice was sharp.

'Ma'am . . .' Harry growled, but Firbank was clearly having none of it.

'You have a job to do, Harry,' she said. 'You cannot, and you absolutely *will* not, just bugger off at a whim to do whatever you want! And that means you will not be on your way back here, in any way, shape, or form! Do I make myself clear?'

'He's my brother!' Harry hurled back, his voice rising now, rough anger rolling out with his words. 'If anyone touches him . . .'

'I said, *do I make myself clear*?' the DSup snapped back.

Harry took the deepest of breaths and muttered, 'Yes, Ma'am. You do.'

'I will deal with this,' the DSup said, her voice hard and unwavering. 'So wind your neck in, Grimm! And I'd advise you against making those kinds of threats.'

'You can't keep me up here,' Harry said. 'I need to be there, to be near my brother. I have to be!'

'No, you do not,' the DSup said, her voice switching from angry to calm in a beat. 'I am on this as a priority. You travelling down here will do nothing. The very best thing you can do is to get on with doing what you are there to do.'

'I'm not needed . . .'

'Damn it, Harry, you're a DCI! Bloody well act like one!'

Harry took a deep breath and massaged his temples with his left hand. 'I'll call in a few hours,' he said.

'No, you won't,' the DSup replied. 'You will focus on your job and I will do mine. Understand?'

Harry mumbled a, 'Yes'.

'Good,' the DSup said, and the line went dead.

Harry dropped his hands to his side, stretched his neck, and stared up into the sky, before closing his eyes and sucking in a long, slow breath. He knew the DSup was right, that driving back to Bristol would solve nothing. But that didn't make it any easier to accept.

Slipping his phone into a pocket, Harry headed off towards the Hawes Community Office, only to see Matt racing towards him from the same direction.

'I'll explain on the way,' Matt said, jangling the keys towards the police Land Rover in front of him, the vehicle parked outside the Bull's Head Hotel, just a few yards away from where Harry was stood. 'Come on.'

'Why? What's happened?'

'Farm accident,' Matt said.

'An accident?' Harry said. 'Then why the rush?'

Matt stopped. 'Jim's out there now.'

'And?'

'He doesn't think it was an accident at all.'

CHAPTER FOUR

'BLOODY HELL, MATT!' HARRY HISSED, AS THE detective sergeant hurled the four-wheel-drive along Beggarman's Road, sending him up and out of his seat to slam his head into the roof above. 'You always drive like this?'

'Yeah, you're right,' Matt said, and sped up. 'That better?'

Harry was pretty sure that Land Rovers weren't supposed to be driven the way Matt was doing so, and he found himself not only hanging on tight to the handle above the passenger door with his left hand, but bracing himself against what was laughingly called a dashboard with his right. And for good measure, he pushed his knees up against it as well, just in case, but all that did was cause some painful chafing.

Matt looked far too relaxed, Harry thought, as he stared at the detective sergeant, who was driving along with only his left hand on the steering wheel, his right arm leaning out of the driver's door window, truck-driver style.

Just a few minutes ago, Harry had been in Hawes marketplace worrying about his brother. Now he was more than a little concerned about surviving a journey out into the wilds of the dales. And wild it was, with Weatherfell looming down over them on their left, its roots stretching out to link with others that Harry didn't yet know the names of.

The dales could be both beautiful and bleak in the same stolen moment, and Harry had seen how a quick weather change could turn a picture-postcard view into a masterpiece of gothic horror, with howling winds churning up rain clouds to send them racing across the landscape to devour the sun.

Right now, the grey of the morning seemed undecided, and Harry wouldn't put money on what kind of weather was on its way later on. Clouds were breaking far off, but over them now sat a plume of sallow white, heavy with the threat of worse to come. And to think it had been all sunshine and wasps just a couple of days ago, Harry mused.

Matt dropped a gear, heaved the vehicle onto another road, and headed off again at speed, all without removing his right hand from the window, Harry noticed, somewhat puzzled as to how the man had managed to change gears.

'Nearly there,' Matt said, nodding ahead.

Smooth, lush fields lay behind the walls which rose like ramparts on either side of the road.

Matt then pointed and chirped, 'There it is!'

Harry saw a gap in the wall, assumed Matt was going to slow down, and too late realised that he wasn't going to do anything of the sort.

'You mad bastard!' Harry yelled, as the Land Rover's tyres squealed on the road, biting into it as Matt swung it left off the road, through the open gate, and up into the field beyond.

'And here we are!' Matt said, as though absolutely

nothing was wrong with his driving. 'Nice little drive that, isn't it? Lovely scenery.'

Harry noticed a couple of barns in the corners of fields further up and wondered if they had stood as long as the walls which hemmed them in. He guessed so, once again amazed at the history of the place, how wherever he looked the landscape stretched away from him not just in distance but time, centuries laying out before him, its ghosts restless.

Parked just a little way off in the field Harry saw PCSO Jim Metcalf's vehicle, which was another Land Rover, only this one proudly wore its farming heritage, with muddy tyres, plenty of dents and scratches, and tufts of hay sticking out from various quarters. The police had a number of vehicles to use, including the Land Rover he and Matt had driven over in, but Harry had come to understand that they weren't always best suited to the weather and the terrain, which was why Jim preferred using his own vehicle. In fact, getting him to part with it in favour of a police vehicle was pretty much akin to prising the lid off a particularly well-gummed-up jar of Marmite.

'Well would you look at that,' Matt said, and let out a long whistle.

The sound drew Harry's attention away from the vehicle and he saw, just a way off in front of them, in the direction they were now driving, the front end of a tractor smashed through a drystone wall. He hadn't noticed it at all from the road and only now, because they were in the field, was it visible.

As they drew closer, Matt, at last, having slowed down to allow the four-wheel drive to do its job and just pull them easily up through the fields, Harry saw that something else was alongside it. He couldn't quite make it out yet, its lines hidden by bits of smashed wall, which stood up like broken teeth from the ground beneath, but it was pretty clear that it, too, was not in good shape.

Matt pulled the Land Rover to a stop, turned off the engine, and half-shoved, half-kicked his door open. 'Best we go and have a gander, then,' he said.

Harry nodded in agreement, pleased with himself for knowing what Matt was actually talking about.

A figure emerged through a gate in the wall ahead, to the right of the crashed machinery, and waved. He was carrying a small rucksack.

'There's Jim,' Matt said, waving back.

'I can see that for myself,' Harry muttered. 'So who called it in?'

'A friend of the deceased,' Matt said. 'Jim was over this way anyway so came over to see what had happened, call the ambulance out, the usual.'

'And now?'

'Let's ask him,' Matt said.

Jim, a Police Community Support Officer, or PCSO, was in his mid-twenties, and as local as you could get, having been born and bred on a farm in Burtersett, a hamlet just a mile or so the other side of Hawes, and just off the main road, which ran like an artery through the dale.

'So, what have we got?' Harry asked as Jim came to a stop in front of him. He could see concern in the young man's face, his jaw clenched firm, eyes dark.

Jim opened his rucksack and handed out some PPE: gloves and facemasks. Jim was already wearing his. Harry and Matt pulled on the gloves, the latex pinging against Harry's wrists as he made sure they were not only tight but that he could still use his hands okay, then slipped the face-masks on over their noses and mouths.

'Got a call about twenty minutes ago,' Jim said, reading from the little notebook in his hand, which all police carried with them. 'Report of an accident. The body was found by an acquaintance of the deceased.'

'Body?' Harry said, then glanced at Matt. 'You said this was an accident. You never mentioned that we'd be dealing with a body. A little bit remiss, wouldn't you say?'

Matt did his best not to look sheepish.

'Who's the deceased?' Harry asked, making a mental note to give Matt a bit of a bollocking for not passing on relevant details about what was now clearly a potential crime scene. 'Why were they here?'

'John Capstick,' Jim said. 'He farms out this way. If you can call what he does farming.'

'And where are we exactly?' Harry asked, having never ventured into this part of the dales before.

'Oughtershaw,' Matt said, and pointed back down the field to a small collection of buildings just down the road. 'Can't say it's a place I'd like to live. No pub for a start.'

'There's the chapel,' Jim offered.

'Methodist,' Matt said. 'Can't even go there for a tipple, what with the wine being non-alcoholic. They actually use Ribena, you know? Ribena! Can you imagine?'

Harry ignored Matt's clearly deeply held issues with what the local churchgoers used instead of communion wine and asked, 'Next of kin?'

'Father died over a decade ago,' Matt said. 'Not exactly a loss either. Right old bastard he was. And his son followed suit.'

'Mother?'

Jim shook his head. 'And no one else, neither. Or if there are, they're not up for admitting to it.'

Harry took a mental note of Matt's judgments on someone long dead and asked, 'Who's the acquaintance?'

Jim's eyes fell back into his notebook.

'Nicholas Ellis,' he said.

'La'll Nick?' Matt said, rolling his eyes. 'Can't imagine he's been exactly helpful.'

'No, not really,' Jim said. 'All panic and screeching if I'm honest. Wasn't really making much sense.'

Harry raised an eyebrow at both men in front of him. 'La'll Nick?'

'Little Nick,' Matt explained. 'Not the nicest of blokes.'

'I'm not nice either,' Harry said. 'In fact, there's a few people I'm sure who think my middle names are *utter* and *bastard*.'

'No, not like that,' Matt said, then started to stumble on his words. 'I mean, it's not that you're not nice, it's just that you can be a bit, well . . .'

Harry let Matt sweat just long enough before he turned to Jim and said, 'Look, best we get eyes on first, right? If this is a Category One, then this is a crime scene and we need to get moving on it fast, sort out a Scene Guard and a Scene Log, the usual. If it's Category Two, then we'll just deal with it accordingly, okay?'

Jim led the way up to the gate in the wall and through to the field on the other side. Here, Harry was at last able to get a good look at what had happened.

The tractor he'd seen when they arrived was a write-off, that much was clear to Harry. The vehicle hadn't so much crashed into the wall as barged through it, spreading shattered stone and bits of itself all around. The front wheels were hanging off, the axle joining them twisted nastily. The engine was leaking oil and diesel, the acrid stink of it polluting the fresh air gusting around them. Behind the engine, the cab was a mangled shell, with glass from the windows dusting the grass like snow. The two huge rear wheels of the tractor weren't touching the ground, thanks to the fact that the vehicle was stuck fast on the rubble of a centuries' old wall. The twin-axle trailer was still hooked into the couplings at its rear, but was on its side and lying to the right of the tractor after it'd jack-knifed at the moment of impact, Harry assumed.

Having taken in the full extent of what had happened, Harry noticed something was missing.

'The body,' Harry said. 'Where is it?'

Jim pointed up the field.

Harry followed Jim's line of sight and was able to make out the scars in the field caused by the out of control tractor and trailer, but nothing else.

'Can't see anything,' he said, then saw a thick grey cloud hovering just above the ground. It was about the size of a children's paddling pool, Harry thought, and knew that the sound of it would be the sickening buzz and hum of blowflies, feasting themselves silly on the corpse which was still hidden from view.

'I'm not sure you'll want to either,' Jim said. 'Come on, it's up this way a bit.'

Harry held back for a second, his eyes still on the flies, his experience giving him a pretty good idea of what awaited them.

'Where's this Little Nick bloke that you mentioned?' he asked. 'I'll need to speak to him once we've had a look at everything, find out why he was out here in the first place.'

'He's back at the farmhouse, just down there near the village,' Jim explained. 'Liz is there to keep an eye on him, try and calm him down a bit, stop him jabbering on and on, which he likes to do at the best of times, so you can imagine what he's like right now.'

'I certainly can,' Matt said.

Liz Coates was the other PCSO in the team covering the dales. She went everywhere on a motorbike, a huge off-road beast which, at a touch over five foot tall, she didn't look big or heavy enough to ride. And yet she handled it with the skill of someone who had clearly grown up riding dirt trails and had somehow managed to not get injured.

'Good plan,' Matt said. 'Though he's probably already nicked most of the cutlery and any booze he could find.'

'I'm getting the impression that you don't like him,' Harry said, glancing down towards Oughtershaw. 'And we'll need to go house-to-house, check if anyone saw or heard anything.'

'Won't take long,' Jim said. 'Aren't that many houses.'

'As for Nick, he's easy to dislike,' Matt said with a shrug. 'But John is . . . *was* worse.'

Harry took a deep breath and looked up the field to where Jim had said the body was. 'Come on then,' he said. 'Let's go see what we've got.'

Halfway up the field, Harry saw blood. Not much, just a dried patch of it pushed into the grass, grown dark over time and under the sun, flies buzzing around, but nothing like the cloud of them further ahead. Walking on, they passed another and another, leading off like some over-sized and grisly Morse Code stamped into the grass at their feet.

'So, come on then, what do you think happened?' Harry asked, as they made their way towards the body, the patches of blood leading the way, and growing darker as they drew closer.

Jim said nothing for a moment then stopped and turned to look at Harry and Matt. 'Look,' he said, 'I guess it could be just an accident. Probably nothing more than John being a victim of his own stupidity. I mean, he wasn't exactly the best of farmers, was he?'

Harry shrugged. 'Can't say that I'd know either way.'

'Well, he wasn't,' said Jim. 'The farmhouse, the yard, it's a mess. No pride in the place. Animals aren't looked after properly. The walls are left to just crumble. He's just carried on like his dad, hating farming and doing nowt to change it. Mad, if you ask me. Actually, just ask anyone around here, and they'll tell you the same, for sure.'

Jim, Harry knew, was talking from experience. He was born a farmer's son, still lived at home, still worked out on the land with his dad, went to the auction mart in Hawes every week if he could. Farming was in his blood. It was also what made him such a good PCSO and, Harry had mused more than once, what would make him a superb police officer, assuming of course that he could get a posting in the area, or at least somewhere similar, once his training was up.

'He was that popular, then?' Harry asked.

Jim's laugh was short and filled with as much warmth as a walk-in freezer. 'There are folk around here who would give their right arm for a place like his, and all he's done is ruin it. So, no, he wasn't popular.'

Harry noticed that the patches of dried blood had turned into more of a smear. Then the smell hit him, as did the sound of the flies. The cloud was close now and he could see a mound beneath it.

'So, what's got you to thinking it's something else, then?'

Harry asked, reaching into his pocket for a little something he always carried with him just in case. It was a pot of vapour rub, the smell of the camphor and eucalyptus oil going some way to disguise the rich, fetid smell of rotting flesh. He popped the lid and rubbed a little under his nostrils.

'Just doesn't smell right,' Jim said, then put his hand over his nose and mouth and muttered, 'in more ways than the obvious.'

'Here,' Harry said, handing the pot to Jim and Matt. 'It'll help.'

They both took some and then as Harry stuffed the pot back into his pocket, Jim led them on for the last few metres to the body.

When they arrived, and Harry finally laid eyes on what was before them, he had the horrible feeling that the vapour rub really wasn't going to be any help at all.

CHAPTER FIVE

'JESUS CHRIST,' MATT SAID, A HAND RISING TO HIS mouth. 'That is rank.'

'I doubt even he could do much about this,' Harry offered. Then, looking at the rather grey colour Matt's face had swiftly taken on, added, 'And if you're going to puke, best you do it away from the body, pal.'

Matt gulped air down, squeezed his eyes tight and rubbed them. 'I'm fine,' he said.

'You don't look fine,' Jim said.

'He's right,' Harry said. 'You don't look fine. The opposite of fine, if I'm honest. Sort of not fine, bordering on really bloody awful.'

'I'm fine, really fine,' Matt said. 'I promise.'

Harry wasn't convinced in the slightest. 'It's the smell,' he said. 'Always is. Dead bodies you can get used to, close your mind to it, but the smell, that's something else. Has the ability to really crawl up your nose and set up shop.'

'You're not helping,' Matt said.

Harry, with Matt and Jim beside him, hung back from

the body for two reasons. One was because if this was a crime scene then he wanted to do as little as possible that could potentially damage any evidence. The other was simply because what lay before them was one of the worst things that Harry had ever seen in his life. And so far, he'd lived one that had seen more than its fair share of violence.

'How long's he been here?' Harry asked, staring at the body, which was a hideously bloated thing, the stomach had swollen up enough to pop a few buttons on the deceased's shirt. The flies were seemingly oblivious to their presence and continued to feast.

Harry had the fleeting image of a badly dressed, sweating walrus basking in the sun, but quickly pushed it to the back of his mind.

The body was covered in flies; huge fat bluebottles, swarming around it in a cloud, thousands of them, and if they weren't flying, they were enjoying the feast, drinking up the fluids of the dead, lapping it up and getting fat, and using it as the perfect place to lay their young. And it wasn't just bluebottles either, Harry noticed. Wasps had come along to join in the party, their black and yellow bodies adding an unnecessarily lurid sheen to the awful vista. They also made it a little more difficult to get close: this was their feast and Harry was pretty sure they wouldn't be too happy at being disturbed. And it was also pretty clear that the body had been munched on by more than a few passing carnivores and hungry carrion, foxes sniffing it out as a midnight snack, crows diving out of the sky to peck at the weeping flesh. The whole scene was, if he was honest, a complete and total disaster when it came to the collection of evidence, assuming of course, that this was a crime scene.

'Not sure,' Jim said, his voice thoughtful. 'Only person

we've spoken to is Nick. He says the last time he saw John was Friday afternoon. So at most since Friday evening, though there's no way he would be up here during the evening.'

Harry turned to face Jim. 'A little something I've learned on the force is the ABC principle.'

'The look of love?' Matt asked.

Harry ignored him, though wondered how anyone could so quickly remember an 80s pop song by that particular band.

'Assume nothing, believe nobody, check everything. We've no reason to believe Nick was telling you the truth so we can't assume John wouldn't be up here in the evening. Everything needs to be checked.'

'No, I get that,' Jim said, 'it's just that John really wouldn't be up here in the evening. And I know that as well as anyone does.'

'Why's that?'

'Too bloody pissed,' Matt said.

'And where did Nick see him?' Harry asked.

'In town,' Jim said.

Inside, Harry smiled. That anyone would refer to Hawes as a town was stretching reality more than a little, but he understood why. It was a bustling place, not just for shops, but with its regular market and the auction mart, and then there were the tourists. It was as much a town as this end of Wensleydale had, and Harry had quickly realised that it punched above its weight. He wasn't quite ready to admit it yet, but he was starting to think the place was growing on him.

Harry stared for a moment at the scene before them,

down towards the crashed vehicles, then back to the corpse at their feet, and something already bothered him.

'This isn't visible from the road, is it?'

'What, the body? No,' Jim said.

'No, I mean any of it,' Harry said. 'The crash, the smashed wall, I only noticed it once we'd come speeding through the open gate like the very hosts of Hell were on our heels.'

'I guess not, no,' Jim said. 'Why? You think someone saw it happen?'

'I'm just surprised no one called it in earlier,' Harry said. 'Visible or not, surely a crash like that makes a hell of a noise. And wouldn't people have wondered where he was?'

Matt and Jim said nothing and just continued to stare at the body.

'Any idea what he was doing out here in the first place?' Harry asked.

Jim pointed into the field around them and, for the first time since they'd arrived, Harry noticed that it was littered with sorry-looking bales of hay. They were scattered about in no real order, most of them sagging and grey, seemingly dissolving into the ground beneath them.

'Out to collect that lot I would think,' Jim said, 'though it's sod-all use now, what with the rain we had last week. What a waste.'

'How do you mean?' Harry asked.

'Hay needs to be dry,' Jim explained. 'You cut the grass, turn it over the course of a week or two so that it's properly dry, then bale it and get it inside quick before the weather changes. And it looks like John didn't. A mix of couldn't be arsed and cheap booze probably. The idiot.'

Harry looked from the body and down the hill to the

smashed-up tractor and trailer. 'You didn't like him much, did you?'

Jim just shook his head. 'No one did. Wasn't much to like.'

'So how did he end up here with that lot down there?' Harry asked, nodding to the smashed tractor and trailer. 'You reckon he was thrown clear?'

'I don't see how,' Jim said then gestured with his right hand at the field around them. 'Not a steep slope really, is it? Assuming he was driving, he'd have been in the cab, so he wouldn't have been thrown clear, he would have had to have jumped out through the door.'

Harry walked around the body to the other side then crouched down to get a better look. It was no better and no worse from any angle. The legs looked undamaged, at least as far as he could tell, seeing as the body was clothed and the trousers were scuffed and worn, but not ripped as would be expected in an accident involving a vehicle. The torso, however, was an entirely different story. The stomach was a swollen thing, almost balloon-like in its repose, but the chest had been not so much crushed as flattened by what Harry assumed was a wheel from the tractor or trailer, perhaps even both. The deceased's body had seemingly exploded violently under the trauma of what had happened, with blood and entrails scattered about like meat left to dry in the sun. Above this, the neck had somehow escaped, but the head must have been caught by another wheel, Harry thought, because there was quite literally nothing left which gave any impression as to what John Capstick had once looked like. The skull was shattered, a fragile vase crushed under a great weight, its contents a purple-black mess thrust out in all directions around it, a halo from Hell. Harry couldn't make out any feature which bore resemblance to what had once been a face.

'And just to be certain,' Harry asked, 'you're absolutely sure it's this John bloke? It's not like you can recognise him, is it?'

'Yeah, it's John alright,' Jim said, then pointed as he spoke: 'His field, his tractor, his trailer.' Finally, he nodded at the dead man's trousers and some muddy orange twine threaded through the belt loops. 'And there aren't many folk left in the world who are happy to keep their trousers up with baler bind. Not anymore.'

Harry rose back onto his feet then walked over to Matt and Jim. 'What do you think?'

'I think it's an absolute bloody mess,' Matt said. 'Poor bastard. And he was a bastard, for sure. But what a way to go.'

'Not exactly helpful, but a fair observation,' Harry said, then he turned to Jim, but it was clear that Jim had nothing else to offer just yet. He looked thoughtful, so Harry left him alone for a moment.

From what Harry could see it looked like a tragic and pretty gruesome accident. Shit happens, and that was a sad fact of life.

'I'm still not getting why you think there's any foul play here,' Harry said. 'I mean, this is farming, right? You work with animals, with huge pieces of machinery, with chemicals, I'm surprised there aren't more accidents like this.'

'You're forgetting the high stress, shit pay, and crippling debt,' Matt said. 'Not a surprise the suicide rate is so high.'

'Could it be that, then?' Harry asked.

'Like this? No,' Matt said. 'Farmers usually go out with a double-barrel under the chin. This? This is way too creative.'

Matt then mimed placing a gun under his own chin and pulling the trigger.

'Unnecessary,' Harry said. 'But thanks for the re-enactment.'

Harry turned to Jim. 'Well?'

Jim didn't reply immediately. Instead, he stepped back from the body and moved a little way up and above it. Harry and Matt followed. From where they were then stood, they could see clearly now the course taken by the tractor and trailer, how it had started to swerve as it gained speed, before slamming hard enough into the wall to break it.

'For a start,' Jim said, 'and like I said when you got here, none of this looks right.'

'Explain,' Harry said.

'Well, there's nowt to suggest that John was thrown from the tractor is there? From what I can see, it was parked up here, right where he's lying, and then it just rolled off down the hill.'

'You mean he got in the way of it?'

Jim shook his head. 'No, I mean it was parked right where John's body is, rolled over him, then headed off down the hill.'

'So, he wasn't in the tractor cab?' Harry said.

'Can't see how,' said Jim. 'But that's not the problem. He could have parked up to check on the trailer before going around to collect the bales.'

'And he'd do that by hand?' Harry asked.

Jim shook his head. 'Front loader,' he said. 'You probably didn't notice it, because it snapped off the front of the tractor when it hit the wall. It's there though. He'd park up, uncouple the trailer, then drive around picking up bales.

Well, that's what I'd do, anyway, if I was out doing a field on my own.'

'I'm still not seeing what you're getting at,' Harry said. 'If we're calling this in as a Category One . . .'

Harry watched as Jim took a moment to compose himself. It was as though Harry could see him sorting things out in his head before saying them.

'Look at the body,' Jim said, nodding at the thing on the ground which had been, just a few days ago, a living, breathing human being. 'Why's he lying on the ground? What the hell was he doing down there in the first place? It doesn't make any bloody sense!'

'Like you said, checking the trailer,' Harry suggested.

'He wouldn't need to do it on his back!' Jim exclaimed. 'It would be a walk around, that's all. Probably kick a tyre or two, nowt else. And this is John we're talking about. He wasn't the kind of bloke who checked his equipment.'

Matt let out the faintest of sniggers.

Harry turned to him.

'Really?'

Matt stifled his laughter. 'Sorry, Boss,' he said. 'It's just, you know, checking his equipment . . .'

Harry stared hard enough at Matt to burn a hole through his skull. He went to speak but the sound of a car racing along the road back down at the bottom of the field drew his attention. He stared down at it, unable to see it clearly beyond the walls, just a flash of some nondescript colour, the sound of the revving engine fading into the distance as quickly as it had arrived.

'He's in a hurry,' Matt said.

'What about the tractor?' Harry asked, keen to keep things moving. 'Could he have been checking that?'

Again, Jim shook his head. 'Ignoring the fact that it's a miracle that it's survived as long as it has, there's still no need for him to be on the ground like that. Doesn't make sense.'

Matt said, 'Perhaps he was knocked down and that's just where he fell.'

'And then he just laid there and let the trailer roll over him?' Jim said. 'Look at him! It's like he didn't fight or couldn't even! I don't know, it just doesn't look right. It *isn't* right! And what's around here to knock him over?'

'Anything else?' Harry asked.

Jim shook his head.

'Matt?'

Matt looked thoughtful, rubbed his chin to emphasise the fact that he was thinking, and then said, 'I'll be honest, I'm with Jim. This doesn't look right.'

Harry took a step back to get a moment alone with his thoughts and looked at the countryside around them. It was, like the rest of the dales, utterly beautiful. Moorlands and rolling hills, crags and ancient walls, all laid out before him. History was here, the land farmed in much the same way now as it had been for centuries, families stretching back generations. The cool air, rich with the scent of fern and heather from the moors, brought with it the faintest tang from the sheep that lived on this land, and their haunting bleats and calls gave the place life. Far off, he heard the rumble of low-flying aircraft, vehicles navigating the lanes. And in the very centre of this, just a step or two away from his own feet, death had come, and in as violent a form as he had ever seen. It was a scene so utterly incongruous to its surroundings that Harry just shook his head and sighed.

'Here,' Harry said, pulling something out of his pocket and handing it to Matt. 'Best make this official then.'

Matt looked at the roll of crime scene tape now in his hands. 'Not sure there's enough, Boss,' he said. 'I'm half tempted to just cordon off the whole field.'

Jim's phone rang. 'Liz?' he said.

When the brief call ended, Jim looked over to Harry and Matt.

'It's Nick,' Jim said.

'What is?' Harry asked.

'He's done a runner.'

CHAPTER SIX

Having left Matt up in the field to not only secure the area, but set himself up as the Scene Guard to log everyone moving on and off the site, and with the crime scene team on their way, Harry and Jim headed back to the farm to see what had happened and to check on Liz. Harry had also demanded that anyone and everyone heading to the crime scene was to meet at the farmhouse first and be directed from there. It would save people getting lost and ending up traipsing through fields at random in some kind of gruesome treasure hunt. It was a formality for sure, but it still had to be done.

There was certainly no need for an ambulance, and with the state of the body, Harry wondered if shovels and a couple of strong plastic bin bags would be more useful than a stretcher for moving it. The coroner had been called, and the pathologist, Rebecca Sowerby. Harry was very much looking forward to seeing her again, in much the same way as he looked forward to having root canal surgery. They hadn't exactly hit it off last time they'd met, so he was quite pleased that she would have a less than pleasant time with the body. Though, Harry wondered how a pathologist would ever be able to class a day as pleasant, up to their armpits in the decaying remains of someone else. Horses for courses, though.

At the farmhouse, Harry saw first-hand what Jim had been getting at with regards to the deceased not being the best of farmers. As they'd approached it from the road in Jim's vehicle, he'd been put in mind of the kind of set used for horror films involving stupid backpacking teenagers and cannibalistic hicks. Horror wasn't exactly Harry's thing, having seen more than enough in real-life to spend his free time watching the fantasy equivalent, but he had a feeling that were Director, Tobe Hooper with them right then, the man would have been chomping at the bit to get back into showbusiness and do a Texas Chainsaw Massacre reboot.

'What a shit tip,' Harry said, as they bounced into the yard in the Land Rover, leaving the road and its smooth, clean surface behind, to be replaced by a mismatch of cobbles, rubble, and patches of crumbling tarmac, all well hidden beneath a blanket of undulating muck and mire. Liz's motorbike was propped up on its stand to one side.

'The man had no pride,' Jim said, pulling them to a stop and heaving the handbrake. He then looked at Harry's feet and shook his head.

'What?' Harry asked.

'Still not bought any, then?' Jim asked, shaking his head, as though disappointed in the behaviour of a child.

Harry said nothing and clambered out, his shoes sinking deep into the stink. He'd been putting off buying some proper farmer-style Wellington boots, because buying them added a sense of permanency to his life in the dales that he wasn't quite ready to accept. But with something indescribably awful now creeping over the lip of his shoes and onto his socks, he made a mental note to get a pair as soon as they were back in Hawes.

Harry looked around the yard. 'I can't believe I'm asking this, but which building is the actual house?'

It was, from where they were standing, impossible to tell which of the buildings that surrounded the yard was the one which was lived in. Harry had been in some rough places, but this was like stepping back in time. There was a mean Victorian dread to the place, as though at any point people in rags would stumble from one of the chewed, rotting doors, their feet bare, their starving mouths begging for food.

Jim gave a nod to their left with his head and said, 'Follow me.'

At the other side of the yard, having negotiated some angry chickens and even angrier dogs, Harry followed Jim through a scuffed, muck-covered door and into a room which clearly served as a living room, kitchen, and dining area. Liz was there to meet them.

'I'd make you a mug of tea,' she said, 'but I don't think any of us want to risk it.'

A quick scan of the room had Harry inclined to agree. Every surface was covered, not just in unclean crockery and tins and packets of food, but equipment and supplies clearly for use on the farm.

Liz was leaning against a sofa, which looked like it should've seen a bonfire years ago, her PCSO uniform hidden beneath her motorbike leathers.

'No milk anyway,' she said, then tapped her right foot against a grubby looking sack on the floor, 'unless you want some of that.'

'What is it?'

'That's dried milk for lambs,' Liz explained. 'You use it if you have to hand feed them. Sometimes mothers reject their own, or you get triplets and have to take one away. Smells great, like really sweet custard powder, or a Caramac bar, but I don't think it would work too well in a brew.'

Harry looked for somewhere to sit down, eventually pulling a chair out from under a dining table, which itself was covered in unopened letters held down with a scattering of shotgun cartridges. The chair looked sticky but Harry went for it and hoped that when he got up he wouldn't leave the place with ruined trousers.

'So then, Liz,' Harry said, as Jim shuffled along and took up another seat, Liz staying where she was against the sofa, 'what exactly happened?'

'All I was doing was talking to him,' Liz said. 'He was in a proper state over what he'd found so I was just trying to calm him down and find out what had gone on.'

'And you met him here?'

Liz gave a nod. 'Jim sent him up here to calm him down and get him away from the accident.'

'And he just buggered off?'

'Yep, out of here, like I'd set a rocket up his arse.'

Harry smiled just a little at that. 'Why was he here in the first place? And how did he know where to find the deceased? Doesn't strike me as all that normal to just walk up into a field to meet a friend.'

Jim said, 'All I know is that when I got to the scene he was in a flap, properly jumping around and not making much sense.'

'Liz?' Harry asked. 'He say anything to you?'

Liz screwed up her face and gave a little shrug.

'What is it?' Harry asked.

'It's just that he said he was out here because John sent him a text,' Liz said, then held up her hands as if to fend off any accusations of making stuff up. 'Don't look at me like that, it's what he said.'

Harry glanced at Jim with a raised eyebrow. 'He mention this to you?'

Jim shook his head. 'He can't have sent one, can he? John's been dead a couple of days, easily. Nick's talking bollocks.'

'And that's your professional opinion?' Harry asked, a crease of a smile in the corner of his mouth.

'It's the opinion of someone who's known him all his life.'

'Exactly my thoughts,' Liz said. 'But that's what he said, or at least that's what I could make out from his hysterics. He said John sent him a text, that he needed help, and when he arrived he found what you've all seen, John not exactly being in a fit state to have sent him a text in the first place.'

Harry folded his arms and felt his brow crease as he tried to deal with what he'd just been told. 'So this Nick bloke reckons he received a text from John, who's clearly dead, telling him to come to the field this morning? You're sure that's what he said? Absolutely positive?'

Liz gave a short, sharp nod.

'And then he just ran? Was there anything you said that set him off?' Harry asked, eyes back on Liz. 'Anything you said or did?'

Liz was quiet for a moment. 'When I arrived, Jim had him pretty calm, so I just took over.'

'He was probably still in shock,' Jim said.

'And having seen the body, that's more than understandable,' Harry agreed.

'That bad?' Liz asked.

Harry and Jim both nodded.

Liz's eyes grew wide at this. 'Anyway,' she continued, 'he was quiet to begin with, so I just tried to keep it like that, but then he started getting agitated.'

'About what?' Harry asked.

'John texting him and John being dead and how could a dead person send him a text, and then he kind of just started leaping about a bit.'

'Leaping about a bit?' Harry said then gestured to the room they were in. 'How does anyone leap about a bit in here without doing themselves a mischief?'

'He had a good go,' Liz said. 'And he's not that big, not much taller than me if I'm honest. It's what he does anyway, never seems to stand still, like he's always agitated, but he was worse than ever.'

'So where is he now?' Harry asked.

'When I said that you and Matt were up there as well, with Jim, he kind of just went silent, then just did a runner, jumped in his van, and buggered off.'

Something jogged Harry's memory. 'When was this?'

Liz checked her watched. 'Twenty minutes ago?'

'That'll be the car we heard then,' Harry said. 'Raced off up the road. Any idea where he was heading?'

'None,' Liz said. 'But we know where he lives.'

Harry fell silent. They had a body in a field which looked like cause of death was a little suspicious. Nothing concrete, but enough to call it in and investigate further. And now they had this Nick bloke going up to meet the deceased at the field because apparently the deceased had sent him a text asking for help. Which was either total bollocks, or something much, much worse. Harry knew he'd be wanting to have another look at the field, that was for sure. If a text had been sent, did that mean there was a phone laying around? And if there was, who had used it? Because if there was one thing he was pretty sure the dead didn't do, it was send text messages to friends.

'So,' Harry said at last, the word rolling out on the end of a long, slow breath, 'and just to make sure we're all absolutely clear on this, so forgive my repeating a few things, we've got the deceased, who is either the victim of a hard to explain, tragic, and particularly gory farming accident, or was murdered in such a way as to make it look like an accident. He's been lying up in the field all weekend, attracting every blowfly from across the dale and no one has done a damned thing about going up to see what had happened because this mess isn't actually visible from the road. And we've got this Little Nick who's up rolled on up here to meet the deceased because the deceased contacted him.'

'You don't think Nick did it, do you?' Jim asked, disbelief clear in his voice. 'Did him over on Friday then came out here today to try and cover things up with his idiotic story?'

'I didn't say that,' said Harry. 'I'm just saying that it's all a bit bloody weird. Could be connected, could be completely irrelevant. I'm just keeping things open. Anyway, he goes up to the field, finds his mate in a pretty poor state of repair, calls the police. Then he gets jumpy and does a runner. Am I missing anything?'

'All bases covered,' Jim said.

'How long before the circus turns up?'

Jim checked his watch. 'Another half hour I'd say.'

'You okay to wait here and direct everyone up to the field?' Harry asked, looking at Liz.

'I know where it is,' Liz said. 'Shouldn't be a problem.'

'Right then,' Harry said, looking at Jim. 'I want the rest of the team over here as soon as possible. We need house-to-house in the local area, and I want us to start tracing Capstick's last few days if we can. Oh, and someone contact his GP.'

'GP?' Jim asked. 'Why?'

'Something Matt said earlier about suicide,' Harry said. 'I get what he meant about it not being the usual way to do it, but stress can really bugger someone up. And someone's medical history can tell you a lot about them.'

Harry stepped outside. 'Come on then, Jim,' he said. 'Let's go and have another look around, shall we?'

'At the field? But what's there to look at?' Jim asked.

'Well,' said Harry, 'if Nick did receive a text, then there's got to be a phone lying about somewhere, hasn't there?'

CHAPTER SEVEN

BACK IN THE FIELD, HARRY WAS SURPRISED TO FIND another vehicle parked up next to the police Land Rover, which had been moved down towards the entrance into the field by the road. Matt was standing by it.

Harry could see that Matt had done a good job of cordoning off the site, pinning the tape down on the grass with rocks. He'd even managed to lay out a route in and out of the site to avoid contamination of the crime scene. It hadn't done much to improve it though. If anything, it had added to the grimness of it all, the tape standing out against the landscape, a sign that here, amongst the beauty, was something pretty bloody terrible indeed.

The vehicle next to the police Land Rover was a black Discovery. Like the Land Rover, Harry saw that it was covered in its fair share of muck and mud, but unlike the Land Rover, it looked comfortable and worth way more than he could ever afford to spend on a vehicle. Hell, it looked worth more than he'd happily spend on a new flat.

'So who the hell is that, then?' Harry asked, winding

down his window to snarl at Matt. 'I mean, this isn't a bring-a-friend party, is it? Or do folk around here just like to turn up and have a look-see at a crime scene, whether they're invited to or not?'

'It's Mike,' Matt said. 'One of the local GPs. I thought you called him?'

'And why the hell would I do that?'

'Confirm death?'

Harry pursed his lips and took a long, slow and particularly deep breath.

'How's about you think about what you just said and try that again,' he said. 'And bear in mind what a live person looks like, so, you know, like you and me and Jim here. And then think about what a dead person looks like, particularly one who's been run over by a tractor and then left out in the sun for a couple of days.'

'You mean you didn't call him?' Matt asked.

'No, I bloody well did not!' Harry roared, biting on his words as he said them. 'It's not like he's needed, is it? Poor old Capstick is a bit beyond CPR and a couple of sodding paracetamol!'

Jim turned the engine off. 'Maybe Nick called him?'

'I specifically said for people to go to the farmhouse first,' Harry seethed. 'Otherwise, this place is just going to end up like a car park at a National Trust site, and before you know it, Matt here'll be charging for parking, and someone will turn up with a burger van!'

'He's a doctor, though,' Jim said. 'Might be useful? And you said you wanted someone to contact John's GP.'

'Look, we've the pathologist on her way already,' Harry sighed, 'And we all know what a pleasure Rebecca Sowerby is to deal with, don't we? We need him gone, you hear? Or she'll simply use this as a grenade to shove where I'd rather she didn't.'

The last time Harry had to deal with her they hadn't exactly got along. And he was already not exactly looking forward to experiencing her particularly spiky approach to developing a good working relationship again.

Harry stared up towards the crime scene. 'So just where exactly is this good doctor, then?'

Harry didn't give Matt a chance to answer and, climbing out of Jim's vehicle, headed straight off up across the field and towards the grisly remains of the late John Capstick.

Matt made to follow but Harry turned on him and stared hard.

'No, you stay here. Scene Guard, remember?' He looked to Jim. 'You got something that'll do the job as the log?'

Jim and Matt both pulled out their notebooks.

'Right,' Harry said, 'names, occupations, times in and out, okay? And as soon as people start arriving, Jim, you take over as Scene Guard. Matt, you get to come up and start using that fancy new detective qualification you're so proud of.'

Matt and Jim both gave firm nods which helped Harry feel a little more confident that things were in control. Then he turned away and headed up the field, muttering to himself, 'Now let's go and see what this doctor has to say for himself, shall we?'

In the distance, Harry spotted the doctor. He was standing on the right side of the police cordon tape, which was at least something, Harry thought.

As Harry drew close, the man turned to meet him. He was tall, Harry noticed, taller than himself by a couple of inches, and altogether exceptionally neat. He was dressed well, inasmuch as he was wearing a pair of good leather shoes, and the kind of trouser, shirt, and jacket combo Harry only ever saw in the expensive clothing catalogues which were sometimes pushed through the door to his flat back in Bristol. He looked fit, too, not bulked up, but wiry, like a runner or a climber, his clothes fitting him well enough in places to show that beneath them lay muscle. He was also not only clean-shaven but completely bald. As to his age, Harry wasn't so sure, but he'd have put him at around fifty, though it was the kind of fifty that he could only ever dream of achieving himself, because Harry figured that when he hit fifty, he would do so with all the weight and care of an out of control articulated truck and make a right proper mess of it.

'Michael Smith,' the man said, placing a worn leather doctor's bag onto the ground. 'I'm the local doctor. Well, one of them. My colleague is back at the surgery.'

Harry reached out with his right hand, expecting a handshake, only to see that the doctor had done the same, only with his left hand instead.

'Sorry,' he said, 'an old wrist injury! And there's nothing worse than a limp handshake, am I right?'

Harry couldn't agree more and swapped hands. The doctor's grip was strong, the smile warm and genuine, and the accent clearly one that said more about where the man had been educated than where he had grown up.

'Grimm,' Harry said.

'Yes, it is rather,' the doctor agreed. 'Can't say I've ever seen anything quite like it if I'm honest.'

Harry smiled. 'No, sorry, I mean that's me, Harry Grimm.'

Harry saw a fleeting look of disbelief flicker across the doctor's face, which then broke into realisation.

'Really? Goodness, I thought that was just someone having me on when I first heard it, your name, I mean.'

'A face like mine usually has the opposite effect,' Harry said.

'IED?'

Harry gave a surprised nod.

'I was army reserve for a while,' the doctor said. 'Did a couple of tours.'

'Para,' Harry said. 'Long time ago now.' He gestured at the body just away from them both on the other side of the tape. 'Don't think we need you to confirm that he's dead, do you?'

'No, not really,' said the doctor. 'Hell of a way to go, though. Any idea what happened?'

Harry declined to answer the question, thinking it best to keep any ideas to himself and his team. Not that he really had any, but sometimes just pretending that he might was enough to keep people on their toes. Instead, he asked, 'Who called you?'

'Nicholas Ellis,' the doctor said. 'Sounded in a real panic so I rushed up here. Didn't tell me what I was going to find, though, just that there had been an accident. I thought he would be here. I didn't expect all of this. You know, you, as in the police.'

'Nicholas Ellis?' Harry said, then realised who the doctor was talking about. 'Oh, right, Little Nick, or whatever he's called.'

'Where is he?'

'No idea,' Harry said. 'Buggered off. So, you knew the deceased?'

'Of course,' the doctor said. 'Comes with the job. I know everyone just about.'

'And what was he like?'

'John Capstick?' The doctor stuffed his hands deep into his pockets and took a long slow breath. 'Accident prone,' he said at last. 'Always knocking and cutting himself or ending up in accident and emergency and getting a cast or stitches. And he had his own problems.'

'How so?'

'Patient confidentiality,' the doctor said. 'Can't really say any more, I'm afraid.'

'He's dead,' Harry said.

'My oath isn't,' the doctor replied.

Harry looked at the doctor and saw that behind the warm smile was a harder edge. Professional.

'When did you last see him?' Harry asked.

The doctor glanced at his watch. 'Look, I need to head off. Got a full day of appointments. It's always busy on a Monday. People seem to save up their aches and pains over the weekend!'

'I'd like to have a chat later,' Harry said. 'If that's okay?'

'Stop by the surgery,' the doctor said, turning to head off back down the field towards Matt and Jim.

'Before you go,' Harry said, 'I need you to keep what you've seen to yourself for now.'

'Of course,' the doctor said, pausing mid-stride.

'This is, as you can see, a crime scene,' Harry explained. 'You shouldn't even be here. And right now the last thing I need is for anything to get out about what's happened. Not until we actually know what happened, if you know what I mean.'

'It's not me you should be concerned about,' the doctor said.

Harry realised immediately what the doctor was referring to. Or, to be more exact, to whom. 'Nick? He's a problem?'

The doctor gave a nod. 'Loves a rumour. And if he can spread it nice and thin, he will.'

'Bollocks,' Harry said.

'Very much so,' said the doctor. 'Perhaps see you later, then?'

Harry waved the doctor off, calling for him to speak with Matt and Jim before leaving, and get signed off the site, then swung around again to look at John Capstick.

The body wasn't exactly improving any, and the flies and wasps were thick, the sound of them a constant buzzing murmur in the air of life feasting on death. He saw no sign of a phone, either by the body or anywhere nearby. And with the pathologist, the CSI team, and the rest, all on their way, he didn't want to go around disturbing the crime scene any more than it already was. But a text sent to someone from a very clearly dead body? It was going to bother him, that was for sure. And he knew he needed to speak to this Little Nick.

Harry looked up from the body and around the field, at the tree just away from where he now stood, its branches home to fat pigeons cooing at the day, then to the barn in the far righthand corner. It all looked so normal and so picturesque and yet there was a mystery here, wasn't there? he thought. And it wasn't just the fact that there was someone dead in the middle of it all either.

'So, John,' Harry muttered to the corpse, 'just how the hell did you send a text to someone when you're dead?' And then he added, just in case, 'And if it's all the same with you, I'd prefer it if you didn't sit up and tell me right now.'

CHAPTER EIGHT

THE CIRCUS, AS HARRY HAD REFERRED TO IT, ALL turned up at once. Which wasn't exactly helpful. Harry was already massively aware that as crime scenes went, this one was pretty awful. What with a body left out to the elements and more than a little nibbled at by nature, the area around it disturbed not just by the weather but numerous animals with the midnight munchies, finding any evidence at all was going to be difficult if not impossible. The one plus was that it hadn't rained, so if there was anything of use, it wouldn't have been washed away. But as positives went, it was a pretty poor one and leaned dangerously close to being a negative.

'Sorry, boss,' Matt said, racing up ahead of the seemingly large crowd of people now crawling into the field. The only thing pausing them on their way was Jim who was at the gate doing his best to give some sense of order to the proceedings as the Scene Guard.

'Not your fault,' Harry said, then gazing past, spotted someone right at the front of the crowd, making their way up towards them with the kind of frighteningly relentless power of an out of control steam train. 'And who's this?'

As the person drew closer, Harry could see now that it was a woman. She was wearing, of all things, a plain blue cassock, which billowed around her Wellington-boot clad feet, which only served to remind Harry that he really had to get some for himself. She already had PPE covering her boots, gloves on her hands, and was still struggling with a facemask when she arrived.

'Well?' the woman said when she finally came to stand in front of Harry. 'Where is it, then?'

'And you are?' Harry asked, stepping back a little from the woman, who was red in the face from the walk up to them from the road, and carrying a ragged looking rucksack over her back.

'Divisional Surgeon,' the woman said, finally managing to get the mask over her face. 'Margaret Shaw. And you're probably wondering why I'm dressed like this.'

'No, not at all,' Harry said, shaking his head unconvincingly.

'I'm a lay reader at the local parish church in Askrigg,' Margaret said. 'This turned up this morning and it's the third I've had delivered in a month, and none of them fit properly!'

She pulled at the blue material which Harry could now see was more than a little tight in all the places it shouldn't be and none of the places it should.

'See? This one doesn't fit either! Blasted thing! Call came in to come over here and I couldn't get it off, could I? And I wasn't about to set to it with a pair of scissors. I want a refund! I ask you, how difficult can it be to make what is little more than a sack with sleeves attached, fit the average human body?'

Harry didn't quite know what to say or indeed where to look. The woman was of average height, but a little on the larger size, and the cassock wasn't doing anything to help, looking as it did like it had been put together with no reference to the human anatomy whatsoever.

'We've not met before?' Harry said, phrasing the statement as a question.

'Not exactly, no,' the woman said, still pulling at the cassock and wriggling uncomfortably. 'I was at Semerwater a few weeks ago, can't remember how many, there was a body found on the shore. You were off busy with something I'm sure. I just sort of turn up, point at the body and say, *Yep, they're dead*, then bugger off.' She stretched, and this time everyone heard a ripping sound. 'Well, that didn't sound good, did it?'

'It's probably nothing,' Matt said, but glanced at Harry and mouthed *it really isn't*.

'I'm not usually this busy,' said the surgeon. 'Not exactly a place rife with murder and intrigue, the dales. But, here we are, once again! Now, where is it?'

Harry nodded just up and away from them, over the police cordon tape, and towards the body.

'Ah yes,' said Margaret. 'The flies are a bit of a giveaway, aren't they? Come on then, let's get this done.'

Harry lifted the tape up to allow the surgeon through, and followed behind, telling Matt to hang back, if only to delay the rest of the entourage now coming up behind them.

At the body, Margaret let out a long, slow whistle. 'Enough to put you off your lunch, isn't it?'

Harry let her do her job in checking the body, which took all of thirty seconds. 'Dead then?' he asked.

'I bloody well hope so,' Margaret replied. 'Don't think I'd

survive seeing him get up and ask me the way to the nearest chemist for a Band-Aid, do you?'

Harry found himself warming to the surgeon. She was clearly someone who spoke first and thought later, but probably without much of the thinking, because she had the air about her of someone who had done so much thinking in her time that when she spoke, she absolutely expected everyone to listen.

'Well, I'll be off, then,' Margaret said, making her way back to the tape. 'Need to get this blasted thing off somehow, fix whatever seam my fat arse just split, and get it sent back. I'm pretty sure God doesn't care whether I wear this or not, but the church is a stickler for protocols and silly uniforms.'

'I hope you get your money back,' Harry said.

'Oh, I will,' the woman said, then having seen who was approaching, she turned and leaned in close to Harry and added, 'good luck with the pathologist.'

Harry's heart sank as he looked past the surgeon to see Rebecca Sowerby striding towards them. She was, just like the rest of the CSI team now approaching, fully dressed up in PPE, the white paper suits making them look like ghosts. 'You know her, then?'

'She's my daughter,' Margaret said, and gave the wickedest wink Harry had ever received in his life.

Harry took a moment, then said, 'Sowerby's her married name, then?'

'Oh, good god no!' Margaret said, the words barking out of her like the cry of a startled wolf. 'Can you imagine? I'm the one who got married! Three times, actually! Seems I can't get enough of it. Anyway, have fun, inspector!'

And with that, she was gone.

Harry watched as Margaret Shaw tacked her way down

the field towards the entrance, and he was put in mind of a galleon sailing off into battle. She paused briefly to chat with her daughter, reached over with an enormous hug, which judging by the reaction it received clearly made Rebecca feel very awkward, then was on her way again.

Harry stepped outside the cordon tape just as Rebecca arrived.

'If this is as much of a shit show as last time . . .' the pathologist said.

'Oh, it's worse,' said Harry. 'Your mother seems nice, by the way. Apple fell far from the tree, did it?'

The face Rebecca then presented to Harry was one of a mix of emotions all fighting for dominance and none of them quite winning. Which made Harry feel a little warm inside.

When they'd first met a few weeks ago, on the shore of Lake Semerwater, following the discovery of the body of local woman, Martha Hodgson, the pathologist had put Harry's back up immediately. And it was pretty clear now to Harry that hadn't been a one-off.

'Where's the body?'

'I'm pretty sure you can see where for yourself,' Harry said, and held up the tape to let Rebecca through, who pulled her mask on and made her way over to the body.

Harry followed as a call came out from behind.

'Hold up!'

Harry and Rebecca turned to watch someone else dressed all in white duck under the tape and jog over.

'He's the photographer,' Matt called over, though that was more than obvious from the equipment the person was carrying.

The photographer came to stand with Harry and Rebecca. 'How long have I got?'

'How long do you need?' Harry asked.

The photographer glanced over Harry's shoulder. 'I'll be taking photos and a video, so maybe ten minutes here, then I can move on down and cover the rest.'

'Right you are,' Harry said, then turned to Rebecca. 'While he's doing that, I can brief you on what we found so far if you want? Might give you a bit of context.'

Rebecca gave a sharp nod and Harry led her back to where Matt was standing. As he did so, something caught his eye, the sparkle of sunshine glinting in the distance, from down among the few houses of Oughtershaw. Harry stared at it.

'What's up?' Matt asked, turning to look where Harry was gazing.

'You see that?' Harry asked.

'See what?'

Harry used his whole hand, held flat and vertical, instead of just a finger, to point, a habit he'd picked up in the Paras and never been able to quite drop. A finger in the middle of a firefight wasn't really very noticeable, but a whole hand was considerably clearer.

The glint came again.

'That,' Harry said.

'It's just the sun reflecting off something,' Rebecca said.

Harry wasn't so sure and called behind them for the photographer. 'You got a zoom lens?'

'Of course.'

'Have a look at that glint over there if you can. Tell me what you see.'

The photographer quickly changed the lens on his camera.

'See anything?'

'Not sure,' the photographer said, then, 'Yep. Got it.'

'Well?' Harry asked. 'What is it?'

'Someone definitely has eyes on us,' the photographer said.

Harry folded his arms and stared down towards the village, giving the okay for the photographer to get back to the job in hand.

'Matt?'

The detective sergeant glanced at Harry.

'I want you to keep Ms Sowerby company for a while. And keep an eye out for a phone, okay?'

'No problem. Where are you off to?'

'I'm going to catch me a spy,' Harry said.

CHAPTER NINE

HARRY WALKED OUT OF THE FIELD, JUST IN TIME TO hear the musical lilt of a female Scottish accent call over to him with the words, 'Aye, that's right, you may as well bugger off home, now that we're here to get on with the real work.'

Harry looked to where the voice had come from to see two women approaching him: Detective Inspector Gordanian 'Gordy' Haig and Detective Constable Jenny Blades.

Harry gave a wave as they approached.

'Busy here, isn't it?' Gordy said, coming to stand in front of Harry, and gazing around to take in the scenery. 'And it's not like there's much to see. Oughtershaw isn't exactly a tourist attraction, now, is it?'

'Not even a pub,' Harry said with a smile, remembering Matt's observation.

Jenny said, 'The DSup is on his way. Can't say he sounded too happy about it either.'

Harry's mind was suddenly filled with the face of his new temporary boss, Detective Superintendent Graham

Swift, and he quickly pulled Gordy and Jenny to one side. The man was already somehow convinced that Harry had brought with him an air of bad luck, seeing as there had been a murder within days of him arriving in Hawes. Another in less than a month would, Harry figured, have the man convinced he was the devil himself.

'Liz, as you already know, is at the house. Jim's on the gate working as Scene Guard, and Matt's up where the body is, keeping an eye on things and hopefully out of the way.'

'So what do you want us to do?' Gordy asked. 'Not that I've got long as I'm expected over in Harrogate on another case later on.'

'We've probably got time to go grab some coffee if you want?' Jenny added. 'It'll be cold by the time we get back, like, but it's the thought that counts, isn't it?'

'You're on door-to-door,' Harry said. 'I can't be arsed with waiting for any uniform to turn up. It's not like the dales is overrun with available police staff, is it? And I'm not going to have us standing around for when Swift turns up to get in the way. It won't take long. It's not exactly a big place, but someone might have seen or heard something.'

'What've we actually got?' Gordy asked.

Harry gave them a quick run-through of what was up in the field. Their expressions were enough to tell Harry that he'd laid it on just thick enough with his description to give them a fair idea of what had happened.

'Hell of a way to go,' Jenny said.

'You could say that,' said Harry. 'What do you know of the deceased?'

Gordy said, 'Not much, but then I've not been around here as long as everyone else. All I know is that he had a bit of a rum reputation. Wasn't liked, that kind of thing.'

'Jenny?' Harry asked, knowing that, like Jim, she'd lived in the area her whole life, so perhaps had a little more to offer.

'Let's just put it this way,' Jenny said. 'The problem we're going to have is finding someone who *didn't* have a motive.'

'You what?' Harry asked, a little shocked to hear such a response. 'There's a big difference between being not liked and everyone wanting you dead!'

Jenny gave a shrug. 'Look, I'm not saying that people actually wanted him dead.'

'Well, you kind of just did,' Gordy said. 'Even used the word motive, if I'm recalling it right, which I am, seeing as it was, ooh, ten seconds ago at best?'

'So what are you saying?' Harry asked. 'Be a bit more specific. People really had it in for him?'

Jenny was quiet for a moment, then looked over at Harry and said, 'Let's just say that come the funeral, the church will be pretty bloody empty, that's for sure.'

'That's not exactly being specific, is it?' Harry said. 'And there's an ocean of difference between not showing up to wave him off to whatever fate awaits him on the other side and crushing him with a tractor and trailer!'

'Perhaps I spoke out of turn,' Jenny said.

'Aye, perhaps,' Gordy said, an eyebrow raised just enough.

With nothing else to say, Harry quickly sent Jenny and Gordy off to go knocking on doors. It was the simplest of all police work, so he was rather pleased to see that Gordy was happy to head off and get cracking, but then she probably knew as well as he did that it usually brought something in. Not always evidence as such, but it often added colour to the setting of the crime, a local flavour. And getting that first-hand was always an advantage.

The glinting which Harry had noticed from the field was gone by the time he got to where he'd seen it come from, which was a large house set back from the road a little, behind a verge of grass. It was obviously a farm, judging by the stack of black-plastic covered bales in front of it on the grass.

Harry went up to the front door and gave a hard, sharp knock, then waited.

Nothing.

Harry looked around the door for any sign of a bell, couldn't see one, so knocked again.

Still nothing.

Harry, working to keep his frustration under control, not just from being spied on, but now from being ignored, raised his fist to knock again, when a voice called out from a driveway leading around to the right of the house. It was quickly followed by a deep, threatening growl, which had an almost prehistoric, flesh-eating monster echo to it.

Turning towards the sound, Harry was met with the sight of a man who seemed to be built entirely of rage, his face a thing of thunder. He was wearing the uniform of the dales farmer: Wellington boots, scruffy denim trousers, and a shirt rolled up to just above the elbows. But what Harry's eyes were drawn to was the huge hound on the end of a thick leash clasped in the man's meaty hands.

'Who the bloody hell are you?'

Harry went to introduce himself, but the man got in first.

'You the police? You don't look like the police, but I bet that's what you are, right? The police? Up here in t' field with that lot, aren't you? And what's up with your face?

Right bloody mess, that. What happened? Fall into a baler or something?'

'I'm Detective Chief Inspector Grimm,' Harry said, but declined to say anything to answer the man's last question.

He didn't move towards the man and his beast of a dog, but instead waited for them to approach him. It gave him time to assess the situation and be a little more in control of it. It was also a little more passive, because here in front of him was a man clearly looking for a confrontation, and Harry figured striding up to him with purpose would only make matters worse.

'Never heard of him,' the man said. 'You must be here about Capstick, am I right?'

Harry was a little taken aback. 'How do you mean?'

'Capstick. Dead I reckon. Up in t' field, like. Couldn't happen to a nicer man, I'll tell you that for nowt.'

Harry gave a nod, hearing the thick slice of disdain in the man's voice. 'Yes,' he said. 'It's about Mr Capstick.'

The dog growled again. God, the thing was massive. Harry could see that it clearly had Rottweiler in there somewhere, which would be reason enough for the size of the thing's head: it was more bear than hound. But it wasn't a purebred, and Harry guessed that whatever else was mixed up in the genes was also probably huge, hungry, and originally designed to scare off humans. Or eat them. Perhaps both.

'About bloody time, if you ask me,' the man said. 'Not that I wish ill on anyone, like, but Capstick was a nasty old bugger.'

Harry asked, 'Can we go inside, please? I have some questions.'

'I bet you bloody well do,' the man said. 'And I'll prob-ably have a few of my own.'

And with that, the man made for Harry with such speed and intent that Harry only just managed to step out of the way in time as he made his way up to the front door.

'Best you come in for a brew,' the man said, then he pointed ahead, down the hall, towards an open door. 'Through there. I'll join you in a minute. And don't mind the dog. He'll only bite if I tell him to.'

The dog stared up at Harry, the look in its eyes not exactly convincing him that it gave a stuff about what the man did or didn't tell it to do, and wouldn't just eat him anyway, just for the fun of it.

'What's it called?' Harry asked, following the man and his dog into his house. 'The dog?'

'Steve,' the man said, and with that, he walked off, disap-pearing with the hound into the darkness beyond.

CHAPTER TEN

HARRY WALKED DOWN THE HALL AND ON THROUGH THE door to find himself in a large kitchen which had clearly not been decorated since the 1970s, even down to the lurid wallpaper.

A door slammed shut somewhere else in the house and Harry was just staring out of the window, which sat above the sink, when the man entered the room.

'Unusual,' Harry said.

'What is?'

'Steve,' Harry said. 'As a dog's name, I mean.'

'Is it?' the man replied. 'It's a name, isn't it? And it's not some stupid bollocks like Fleck or Fly or whatever else folk seem to want to call their dogs. Wife wanted to call him Tiny, but I was having none of that, like. Steve? It's a proper name, isn't it? Tiny! I ask you! I mean, you've seen him. He's huge! So why would I call him Tiny? I wouldn't, would I?'

Harry shook his head pretty sure there was no arguing with the man. 'Is your wife home?'

'Out,' the man said. 'Put the kettle on, then! Tea won't brew itself, you know.'

Before Harry knew what he was doing, he had filled the kettle and switched it on.

'Biscuits are up there,' the man said, pointing at a cupboard, 'teabags are on the side by the teapot. Milk's in the fridge.'

The man sat down at the large dining table, which took up the centre of the room. Harry, with little option now but to just go with the flow and make the tea, grabbed the biscuits and, by sheer luck, opened the cupboard with mugs in it, removing two and placing them by the kettle.

Once the tea was made, Harry sat down at the table, opposite the man. 'Here you go,' he said, handing a mug over. 'Hope it's drinkable.'

The man stared suspiciously into the mug, then took a lengthy slurp, the sound of it as loud as water draining down a plug hole.

'Well, looks like you make a decent brew, so that's something,' he said. 'I'd heard southerners liked it all weak and flavoured with almond milk or whatever other kind of nonsense you can get now instead of actual real proper milk.'

Harry took a sip from his own, nibbled a biscuit. 'The accent gave me away, then?'

'Just a bit,' the man said.

'I didn't catch your name,' Harry replied.

'Well, you wouldn't have, because I didn't give it, did I?' The man blew at his tea, then took a gulp. 'I don't go around handing out money to strangers, so why would I give my name out as well?'

Harry was sure there was logic in there somewhere, but

he didn't have time to look for it. 'Well, we're not strangers now, are we?'

The man harrumphed. 'I suppose not. Name's Dinsdale. Bill Dinsdale.'

'So, Bill,' Harry began, 'can I ask why you were having a look at us from here with your binoculars?'

'I haven't got any binoculars,' Bill said.

'The sun caught the lens,' Harry explained. 'I spotted it from the field. You were looking out from one of the windows upstairs.'

'That bit's true, but I wasn't using binoculars. Don't have any. Do I look like someone who goes sight-seeing and bird watching? Do I bollocks, like!'

Harry took another sip, if only to try and gather his thoughts. Bill here was certainly an interesting character to deal with. Harry had the impression the man wasn't about to offer any information up without it being prised from him first. 'So, can I ask why you were looking out over the field?'

'I used my scope,' Bill said, ignoring Harry's question. Then he stood up, grabbed some keys from a hook on the wall, and disappeared through the kitchen door, only to return a minute or so later with a rifle, on top of which was sat the kind of scope that Harry figured any sniper would be proud to own.

'You looked at us through that?' Harry asked.

'Don't worry, it wasn't loaded,' Bill said, his words curling around a laugh. 'And it's all kept under lock and key. And my firearms licence is up to date. I'm not a total bloody fool, you know!'

'There's a need for that around here, is there?' Harry asked. 'A firearm, I mean.'

'Why else would I have it?' Bill asked. 'It's only a two-

two calibre, nowt too powerful. Much better for rabbits and pigeons and crows than an air rifle.'

Bill rested the rifle on the dining room table.

'You've not answered my question,' Harry said.

'I knew something was up,' Bill said. 'Saw John had smashed up his tractor. Not the first time, neither. Couldn't be arsed with going over to be told it was none of my business, either. So thought I'd just have a look. There a law against that?'

Harry knew full well that there were plenty of laws about where exactly you should and shouldn't point a firearm, but now wasn't the time.

'The accident isn't visible from the road,' Harry said. 'How did you notice it?'

'Upstairs bathroom,' Bill said. 'Had to open the window, if you know what I mean. Breakfast came back at me with a vengeance, but that just serves me right for having bacon and eggs. I'm not supposed to, but I was hungry, wasn't I? The stink was thick enough to carve with a knife.'

Harry got the picture and very much wished that he hadn't.

'Right, so you saw it from upstairs, then?'

'Which was where you saw me earlier, with the rifle scope. Heard all the noise, thought I'd have a gander at all you lot.'

'So, was there a reason why you didn't go to see John after you'd noticed the accident?'

'Like I said, it's not the first time something like this has happened,' Bill said. 'And if I'd spent my life going to see if he was alright after every prang that he'd had, then I'd have never got my own work done now, would I? I've my own farm to be worrying about, you see, and helping someone like old Capstick generally comes back and bites you on the arse.'

Harry asked, 'Did you notice anything else, last week, or over the weekend, at all? At his house, out in the fields?'

'So, he is dead then, is he? Thought so. Knew you lot were over there for a reason, like.'

Harry neither confirmed nor denied it, but knew his silence was enough. 'All I can say right now is that there's been a very serious incident,' he said. 'And myself, and my fellow officers are now attempting to collect as much information as we can to find out what actually happened.'

'Fancy way of saying that old git is dead,' Bill mumbled to himself as much to Harry. 'So, how did he die, then?'

'I'm afraid I can't provide any further information,' Harry said.

'Well, however it happened, Capstick had it coming, that's for sure.'

'How do you mean?' Harry asked.

'The man was born with a mean streak in him as wide as the Ure!' Bill said.

'Ure?'

'The river that runs through Wensleydale. You should see it when it's in full spate after a storm. Terrifying! You should've met his dad, though. Even worse! You've seen the farm? Awful, isn't it? Total bloody disgrace!'

'So, did you notice anything?' Harry asked again. 'Anything suspicious? Any visitors? Anything in the way John behaved?'

Bill leaned back in his chair and knocked his head back to drain his mug of tea. Then he leaned forward on his elbows, his huge, weathered hands clasped together. 'Suspicious? Everything Capstick did was suspicious!' he said, anger creasing the corners of his mouth as he spoke. 'There's not a farm around here that hasn't lost something to Capstick. Never any proof, mind, but stuff went missing. Bits of equipment, deliveries, even stock. We all knew it was him, but nowt was ever found so he just got away with it. Usually flogged the stuff we reckon. Not daft enough to rub our noses in it. Better to have some cash.'

'He was a thief?'

'He was a bastard!' Bill said. 'And a right proper one at that. If you ask me, the dale's better off with him out of it! Just a pity it hadn't been sooner rather than later, like.'

Harry finished his own tea, then stood up. 'Look, I'll be sending a couple of my officers around to ask a few more questions, take a statement. I hope that's okay. It's just routine. But best you have that rifle of yours locked away before they come around.'

'I'm not a total bloody idiot!' Bill snapped, rising from his chair and grabbing the rifle. 'You leaving, then?'

Harry gave a sharp nod and made his way back out into the hall and towards the front door.

'You want to find out what happened, then best you speak to La'll Nick,' Bill said. 'He'll know. If you want suspicious, that's right where it is, I'll tell you that. Gossip and rumour spin around him like a whirlpool of shite.'

Harry stopped, turned. 'Why's that?'

'Saturday morning, around six I think,' Bill said, his voice lowering to a conspiratorial whisper. 'I mean, I was pretty surprised to see John up that early as it was, and heading out into the field, and all, but with Nick as well?' He gave a conspiratorial nod, then tapped the side of his nose with a finger and pointed at Harry. 'He'll know what happened.'

'You mean he was there?' Harry asked, wondering why

Bill had said nothing earlier when he'd specifically asked if the man had seen anything strange.

Bill shrugged. 'There were two of them in the cab,' he said. 'Saw them drive up into the field, didn't I? I was off on a walk around with the gun, you see. Me and Steve do that most Saturday mornings, like.'

'You mean you saw the accident?'

'I didn't see anything!' Bill growled. 'All I'm saying is that I saw two people in that cab driving up into the field. And Nick's the only bugger on earth who'd be with John, so it wouldn't be anyone else, would it?'

Harry really wanted to find Nick now more than ever, and reached out for the front door. 'Thanks for your time,' he said, stepping out into the day once again.

'No need to thank me,' Bill said. 'I went to school with Capstick. Never liked him then. Never liked him since. I'm not usually one to wish ill of the dead, but with him, I'll make an exception. And I'm not the only one, you'll find that out, soon enough.'

Harry stepped away from the house as Bill closed the door behind him. He then stared back up the road to where he could see the field where John Capstick had been found. A white tent had been erected over where the body lay, and little white-suited bodies moved around it like maggots crawling over a carcass.

Harry's phone buzzed. 'Grimm,' he answered.

It was Matt.

'We've found something, boss.'

'What?' Harry asked, moving off quickly now, back towards the field. 'The phone?'

'No,' Matt said. 'A feather. Stuffed in Capstick's mouth.'

CHAPTER ELEVEN

Back at the field, Harry was met at the gate by a group of stern faces, two of which looked about as happy to see him as he would be a toenail in his breakfast cereal. The sky was darkening, and the wind was certainly getting up. So much for the nice weather then, Harry thought, smelling rain in the air.

'Ah, Grimm,' Detective Superintendent Graham Swift said, stepping in front of Harry as he made his way into the field. 'So there you are. I was beginning to wonder if we'd lost you for good.'

The way the man said it, Harry was pretty sure there was a little hint of hope in the words.

'Sir,' Harry said, offering no explanation as to where he'd been, his attention drawn to the woman beside Swift.

'DC Metcalfe tells me you've found something.'

'Does he, indeed?' said Rebecca Sowerby, the pathologist. 'And what would that be?'

'I was kind of hoping you would be able to tell me that,' Harry said.

'Well, it sounds like you already know, so . . .'

'A feather,' Harry said, cutting in before the pathologist could finish what she was saying. 'But what about a phone? Has one been found?'

Sowerby glowered for a moment at Matt, who was standing with Jim to one side, then was back on Harry.

'No phone,' the pathologist said. 'And to be honest, I'm surprised you didn't find the feather yourself!' The woman's eyes were as narrow as a hawk's. 'Do you have any idea how much potential damage you did to the crime scene? Why didn't you call it in immediately? From what I can see, you've walked up and down and around like you were all in a dance competition!'

Harry sucked in the deepest of breaths then let it out real slow through his nostrils. 'It was called in as soon as we regarded it as being potentially Category One.'

'And you couldn't tell that just by looking at the body?'

'The report we received was that there had been an accident. That's how the scene was initially approached. It was only after investigating that—'

The pathologist pulled out a transparent plastic bag. Inside it, Harry could just about make out a scrunched up lump of something, which looked moist and black and revolting.

'This was in his mouth,' she said, holding it up in front of Harry's face. 'No idea what species right now because, as you can see, it's a total mess. Like this crime scene.'

'We think whatever happened here occurred around two days ago,' Harry said. 'So everything has been out in the open ever since. If you want to blame anyone or anything for the mess, how's about you have a chat with some of the local wildlife? There's a few foxes and buzzards I'm sure who could give you a little run-through of just how tasty the victim is! Crows and pigeons, too, I'm sure, and they'll eat just about anything.'

'Enough, Grimm,' Detective Superintendent Swift said. 'Ms Sowerby is only trying to do her job.'

'And I'm only trying to do mine,' Grimm replied, his voice a guttural growl.

'She has every right to question how things are done, especially when working with someone new.'

'New?' Harry laughed. 'And what's that supposed to mean?'

'It means,' Swift said, 'that an experienced detective wouldn't have allowed someone who has nothing to do with a potential investigation to go wandering around a crime scene!'

'You mean Doctor Smith? He was here when we arrived!'

Rebecca Sowerby stowed the bag containing the feather away, frustration clear in her every move. 'The Scene of Crime officers will finish off and then I'll have the body over to do the autopsy,' she said, pushing past Harry to head towards the road.

'Think you'll find anything?' Harry asked.

'I always find something,' she replied. 'Always.' And was gone.

For a while, no one said anything. Harry could sense that Detective Superintendent Swift was continuing his grumbles in his head, but he didn't care. Jim and Matt were simply staring at him expectantly. Up in the field, things were starting to quieten down. Soon the body would be removed and would chase the pathologist back to Harrogate and into a sterile, stainless steel chilled freezer drawer in the mortuary.

Then there would be a final sweep of the scene to see if anything else could be found, and that would be that. The place would be off-limits to the public though for a good while, at least while the investigation was in its early stages. And that, Harry knew for certain, would be more than enough to bring the press sniffing around.

'This is just the kind of thing I was worried about,' Detective Superintendent Swift said, breaking the quiet.

'How do you mean?' Harry asked. 'It's not like I came here and murder followed me from Bristol like some stink on my shoes!'

'I didn't say that,' Swift replied, 'but if there's something I've learnt in my years on the force, it's that some people just attract the worst of it, if you know what I mean.'

'No, I don't,' Harry said.

'And that's the problem,' Swift snapped.

Harry breathed deep, searching for some calm so that when he spoke next, his voice didn't give the senior officer cause to think he was about to rip his head off. 'I'm the senior investigating officer on this and I know what I'm doing,' Harry explained. 'As do the team. They're good. You have nothing to worry about.'

'Then convince me,' Swift hissed. Then he, too, was gone.

Matt and Jim shuffled forward.

'So where did you go, then?' Matt asked.

Harry gestured over to Bill's house.

Jim said, 'Was Steve there to meet you?'

'You know him, then?' Harry asked. 'Bill, I mean.'

'Everyone knows pretty much everyone else around here,' Jim said. 'Bill's alright, though. Bit blunt, but that's just his way. And Steve is all mouth and no trousers, if you know what I mean. The worst that dog would do is lick you to death. Spoiled rotten.'

'Thought I saw someone looking at us in the field with binos,' Harry said. 'Turns out it was Bill through a rifle scope.'

'Just being nosy, then,' Matt said. 'He see anything?'

Harry was about to mention what Bill had said about seeing Little Nick in the tractor cab with John Capstick, when Gordy and Jenny turned up.

'Anything?' Harry asked.

Jenny pulled out her notebook and flipped it open. 'It's like I said before, no one is exactly queuing up to attend his funeral,' she said. 'Other than to cheer maybe.'

'Only reason I can see right now for anyone going,' Gordy added, 'is to make sure he's actually dead.'

'And Bill?' Harry asked. 'He say any more about seeing Little Nick with John?'

Liz read her notes out, which confirmed what Harry already knew.

'Not much is it?' Matt said.

'Well, I look forward to hearing more later on,' Gordy said. 'I'd best be off. But I'll be over tomorrow morning, first thing, if only to check up on the board.'

'No need,' Jenny said. 'I'll be all over it like a rash.'

'Let's hope we've got something to actually put on it, then,' Harry said, as Gordy walked off. 'It's not like we've got much so far, beyond the corpse of a man no one liked and a feather in his mouth.'

'At least it wasn't up his arse,' Matt added.

'Doubt we'll get much more, either,' Jim said. 'Been too long since whatever it was that happened, happened, if you know what I mean.'

'Hasn't rained yet, though,' Matt said. 'And that's something.'

Which was when the dark sky above gave up at last, and sent a grey sheet of rain to fold itself across the earth below.

Harry took another look at the field in front of them. The change in the weather had lit a new sense of urgency in the work of the SOC team and Harry could see that they were now hurrying to get as much evidence as they could before the rain washed away any possibility of finding even the faintest hint of DNA or anything else for that matter.

'Back to the office, then?' Harry suggested.

'First one there puts the kettle on,' Jim said.

'Last one there buys the cake,' Matt added with a hungry-looking grin.

CHAPTER TWELVE

THE DAY HAD ROLLED INTO EARLY EVENING WITHOUT Harry even noticing. And he hadn't yet even had a chance to visit his new flat to properly move in. The rain had chased them all the way back to the community office in Hawes, where the permanent police presence was housed all comfortable and cosy with, among other things, the local library and a community information hub. It was unlike any police station Harry had ever worked in because it wasn't really a police station. He wasn't one for getting all political, but it struck him as a bit dim-witted to think having interviews and cells and all the other police gubbins over an hour away in Harrogate made sense. Couldn't even lock someone up to allow them to cool off. Nope. Instead, they had to be driven all the way across the dale.

Imagine that, he thought, racing down all those twisty lanes and roads, with a van full of abusive pissheads, all vomiting up their liquid refreshment, when instead they could've been just given a room to sleep it off in all but a few steps away. Where was the sense in it? But Harry wasn't in politics and never would be. The world, he thought, was an increasingly angry, shouty place, and more and more the people in power were taking advantage of the popular vote, taking the easy route.

The world needed, in Harry's mind at least, a little bit more gentleness and understanding, which was exactly why he was never going to get involved. Yes, he knew that was what the world needed, but he also knew that he was some-what lacking in those areas. So he would do his bit where he fitted in best. As far as the resources in Hawes were concerned, they would have to do because that's all they had. And if he was honest, Harry didn't exactly miss the warren of rooms and corridors he was used to back at the station in Bristol, it was just a bit strange to not have them to get lost in if he wanted to.

'Here you go,' Matt said, handing Harry a mug of tea. 'Can't remember if you take sugar.'

'I don't,' Harry said. 'And before you say it, don't.'

'Wasn't about to,' Matt said. 'Me though, I'm never going to be sweet enough, so in goes a couple of teaspoons of the good stuff.' He shovelled in the sugar. 'And a couple more, just in case.'

Harry watched as Matt added enough sugar to his tea to keep a class of six-year-olds awake for a week.

'Sure you don't want any more?'

'No, I'm good, thanks,' said Matt, taking a sip. 'Yummy.'

Harry leaned back into his chair as around him the rest of the team busied themselves with getting comfortable. Gordy had managed to get back from whatever case had called her away earlier, and Liz had followed them over from the farmhouse, leaving the SOC team, and anyone else, to clear up after themselves and find their own ways home.

Matt was now slumped down in a chair and tapping away at a computer. Next to him was Jim, and Jenny was standing up in front of a whiteboard, which was bare except for a name in the very middle of it: John Capstick.

'So, what have we got?' Harry asked.

'About as much evidence as I've got for Nessie,' Gordy said. 'Anything from the CSI bods?'

The room fell silent.

'HOLMES is coming up with the usual ABA,' Matt said, pointing at the screen in front of him.

'ABA?' Harry asked. 'And what's that?'

'Absolutely bugger all.'

As acronyms went, the Home Office Large and Major Enquiry System, was a world-beater, Harry thought, and had often wondered how many focus groups and millions of pounds were spent coming up with it. Commissioned by the Home Office to provide a computer solution to the vast amount of data being held by the police across the country, it hadn't exactly gone smoothly. Numerous systems were developed by different companies and all implemented at different times, and the reassurances given by the smooth-talking salespeople had turned out to be little more than smoke and mirrors. Things had improved over the years, with different systems actually being able to communicate with each other, but it was still a monster to get to grips with. It was accessed through a private cloud service to ensure that individual forces could use it and security could be maintained.

Harry was pretty surprised to see Matt deftly searching through what HOLMES was, or wasn't, giving him. 'How do you mean?'

'Well,' Matt explained, 'we've got nothing really to lead

with, have we? No one saw anything, no one found anything, blah blah blah.'

'What about the pathologist?' Jim asked.

'She'll be on with the autopsy,' Harry said, 'though I doubt we'll hear much till tomorrow morning. She's not got an easy job of it, what with the state of the body.' He looked over at Jenny and Gordy. 'Anything from the door-to-door?'

'No one liked him,' Gordy said. 'And that's about it.'

Harry leaned back, letting his head fall so that he was staring at the ceiling. Then he pulled his head forward again to stare at the board in front of Jenny. 'Bill reckons he saw John driving up the field early Saturday morning, with Nick in the tractor cab. So, where the hell is he?'

'Still missing,' Jim said. 'No one's seen him.'

'So what do we know about him?' Harry asked. 'Friends? Family? What does he do?'

Liz jumped in. 'Nick's just a bit dodgy, I guess,' she said. 'One of those people who's always been around and always been into things that he shouldn't.'

'Like what?' asked Harry.

'Nothing big,' Liz said. 'He's been done a few times for possession, got beaten up once by a parent or two for supplying their kids with booze and a few joints, that kind of thing.'

'Rough justice, there, then,' Harry said.

'Yep, and no one was charged because he wasn't about to go grassing someone up, because then everyone would know and well, I guess he figured it was just easier to let it go.'

'Well,' Jim laughed, 'Wensleydale is a bit like the Wild West of Yorkshire! Oh, and the doctor dropped off John's medical stuff. Doesn't tell us much other than the fact that he was physically a bit of a mess, drank too much, didn't eat properly, was over-weight, and had a few broken bones.'

'Can't say I give a stuff about what the doctor dropped off,' Harry said, his voice growing louder, like the rumble of an approaching rockfall. 'We've got Bill's possible sighting of Nick, who just sounds dodgy anyway, with the deceased on Saturday morning. We know Nick found the body earlier today. And we've also got the message that he said he received from the deceased. Whatever his involvement, it isn't good, is it?'

Harry knew he was shouting, but it wasn't at anyone in the room, more at the situation they were facing.

'Remember that little fact?' he continued. 'The weird and impossible call from beyond the grave? It's not something someone would lie about, is it? And it's basically the single sodding reason we're here in the first place and why we had everyone out in the field today! We need Nick and his phone so that we can check that he actually received a call at all, and if he did, to see who the hell sent it. Because it's pretty bloody clear that Mr John Capstick didn't!'

Harry rose to his feet, weariness suddenly swooping in from all around and making him feel a little bit unsteady on his feet.

Jenny quickly wrote on the board about Bill seeing Nick on Saturday morning, the call Nick had supposedly received Monday from John, despite him being dead, and that Nick was still missing.

'Right now, I reckon we all need to sleep on it,' Harry yawned, moving away from his chair and resting his now empty mug on a table. 'Go home, all of you. Watch television. Have a beer. Come back tomorrow with fresh heads. By then, we should have at least something from the pathologist.

And I'll want a renewed effort on finding this mysterious Nick bloke.'

Harry was now at the door but before he left, he eyeballed everyone in the team.

'Let's not give old Swift any reason to think we can't handle this,' he said. 'We all know when something doesn't smell right, and John Capstick dead in a field doesn't, and not just for the obvious reason either. Nick knows something. That phone call doesn't sound right at all. And hopefully, we'll have something from the pathologist.'

Jim then asked, 'What about that feather?'

Jenny added that little nugget to the board.

'And there's that as well,' Harry said. 'Maybe when we know what species it is or whatever, we'll have something to go on, perhaps even some DNA. Anyway, get yourselves home and I'll see you in the morning.'

Harry made to leave, then something that had been said earlier about Nick resurfaced. He looked over at Liz. 'You said he deals a bit?'

Liz gave a nod.

'So I'm assuming there's somewhere around here folk go for a fly smoke, am I right?'

'Down by the beck,' Liz said. 'You know, the path between Gayle and Hawes? Why?'

'Might go for a little stroll later,' Harry said. 'You never know.'

It was a longshot, but he was happy to take it.

Harry left the office then, striding out into the evening with the purpose of a man whose energy has gone, but he still wasn't home, and the only thing moving him at all was the promise of a comfy sofa, a pizza, and a beer.

CHAPTER THIRTEEN

Harry's evening was a restless one, his mind caught between concerns for his brother, and pent up rage at their dad resurfacing, and the start of a case which already looked like it was going to be a pain in the arse. Right now, the whole thing was much like starting a jigsaw puzzle without any idea what the final picture was supposed to be. What they had so far didn't make much if any sense, but somewhere someone knew something, and Harry had to have faith in his team that they would get moving on it the following day.

Having grabbed a Pizza from the Spar in Hawes market-place, along with some essential items, like bread and milk, and some non-essential items, like a few beers and a couple of chocolate eclairs that had pretty much screamed at him to buy them, Harry had headed to his new flat, very much aware that his fare for the evening was in no way going to help his weight loss. But he didn't care. He was tired. He was hungry. And that was all there was to it.

Later, with the food demolished, along with a couple of beers, Harry found himself channel-surfing and getting increasingly annoyed with either dropping in on programmes already partway through, or into yet more adverts. There was only so much he could take of people buying things at antique fairs to sell at other antique fairs, of gameshows and cookery, and of sodding celebrities famous for being on programmes about being famous, for being on programmes about being famous. Which was when he remembered what Liz had said about the beck being a place used for sneaking a toke on a fat reefer. So, with all the energy he could muster, which wasn't much at all, Harry headed out to get some fresh air and hopefully a fresh perspective on what had happened that day.

The path he took was an ancient one. It slunk out of the middle of Hawes, just up a little hill from the cobbles which rode past Cockett's Butchers. It was a thing of old flagstones stitched into the earth, the path pinned into place by stone stiles, which allowed walkers through, but kept the sheep where they were meant to be. The path was, Harry thought, perhaps some ancient lifeline, no doubt having seen centuries of lives flowing along it between Hawes and Gayle. That evening, though, it was quiet, and Harry meandered along, working as best as he could to clear his mind and just relax a little.

Harry stopped.

For a moment, he wasn't sure why, but something had brought him up sharp. He stood statue-still, focusing, even though it was the last thing he actually wanted to do.

Then he caught it, just on the edge of wind slipping around him, a scent drifting up from his left, the slope which led down to Gayle Beck, a babbling brook with rocks carved into scalloped waves by thousands of years of moorland-born water dancing across them.

The smell was one Harry was used to catching back home on the streets of Bristol: pot, cannabis, weed, whatever you wanted to call it. Back there, it wasn't exactly smoked openly in public, more that there was just so much of it about, being enjoyed on balconies, in parks, in gardens, that you just couldn't get away from it. But here, it seemed a little out of place, and although Harry was pretty sure that he wasn't in the best frame of mind to go and have a word with someone sparking up a fat reefer, he knew there might be a slim chance of a lead on the, so far, highly elusive Little Nick. And anyway, deep down, he knew he couldn't let it lie, the sweet, perfumed scent of the stuff taking him years back, to his brother, and to what had sent him even more off the rails than he'd already been, to finally land him behind bars.

Down by the beck, Harry spotted a group of teenagers. They were sitting in a semi-circle on its edge, four girls, three boys. Two of the girls had their feet in the no doubt cold water. Standing in the middle of the group was a gangly looking teenager. Whatever he was talking about, it certainly required lots of arm movements, Harry noticed, as the boy laughed then pulled his left hand to his mouth, a few seconds later sending out a fat, grey plume of smoke.

Harry walked towards the group and when the boy in the middle spotted him, he raised a hand as a non-committal attempt at a greeting.

The rest of the group, seeing their friend pause his jigging around, turned to stare.

'Evening,' Harry said, bringing himself to a halt barely a metre away from the group.

No one spoke, just stared.

'Been out long?'

Still nothing.

The boy in the middle took another draw of the joint then exhaled theatrically, blowing the smoke up into the air.

'Something up, mate?' the boy said.

'I'm not your mate,' Harry said, a little more gruffly than he'd planned, but if he was honest, the effect was worth it, as the group looked suddenly a little more spooked, staring at him, at his face. So he curled his lip just a little, adding to the overall image of menace. It wasn't that he wanted to frighten them as such, but on the other hand, he didn't want them thinking that what they were doing was fine and dandy. Because it wasn't. And Harry had seen where all this could lead. A brother in prison was a fairly hefty reminder of the fact that drugs didn't actually pay.

'You got that right,' the boy said. 'What happened to your face?'

'Bear attack,' Harry said, not a hint of humour in his voice. 'Ripped it off in one swipe.'

A splutter of nervous giggles bounced around the group.

'Best you jog on then, before I make it even worse,' the boy said, displaying surprisingly more bravado and balls than Harry would have given him credit for, seeing as he was about as physically threatening as a streak of piss.

The other two boys high-fived each other, also very impressed.

Harry stared at the boy who was now clearly not only sporting a spliff, but also an attitude, and pulled something from his pocket to show him.

'What's that?'

'Look closely.'

The boy did exactly that.

'You're police?'

'Give the lad a coconut.'

'What?'

'A coconut. A prize, son.'

The lad took another fat drag from the spliff, then flicked it over his head and into the beck, before shoving his hands in his pockets.

'Nowt to see here, is there?' he said. 'And I'm not your son.'

Harry watched the now-dead spliff drift off down the beck towards the bridge just off in the distance. 'Can you tell me where you live?'

'Yes I can,' the boy said. 'But I'm not going to.'

'I think perhaps you should.'

'And I think perhaps you should piss off.'

Harry stuffed his ID back in his pocket and rubbed his chin, as the boy spent a few moments soaking up the misdirected praise and adoration of his friends.

'Look,' Harry said, 'I just came down here to have a quiet word, okay? I could smell you up there, so you're not exactly being discreet, are you? I'm not here to make an arrest. Just want to ask you a few questions. How does that sound?'

The boy looked thoughtful, rubbing his chin, mocking Harry's body language. Then he held out his right fist, middle finger pointing to the ground. 'How does it sound?' he said. 'What, you want me to turn it up for you?' The boy swivelled his fist so that it was palm up, the middle finger raised good and proud. 'That loud enough?'

More squawking and laughing from the rest of the gang. God, Harry thought, these kids haven't the faintest sodding clue, did they?

'So, what was it?' Harry asked. 'Resin? Bud? Skunk? No,

I doubt it was skunk, didn't reek like that stuff does. And you couldn't handle it anyway. Not someone like you. But you enjoyed it, right? Made you feel on top of the world, am I right? Relaxed? Because that's how it starts, yeah? It's why it's called a gateway drug. And that doesn't just mean a gateway to other drugs, like this time next week I'll find you dead in a barn, having shot yourself up with some badly cut heroin, bleeding from your eyes and your arse, vomit all over your shirt, your parents screaming at your pale, cold body, wondering just where the hell they went wrong to have you go and do something so bloody selfish and stupid.'

Harry paused briefly. He had them now. The laughter was gone. They were staring.

'The fuck you on about, old man?' the boy said. 'It was just a joint, that's all. I'm not dealing.'

'Not yet you're not,' Harry said. 'Gateway, remember? Who did you buy it from, then? That's what I want to know. Was this a first time? I don't think so. You seem to know what you're doing. You're showing off with it, like you're king of the hill. So you have a relationship with whoever it is, right? Think you're almost mates, probably have some shitty little special way of greeting each other, don't you? Handshakes and fist bumps and a manly hug? They asked if you want to sell a bit yourself?'

The boy went to nod, then shook his head. 'Yeah, I mean, no, not really. None of your business anyway. Why haven't you fucked off yet?'

'So you'll sell a bit, you'll become the easy way to get product around, a nice *in*. And you'll get a taste for it, the money as well as the drugs. More will be offered, more will come. You'll widen your distribution. Before you know it, everyone will know who you are. The flash kid with the money. The one with the good stuff. You'll get noticed up the chain and they'll call you in. Then what, kid? What do you think?'

Harry stared hard, knowing full well that the look on his face right there and then was all dark threat and horror.

'You'll get the car, the house, the girls. Move on to dealing other drugs. But that's when things get a bit more sketchy, because this isn't just business, it's war. You'll get threats, you'll want protection. For all we know, it could go well for you, make it big, yeah? The big man who started off with a spliff on the banks of a river in the dales! What a story! Until the day something goes wrong, and it always does. Bad stuff happens in a very bad way in this particular world, you know? Very bad indeed.'

Harry stepped forwards and the boy's friends parted to allow him through. And now he was face to face with the teenager. Couldn't have been more than sixteen. Same age his brother was when it started to go wrong for him.

'I remember this dealer,' Harry said. 'Few years older than you. Doing well. Clever lad he was. Never could get much to stick. Always clean. Then we got news something had gone wrong. The details don't matter, but what we found does, so I hope you're listening.'

The boy stepped back, but had nowhere to go, the beck directly behind him, Harry directly in front.

'I found him,' Harry said. 'What was left, that is. It was a room on the top floor of a deserted tower block, which was why no one had heard the screams.' Harry paused for effect. It worked. 'He'd been tied to a chair with wire so tight it had cut into his wrists, his ankles.' Harry drew an invisible line around his wrist with a finger. 'Nails had been driven into his knees. They'd gone at him with a welding torch, and you could smell it in the air, the skin they'd burned off. Poor kid.'

Harry held the boy's eyes with his own. 'That what you want, son? Well, is it?'

The boy said nothing, his mouth opening and shutting like a fish gasping for air.

'I'm not arresting you,' Harry said. 'But here's what's going to happen instead. One, you're going to tell me who sold it to you. Two, you're going to tell me where you live. Three, you're going to never, ever do this again, you hear me? Because I do not want to be the one responsible for turning up at your parents' door to deliver the news that their son has just got slammed into the freezer drawer at the mortuary!'

Harry didn't move as he waited for the boy to speak.

'It was Nick,' the boy said. 'He gave it to me! Got it off Reedy, he said!'

'Nick? Nick who?'

Harry guessed it was the same Nick, but always best to be sure.

'Little Nick,' the boy said. 'Gets us beer, too, if we want. Cigarettes. Anything.'

Harry jumped at this. 'When did you last see him?'

'Who?'

'Nick!'

The boy scratched his head and Harry thought how funny it was that people really did do that when they were thinking.

'Earlier,' the boy said. 'He was late. We was supposed to meet at twelve, like, but he was late. Three? Yeah, three.'

'Where?'

'Here.'

'But isn't it school?'

The boy shook his head. 'Summer holidays.'

'Do you know where he went?'

The boy shook his head once again.

'You sure?'

''Course I'm sure! Probably to see Reedy, though. Get some more. I've not done it much, none of us have. It was Nick and Reedy!'

'And who's this Reedy, then?' Harry asked, pulling out his little notebook.

'Lives over in Swaledale, near Reeth,' the boy said, his words starting to tumble into each other a little. 'Drives a Subaru Impreza. Red one. Well posh. Goes like stink.'

'Lucky fella,' Harry said, then offered the boy his notebook. 'You got Nick's number?'

The boy jotted a mobile number down on the open page.

'And what about Reedy's?'

The boy shook his head.

'Don't know it or don't want to give it to me?'

'Yes, I mean, no, I don't know it,' the boy said. 'He doesn't give his number out. It's all in person, or he calls you, or uses someone else, like Nick, but the number doesn't show.'

Harry slipped his notebook away again. A red Subaru Impreza, eh? Nice wheels. Probably very easy to spot as well. So he'd be taking a trip out there later, that was for sure, even though the evening was drawing on. Wasn't like he had much else to do. And Nick was certainly becoming more interesting the more he heard about him.

'And now for your address. Don't think I'll need to write it down, seeing as I'll be accompanying you.'

'What? You're taking me home? My parents will kill me!'

'They won't,' Harry said. 'But I'm hoping it'll be just

close enough to make sure you adhere to point number three.'

The boy visibly shrunk in front of Harry, and the rest of his pals upped and left.

'Well, come on then,' Harry said. 'Let's get you home, shall we?'

'You can't be serious!'

Harry leaned in. 'Trust me, I'm rarely anything else.'

CHAPTER FOURTEEN

Outside the boy's house, which was a rather grand place, with sweeping gardens and a double garage, the teenager was moving around nervously, like he either really needed to relieve himself, or his boxers were full of itching powder. Harry couldn't blame him. Being brought home by the police was never fun, and even less so if drugs were involved. But as Harry's sole aim here was to scare him into not being an idiot, so be it.

The front door opened and Harry was staring into a face he recognised.

'Mr Adams,' Harry said, doing his best to smile. The trouble was, with a face like his, a smile often made the scarring just look even worse.

Harry had met Richard Adams on his first day in Hawes. The man was a businessman who had moved to the area with, it seemed, the intent of running for mayor, even if there wasn't one. He hadn't exactly made friends with all the locals thanks to his plans to replace a nice bit of woodland with a building project. Harry couldn't quite remember the details and didn't really care. It wasn't going anywhere fast, not least because that little bit of woodland was currently under occupation by some tent-dwelling folk who'd taken it upon themselves to make sure the trees stayed exactly where they were.

'Ah, Constable,' Mr Adams said. 'You here about those blasted tree huggers?'

Harry let the constable thing slide and eased the boy forward. 'This is yours, I believe?'

Mr Adams stared at the boy. 'Christian? What's wrong? What's happened? Are you okay?'

'Can we go inside, please?' Harry asked.

'Whatever it is, you'll tell me here and now!' Mr Adams said, his face growing a little flush.

Harry sighed. 'Right now, this is just a warning, okay? A friendly nod, that's all.'

'What is?'

'Christian here,' Harry explained, 'and a few of his mates, well, I found them down by the beck, smoking.'

'Smoking? Smoking!'

Mr Adams was indignant, his flushed face growing redder by the second.

'A spliff,' Harry said. 'Cannabis? I could smell it up on the path.'

'Rubbish!'

The word blasted out from Mr Adams, not as disbelief, but the absolute conviction that what he'd just been told was so wrong as to be laughable.

'He said that he got it from someone called Nick, and he mentioned someone else called Reedy. Drives a fancy red car by all accounts. It's them I'm after. But thought it best to bring Christian home to you, so you're aware of what's happened.'

Mr Adams stepped forwards, pushing Christian behind him. 'Now, you listen here,' he said, his voice battling through his gritted teeth, 'there is no way on earth that a son of mine would be stupid enough to take drugs, do you hear? And as for having anything to do with this Nick person? He wouldn't be that stupid!'

'Every parent says the same,' Harry offered.

'And I am not every parent!' came the reply. 'Where's your evidence?'

Harry knew then that he was arguing with the deliberately deaf. 'He threw it away. But like I said, that's not what this is about. I'm just intervening before something worse happens.'

Mr Adams leaned in close, doing his best to intimidate Harry. It didn't work. Then he poked Harry in the chest with a finger.

'I think you should sod off now, don't you?'

Harry stared at the finger. 'Please don't do that, sir,' he said.

The man poked Harry again and said, 'You're on private property. Leave immediately!'

Harry stepped back, just out of reach. 'I've seen what can happen,' he said. 'It destroys lives. It destroyed my brother's life. I'm just trying to help, that's all.'

Mr Adams walked towards Harry poking him once again.

Harry held up his hands. 'Please, sir,' he said. 'Stop now. I'm going, okay? I've done my bit. Next time, I just hope it's not an arrest.'

'An arrest?'

Mr Adams' voice was a high-pitched screech and he came at Harry with rage in his eyes.

Harry stepped to one side just enough to let the man stumble past him and onto his knees. What the hell was the idiot thinking? That he could take him on? That a fight was the best solution here?

Harry backed further away, then as he turned to go, glanced up at Christian who was still standing in the doorway.

'Stay away from it, okay?' Harry said.

Then he was gone, and the bellowing threats of Richard Adams chased him further down the street than he'd expected. Which was why he pulled out his phone and punched in a call to Matt, if only to drown the man out.

'Boss?'

'I've got a sighting on Nick,' Harry explained. 'You know anything about someone called Reedy? Just wondering if that's where he's gone.'

'Reedy?' Matt replied. 'Lives over in Swaledale. You want to head over now?'

'You busy?'

'Nope.'

'Good,' Harry said. 'What say we go and pay him a surprise visit?'

SWALEDALE, from what Harry could see in the fading light of the late summer evening, was as beautiful as Wensleydale, but in a way all of its own. He wasn't exactly sure what the difference was, whether it was a little more wild, perhaps, or that it somehow seemed even older than its sister valley over the hill, but he found himself almost forgetting Matt's mad driving as they sped over the moors, which lay between Askrigg and their destination.

'Crackpot?' Harry asked, spying the odd name on a sign-post as they swept down into the bottom of the valley and through a small clump of houses.

'Great name, isn't it?' Matt said.

'What does it mean?'

'No idea,' Matt said. 'Probably something to do with all the caves and whatnot. And all the lead mines in the area.'

'Can't say I've ever fancied caving,' Harry said. 'Not a fan of enclosed spaces. I'm more your staying up top in the open air kind of person.'

'Ah, Crackpot's fine,' Matt said. 'I'll take you down there if you want?'

Harry laughed. 'What? You're a caver?'

'I am that,' Matt said. 'Member of the Cave and Rescue Team as well. Multi-talented!' He nodded ahead. 'Here's Reeth. Pity we're on duty. The Black Bull is a fantastic little pub. Mind you, they all are. Love it here. Might move over one day, you never know.'

Matt pulled the Land Rover up in the middle of the village, which was a huge expanse of green surrounded by stern-looking buildings, each one staring down at him ominously.

'So where are we likely to find this Reedy, then?' Harry asked, meeting Matt at the front of the vehicle.

'The King's Arms,' Matt replied, and headed off. 'Come on.'

Entering the pub, Harry immediately wanted to just sit down and stop. The place was old fashioned but not dated, if such a thing was possible. It was homely and warm and smelled of comfort food and good conversation, with the faintest hint of dog.

Matt walked up to the bar and waved at the barman, a

man who seemed far too tall to be working behind it, as he stooped down to see who had called to him. He rather reminded Harry of Lurch from The Addams Family, only not as smiley.

'Now then, Brian!'

''Ow do, Matt,' the barman said. 'What can I do you for, then?'

Matt held up a hand and said, 'Sorry, on duty tonight.'

'Pity,' the barman said. 'Got some new pickled eggs out. Your lot been out on the fells at all?'

Matt shook his head.

'Rescue team's been pretty quiet to be honest. Folk must be taking care of themselves for a change! And I'll still be having a pickled egg, that's for sure.'

'It's that caving I don't get,' the barman said. 'Why the hell anyone wants to do that is beyond me.'

'Couldn't agree more,' Harry said, approaching the bar.

'This is DCI Grimm,' Matt said, introducing him to the barman. 'Boss, this is Brian.'

Harry gave a nod, then said, 'Couple of cokes and some crisps, please. Cheese and onion.'

'I'm more of a peanuts man,' Matt said. 'And that pickled egg, Brian, thanks.'

As the barman made off to fetch Harry's order, including Matt's peanut preference and pickled egg, Harry asked Matt if Reedy was in.

'Sure is,' Matt said, then gave a faint nod behind him.

Harry turned just enough to have a look without it being obvious. In a far-off corner he saw three men talking around a small table, on top of which were a number of empty pint glasses, and three which were not so empty, but probably soon would be. One of the men stuck out enough for Harry to guess which one was Reedy, thanks not only to the glint of light shining off the bad taste chains around his wrists, but also the sunglasses slapped across his face.

The barman returned with the order and Harry paid up, handed Matt his drink and snack, then turned towards Reedy.

'Time to go and introduce myself,' he said, then nodded back to the barman and handed him his bank card, gesturing towards the three men, 'And bring over another round of whatever it is they're drinking . . .'

CHAPTER FIFTEEN

HARRY WALKED OVER TO THE TABLE AND STOOD BEHIND the man whom he was pretty sure went by the name Reedy.

'Hello, boys,' he said. 'Mind if we join you?'

With Reedy having his back to him, the other two glanced up and Harry caught their irritated stares which were thrown up at him with mean intent.

'Yeah, actually, we do,' one of them said. 'Private conversation.'

The other mouthed something at Harry.

'Sorry, I didn't catch that,' Harry said and leaned in across the table. 'You mind speaking up?'

'I said piss off,' the man said, the words spitting from him like sparks from a fire. 'That clear enough for you?'

The barman arrived carrying three pints and set them on the table, giving Harry back his bank card. The two men stared at the drinks, uncertainty drawing lines of confusion across their faces.

Harry watched as Reedy finished his own pint then reached out for one of the fresh ones in front of him. He drained it in one go, resting the empty glass back on the table barely ten seconds later.

'I'll grab a couple extra chairs,' Matt said, and rested his own drink and snacks on the table.

When Matt came back, Harry took a chair, placed it next to Reedy's left, and sat down, leaning back with a long, back-creaking stretch.

'Thanks for the drink,' Reedy said, for the first time turning to look at Harry. 'Much appreciated.'

'Well, there's no point in being rude now, is there?' Harry said. 'And I was just coming over to introduce myself, that's all. Get my face around, if you know what I mean.'

'Face like yours isn't exactly difficult to forget,' said the man who'd just told Harry to piss off. Harry stared at him over his own drink before reaching for his packet of crisps and opening it, taking a nice handful and stuffing them into his mouth, all the time never letting his eyes drop, or blink.

The other man laughed, but the sound of it soon died, and dropping his eyes from Harry, he sunk the rest of his pint.

'So,' Harry said, 'how's about we all start with our names first, eh? How's that sound? My name's Grimm. Harry Grimm. No, sorry, DCI Harry Grimm. The face makes it easier to remember, I think, seeing as how I look like my name. It's not something I did on purpose, but it comes in surprisingly useful. The ultimate poker face you might say.'

'DCI?' Reedy said. 'You wouldn't be trying to harass us now, would you, Mr Policeman?'

Harry ate more crisps, this time as loudly as he could.

'I don't think buying someone a drink can be regarded as harassment, do you?' Harry glanced over to Matt. 'What do you think, detective sergeant? Is buying beer a crime at all?'

'Not that I'm aware of, no,' Matt replied, popping a peanut in his mouth before chomping into his pickled egg. 'I think it's generally regarded as being a nice thing to do. A very nice thing to do, actually. And usually gratefully received.'

'Really, now? Is that so? You hear that, gentlemen? It was a nice thing to do! Isn't that just wonderful?'

Reedy turned to Matt who had parked himself at the man's other side. 'This your new boss, then, is it?'

'He doesn't think so,' Matt said, finishing off his egg, his eyes on Reedy.

'You ever find out what happened to the last one?'

Harry spotted something scratch its way across Matt's generally genial, friendly demeanour, and a dark shadow flitted in his eyes.

'Not yet, no,' Matt said, his voice quieter than before, his eyes on Reedy. 'But we will.'

Harry finished his crisps then spent a few seconds quickly folding the packet into a little triangle, before popping it onto the table in front of them.

'Right then, I'm looking for a friend of yours,' Harry said, his attention now fully on Reedy. It was all he could do to not reach out and just yank the stupidly unnecessary sunglasses from off his face. 'Nick Ellis.'

Reedy, Harry saw, remained calm, but the other two suddenly looked a little on edge.

'He in some kind of trouble, then?' Reedy asked.

'That's what we need to find out,' Harry answered. 'Don't suppose you've seen him at all?'

'Can't say that we have.'

'And you're sure about that, are you?'

'Must be if I said it.'

Reedy said nothing more as the man sat opposite Harry, and on Matt's right, took a deep pull on his drink, then stood up, before heading off towards the toilets.

Harry reached for a beer mat, pulled a pen from a pocket, then wrote down a number. 'Well, if you do hear from him or see him, can you give him this number, please, and tell him to give me a call?'

Reedy ignored the beermat.

Harry reached for the beermat and placed it in front of Reedy's face. 'That number look readable to you?'

'Just about,' Reedy said.

'You're sure, now?' Harry asked, and moved the beermat in just a little further, forcing Reedy to lean his head back. 'I wouldn't want to think I'd written something down you couldn't read.'

'Yeah, it's clear,' Reedy said.

'Well, that's good then,' Harry said. 'So, if you wouldn't mind?'

Reedy didn't respond, so Harry once again moved the beermat close to the man's face, this time to touch the end of his nose.

With a huff, Reedy snatched the beermat from Harry's hand and stuffed it into a pocket.

Harry stood up, with a nod to Matt to follow suit. Then, before they moved away from the table, Harry rested his right hand on Reedy's shoulder, squeezed it just hard enough to make him flinch, and leaned in real close. 'Thanks for your help,' he said. 'I'll be making sure everyone knows how helpful you were.'

Reedy turned and Harry saw a faint crackle of fear at the corner of the man's eyes, just visible at the edge of his sunglasses. If he'd managed to unsettle him, Harry thought, then at least there was a chance that he would pause on supplying cannabis to kids, so that was something. And he might even flush Nick out from wherever he was holed up.

'Come on, then,' Harry said, tapping Reedy on his shoulder in a friendly fashion, 'best we be off.'

Matt rose to his feet and followed Harry to the door, but before they got there, Harry said, 'You see where that other one went?'

'Toilets, I think,' Matt said.

Harry wasn't so sure. 'Seemed to suddenly need it didn't he? After I mentioned Nick . . .'

Matt glanced over to the other side of the pub, to the toilets. 'What're you thinking?'

Harry rubbed his forehead. He was tired. It was late. He needed to get some sleep. And he knew he wasn't getting any soon. Then, through the windows in the pub door, he saw a flash of movement. It was someone running across the village green.

Harry pushed through the door and out into the fresh air. 'Nick?'

The man turned mid-run and at the sight of Harry almost tripped.

'Nick! Stop!'

Harry was running before he even realised he was moving. Then the sudden burst of movement caught up with him, with the sensation of his supper swilling around in his stomach, as his feet pounded the ground.

Matt was on Harry's heels and they made chase.

'Where the hell's he going?' Harry hissed out between hard, painful breaths.

Harry saw Nick disappear down a small lane, the darkness of the evening skulking in it. He followed, his lungs burning, legs feeling the pain of trying to run in shoes designed for a nice, casual stroll, not a race.

'Footpath ahead,' Matt said, 'I'll see if I can cut him off.'

With that, Matt skidded to a halt and took another path, which led down between two quaint little cottages.

Harry did his best to maintain his pace. Nick wasn't exactly getting away, but neither was he getting any closer.

The darkness of the lane closed in. Harry's throat was burning now and he hacked up a glob of phlegm and spat. He felt sick, dizzy with the chase, but if Nick was running, then there had to be a reason for it and he wanted to find out exactly what that was.

Nick was only about twenty metres away and Harry watched the man, who looked skinny as a runner bean, leap over a stile in the wall, and on into a field beyond.

Harry got to the stile a few seconds later, decided against going for the jump, squeezed through, and continued on.

Sheep scattered and bleated. The moon was high now, though the night still wasn't full-dark.

Harry's feet slipped and he only just managed to catch himself from losing his footing and ending up on his arse.

A shout from ahead and Harry saw Matt hammering his way across the field from another direction, and on seeing him, Nick changed route, heaving a right to head off the path and across the field.

'Nick! It's Matt! Stop running, you mad sod! We just need to talk! Stop!'

But Nick wasn't going to stop, that much Harry was sure about, though he was slowing now. Harry was gaining on him, which actually rather surprised him, considering how his own attempt at getting back into running as a keep-fit activity was going.

Harry coughed. He managed to dig just a little bit deeper, imagined that he was dumping fuel into his muscles to burn, and that's why they were on fire right now, because they were working hard. Harry wasn't going to stop, not this close, not a chance.

Nick tripped. Harry watched the man cartwheel through the air, arms and legs flailing. He let out a cry like a frightened animal, then slammed into the ground face first.

Harry and Matt arrived together, both sucking in great lungfuls of air.

'Seriously, Nick,' Matt said, leaning forward, his hands braced against his knees, 'the hell did you think you were going, anyway?'

Nick tried to get up and flopped back down into the grass, but then Harry stepped in close and gave him a helping hand. The man struggled to both stand up, and at the same time, get away, but it was no good, Harry's grip was iron.

'You can't arrest me!' Nick yelled. 'I've not done nowt, I tell you! Nowt at all!'

Harry ignored the double negative. 'I'm not arresting you,' he said. 'But if you run again, trust me, I bloody well will do!'

Again, Nick tried to pull away.

'Matt?' Harry managed to say, his breath still not coming easily.

Matt leaned in to help. 'Come on, Nick,' he said, 'we just want to have a chat, that's all, okay?'

'I didn't know he was dead! I didn't! And I didn't do it! I'm not lying! I'm not! You've got to believe me! He was dead when I got there!'

'Come on,' Harry said, a yawn cutting through his urge to throw up. He turned Nick around to face back the way they'd come, and with Matt having a tight hold of him on the other side, started walking back towards Reeth.

The journey back to Hawes didn't take long. Not just because Matt raced along the lanes like an idiot, but because Harry was so tired that he soon nodded off, his head ricocheting off the passenger-side window with a dull thud, and the rattling heater between him and Matt turning the Land Rover cabin unnecessarily toasty and warm. It brought back memories of his Para life, thundering along in the back of a truck, his body suffering from levels of exhaustion he never thought possible. They were good days, Harry thought to himself, and with that, his eyes closed, and he was gone.

CHAPTER SIXTEEN

'So if I'm not under arrest, then why am I here? And it's a bit bloody late, like, isn't it?'

Harry looked at his watch. Nick had a point. It was nearly ten-thirty. And here they were, sitting down around a table in the police office at the Hawes Community Centre, helping themselves to a plate of chocolate bourbons. Three mugs of tea also sat on the table, but they were still too hot to enjoy.

'You ran off,' Harry said. 'If you hadn't, if you'd just come in for a chat, we could have got this over and done with at the pub. So we're here, right now, because of you.'

'You can't blame me!'

'I'm not blaming you,' Harry said. 'I'm just stating a fact. You ran off. We persuaded you to stop doing exactly that. And now we're here.'

'I didn't know who you were!' Nick said. 'And you didn't persuade me about anything, did you? You just ran out of the pub and charged at me!'

Harry sighed. 'You were already running. I made chase.'

'You charged me!' Nick shouted, repeating himself. 'That face was like the devil coming at me! I was scared for my life!'

'And why would that be?' Matt asked, jumping in.

'You could've been robbers!'

Harry coughed on his biscuit and turned an eye to Matt. 'Did he really just use the word *robbers*?'

'I believe he did that,' Matt said. Then, to Nick, 'You've still not told us why you were running, to begin with. Or to where. It's not like you live in Reeth, is it? So why were you over there?'

Harry tried his tea. It stung his mouth, but not enough to stop him from taking a gulp. 'Look at it from our point of view, Nick,' he began. 'You find John dead, and you do the right thing and call it in. Then we hear that you've done a runner, but not only that, we also hear that you didn't just find John in the field, did you? No. You received a text from him, which we all know is pretty hard for someone to do when they're dead. And John was a little more than just dead. It's now taken us all day and most of the evening to find you. And when we eventually did, through luck more than anything, you hot-footed it out of there and tried to run off! If you were wanting to give us the impression that something is amiss, then you did a bloody good job!'

There was something else Harry wanted to ask Nick as well, about what Bill had said he'd seen on Saturday morning, but he was saving that for later. Didn't want to spook him too early.

'Suspicious, that,' Matt muttered. 'Very, very suspicious indeed.'

'You can't think it was me!' Nick said, panic in his voice.

'I already said I didn't do it! I didn't! I couldn't have! And I wouldn't have, neither!'

Harry leaned forward to rest his hands on the table. 'If that's so, then why didn't you just come in and tell us? I'd have forgiven you being a bit spooked and nicking off for a while if you'd have come back. But you didn't, did you? And from what I can tell, you had no intention of ever doing so. Running away is not the best way to make a good impression with the police!'

'Still not shown us that phone of yours either, have you?' Matt added. 'Why's that, then?'

Nick, Harry could see, was displaying all the behaviour of a trapped animal. Part of him wanted to see what would happen if they really pushed him, but he wasn't quite sure that it was the best approach.

'Look,' Harry said, working hard to look relaxed and unthreatening, which wasn't all that easy with a face from Hell and a voice that even when it was being friendly came across a little like the rough growl of a bear with a sore head, 'we just need your help, Nick, that's all, okay? The last thing you want is to be caught up in something that has nothing to do with you, right? You found your friend dead, and I understand that's difficult to deal with, I really do. I've been there, I know.'

At this, Harry saw Nick visibly relax. They had a connection now. That was good. 'You're worried about showing us your phone, right? Well, how's about DS Dinsdale and I promise that we won't go snooping around? In fact, all I actually want to see is the text that you received and the number. How does that sound? Actually, you know what? Don't even give us the phone! Just show us the text, the time you received it, the number, and we're good. How's that for a start? Make you feel any happier?'

Nick took a nibble from a biscuit. From outside the building came the sound of laughter. Voices rolling along the road between pubs, Harry guessed. Folk out enjoying themselves, blissfully unaware of the darker goings-on being dealt with just a few steps away from them behind closed doors.

'It's got private stuff on it, that's all,' Nick said, pulling out his phone. 'And I'm a private person, you see? You can understand that, right?'

'Aren't we all, Nick?' Harry said, putting his hands out as though by doing so he was lumping them all together.

Nick's fingers danced around on his phone for a few seconds, then he turned it around and showed Harry and Matt the screen.

'That's what I got,' Nick said, pointing a thin, bony finger, which resembled a sun-bleached twig at the screen. 'And that's the number there, see?'

Both Harry and Matt jotted the number down quickly, and the message.

'And that's all you got?' Matt asked. 'Nothing else? No other messages?'

Nick gave a nod. 'Got it early morning. Woke me up.'

Harry asked, 'And what time was that?'

'Says on the message,' Nick said. 'Seven fifteen.'

'And where were you when you received it?' Harry asked again, trying to keep Nick moving now, not wanting to give him a chance to stop and think.

'Home,' Nick replied, pulling his phone back and stuffing it back into a pocket.

'He lives just off Brunt Acres Road,' Matt explained. 'On the road out towards Hardraw.'

Harry nodded as though he knew exactly where that was, which he didn't. He was still thinking about the message he'd just read on Nick's phone. 'Not much of a message, is it?' he said. "'*Need a bit of a hand. Can you help?*" You often get messages like that from John?'

'No,' Nick replied. 'That's why I went out there, like. See what was up.'

'And you just headed off out there, did you?' Matt asked. 'Jumped out of bed, and into your car?'

'He's a mate!' Nick said. 'Of course, I did! Wouldn't you?'

Harry wasn't convinced Nick was the kind of person to jump out of bed for anyone or anything unless there was something in it for him. He didn't exactly strike him as the Good Samaritan type. 'So what did you think when you got there?' he asked. 'About the message, I mean.'

Nick shrugged. 'I just saw that John was in a bad way so I called nine-nine-nine.'

'And didn't mention the message.'

Nick shook his head.

'And you're sure that's John's number?'

'Yes,' Nick said. 'He's in my contacts. It was him who sent it alright.'

'Well, it was his phone, at any rate,' Matt said.

Harry's head was starting to hurt. He'd hoped for more from Nick, but so far they'd got nothing more than what they already knew. 'So you're good friends with John, then?'

Nick gave a nod.

'Does he have many other friends?'

Nick actually laughed. 'John? You're having a laugh, aren't you?'

'This look like a face that laughs much to you?' Harry asked.

Nick's laugh died as quickly as it had started. 'It's just that he's a bit of a rogue, you see.'

'A rogue? You make him sound like Han bloody Solo!'

And just what was it with Nick using words he'd not heard in decades? Rogue? Who the hell says, rogue?

'You know, bit of a rum 'un. I mean, he's not bad, not really.'

'What about enemies, then?' Harry asked. 'If he's running low on numbers when it comes to people who like him, then I'm guessing there are plenty who don't.'

'John doesn't, I mean *didn't*, care,' Nick said, slumping on his chair now, and Harry heard the sadness in the man's voice. 'No one liked him, not since he was a kid. Well, a few of us did, but the rest? No chance. They didn't know what it was like for him at home, did they?'

'So you've been friends since school?'

Nick gave a shallow nod. 'We had our own little gang in the end,' he said. 'Used to play together a lot, like. You know, games like Kick the Can, Tag, Cowboys and Indians, that kind of thing. We were always the Indians, though. Named ourselves after them, didn't we? They were John's favourite.'

'Why's that?'

'What does it matter?' Nick snapped back, and Harry sensed there was more behind those words than Nick was letting on. 'It was years ago! Can't bloody remember much of it anyways.'

'And I think it should be Cowboys and Native Americans now,' Matt said. 'And you were the Native Americans, Nick. Not Indians.'

'Do I look like I care?' Nick grumbled. 'There's nowt else I've got to say. John's dead. That's all I know.'

'From what I've heard, he was a bit of a bully,' Harry said. 'Was he like that at school, as well?'

Nick let out a short bark of a laugh and rolled his eyes. 'It was tough back then,' he said. 'School was hard and so was John. Simple as that.'

'So he was a bully, then?' Harry asked.

'Kids are cruel,' said Nick with a shrug. 'Everyone got it bad at some point. Bet you did too, right? Didn't matter if you were local, new to the school, rich or poor, you had to stand up for yourself. Some got it worse, mind, but what can you do?'

Matt leaned forward and said, 'I know as well as you do, Nick, that people won't be exactly lining up to mourn John, sad as it is for the few who liked him, including you. But did you know of anyone who really had it in for him? Enough to do him harm?'

'Plenty,' Nick said, 'and he'd have had them all!' He was on his feet suddenly, thumping his fist on the table. 'Take anyone on, would John, no bother at all! And if I find who did this to him, I'll have 'em, you hear? I will!'

Harry waited for Nick to sit down again, then asked, 'Any names? Anyone specific?'

'I'm not a grass.'

'I didn't say that you were,' Harry said. 'But if someone was involved in John's death, wouldn't you want to help us find out who? Isn't that what you'd want to do for John, what a friend would do?'

Nick fell quiet and Harry let the conversation die, punctuating the silence with a yawn that came out far louder than he'd expected.

'Whatever anyone says about John, he wasn't all bad,' Nick said. 'He got blamed for a lot of stuff, but it wasn't all him, right, you hear? It was everyone! They all did it!'

'What was?' Harry asked. 'What do you mean by *it was everyone*? They all did what? Did something happen, Nick?'

Nick's expression turned from anger to worry. 'No, look, what I mean is . . . I'm just saying . . .' he stuttered, trying to find the right words, 'I'm just saying that John wasn't the only one who got into trouble. We all did. Everyone did. Kids is kids, like, and, well, you know . . .'

'No, I don't know,' Harry said. 'Are you saying John got blamed for something at school? What was it?'

Nick shut down, didn't say a word.

'If you know something that you think can help,' Harry said, 'you need to tell us, Nick.'

'Nothing happened!' Nick yelled, spit flying from his mouth. 'School was years ago, wasn't it? Years ago! What happened to John, well that happened now, didn't it? And my mate's dead and you're asking me about what it was like when we were kids, like? It doesn't make sense! None of it does! It's got bugger all to do with now! Bugger all!'

Harry gave Nick a moment or two to calm down. 'Right, I think that's all for now, Nick,' he said, as the yawn from a few minutes ago threatened to come along again for another go. 'We'll give you a call if we want another chat, okay, Nick? But it's probably best for all of us if you don't go running off again.'

'So, I can go? That's it for the questions?'

Harry nodded at the door and Nick stood up. Then, as Nick made to move, he said, 'Just out of interest, Nick, can you tell me where you were Saturday morning, around six?'

'What? Why?'

'Answer the question.'

'I was in bed! Where the hell else do you think I was?'

'You sure about that?'

'Yes! Of course, I'm bloody sure!'

'You weren't round with John driving up into the field with him?'

'What? On a Saturday? Sod off!'

'Can you prove it?'

Nick's eyes grew wide, his mouth thin and Harry knew from that alone that he probably couldn't.

'Someone saw two people in John's tractor heading up into the field,' Harry explained. 'Was that you and John? Because if it was, we need to know.'

'No it bloody well wasn't!' Nick shouted, the words flying from his mouth, hot and angry. 'I was too pissed still from Friday night at the pub! Didn't get out of bed till midday!'

'You sure?'

Nick's mouth fell open and he snapped it shut immediately, rage burning in his eyes. Harry found himself believing him, which was annoying really, because it would've been nice and neat for it to have been Nick that Bill had spotted. The thought that it wasn't, that it was someone else who had driven John up into the field? Well, that just made this whole case considerably more complicated, didn't it?

'It wasn't me,' Nick said, clearly fighting to keep his voice calm. 'John was a mate. Look, I know, most folk didn't like him, but then most folk don't like me either, do they? So why the hell would I go and kill my only friend, hmm? You tell me that!'

Nick stared at Harry for a while after speaking then

finally his eyes dropped and to Harry, it was almost as though the man shrunk a little in front of them.

'If you do think of something that might be important, a name, anything, you'll let us know, won't you?'

Nick gave a nod then headed back to the door, before turning around one last time.

'What happened, to John? You think someone did that to him? On purpose, like? Murdered him?'

'I really don't know,' Harry said. 'And that's the honest truth, Nick. But if you know anything, even if you don't think it's important, you need to tell us, right? Whatever happened to John, we need to find out.'

Nick said nothing more and left the room, the door swishing shut behind him like it was shooing him out of the room on Harry and Matt's behalf.

With Nick gone, Matt stood up next and stretched.

'You don't think he did it, do you?' he asked, relaxing from the stretch. 'You know, clobbered John a couple of days ago, took his phone, used it to send a text to himself, then drove out there, and hey-presto, he's got an alibi?'

A wave of tiredness hit Harry. He screwed his eyes up tight, then opened them again, and they took longer than they should to focus on Matt. 'We need the pathology report,' he said. 'Hopefully that'll tell us something. And a location request will have been put through to whichever phone network Capstick was with. So hopefully we'll at least know where that message to Nick was sent from, but it sure as hell wasn't sent from the field by him, was it?'

'Reckon sleep is in order before then,' Matt said. 'I'll lock up. What do you think about what he said about school?'

Harry really wasn't sure. 'I think John had a little gang and that, like Nick said, school was probably pretty hard.

Kids pick on each other, that's what happens. Linking what happened to John to primary school just seems like a massive stretch.'

'Yeah, I can see that,' Matt said. 'But some of what he said, it sounded like something happened back then.'

'Yeah, it did,' Harry pondered.

Outside, with the office locked and Matt on his way home, the night had fallen to full dark. Harry wandered back to his new flat, feeling no further on with what they were dealing with than he had been when the call had come in that morning. They had a dead body, a weird death, a missing phone, a mysterious text, no suspects at all—unless he counted Nick, which Harry's gut told him was complete and total nonsense—and the general impression that John was a man no one was going to mourn, a boy bullied by his dad, who became a bully at school with his own little gang, and since then, a life lived not that well or that happily. So, just what the hell had happened? The man was dead and someone seemed to have gone a long way to ensuring that the death had happened in a very specific way. But it was the why that was really bothering Harry, gnawing at the back of his mind like a starved dog. Why would someone go to all that trouble? Just what the hell was it all about?

Tomorrow is a new day though, Harry thought. Perhaps then, some answers would come. Until then, he would sleep.

CHAPTER SEVENTEEN

HARRY WOKE TO THE SOUND OF HIS MOBILE PHONE crashing through his skull with all the loving, affectionate tact of a pneumatic drill in the hands of a murderous dentist.

'Yes, what?' Harry answered, catching sight of the time, his voice broken by a cough brought on by the chill of the morning air. 'And this had better be good seeing as it's only just gone six!'

'Harry, it's Jim . . .'

Harry was suddenly very, very awake. 'Jim? What's up? What's happened?'

Light was streaming in through a crack in his bedroom curtains to blind him and Harry had to shield his eyes with a hand.

'We've, well, it's just that . . .'

Jim's voice was stumbling over whatever it was he was trying to say and that unnerved Harry.

'"Just that" what, Jim? What's up? What's happened?'

There was a pause down the line and Harry felt himself being sucked into it, the ominous threat of the unknown something he was pretty damned sure was about to give him a mule kick in the shins.

'We've had another call,' Jim said. 'A . . . Another one's been found. Another body, I mean.'

Harry was now on his feet, using his free hand to try and get dressed, the sun in his face again, sending his view of his bedroom hazy. 'What? Where? What do you mean, a body's been found? How? I mean, what the—ah, bollocks!'

Harry, with only one leg in his trousers, his eyes blinded by the sun, managed to get his other foot caught up in his belt, and tripped and fell mid-sentence, landing first on his bed, before rolling onto the floor, his phone skipping out of his hand.

'Harry? You okay?'

'I'm absolutely fine and bloody dandy!' Harry shouted back as he scrabbled across the floor for his phone and pulled it to his ear. 'A body? You're sure? Where? How?'

'Up Widdale,' Jim said. 'Gordy just rang to say she's on her way. She'll pick you up in fifteen and tell you what she knows.'

Harry didn't know Gordy as well as the others quite yet. As the Detective Inspector for the area, she was based down dale, and usually busy with things that way. And if she was only fifteen minutes away then that meant she'd set off a while ago now. The towns of Leyburn, Richmond, and Bedale had their own troubles, and with Catterick not too far away, which was a garrison town, her life was a busy one, to say the least. There were other officers down that way, but they didn't generally end up at the Hawes end of things.

'Can't you pick me up?' Harry asked. 'Actually, what am I on about? I can drive my own car, can't I? Where's the body?'

'I'm already at the scene,' Jim said. 'I'll see you when you get here.'

Jim hung up.

Harry finished getting dressed, nipped to the bathroom, then just as he was sorting out some toast, scraping off the burned bits because he'd left it in too long, there was a sharp knock at the door.

'Just a minute,' Harry called, stuffing the toast into his mouth, then racing to the door, grabbing his jacket on the way.

Gordy looked him up and down, shaking her head. 'Aye, well aren't you a sight for sore eyes? By which I mean, eyes so sore they never want to see anything ever again! And still no boots, then, I see? Were you born stubborn and stupid, or have you developed those traits all by yourself?'

Harry shuffled his feet into his shoes. 'I've just not got around to it yet,' he said, pushing himself out of the door. 'But I will. Now, what's going on?'

'Well, after today, you make sure you do, you hear?'

Harry liked Gordy because she had no filter. What was in her head came out of her mouth. That she had just made him feel like she'd given him a little bollocking for not having appropriate footwear only added to her charm. At least he thought it did. Right then, he wasn't so sure.

'Why? Where are we going?'

'Oh, you'll see soon enough,' Gordy said. 'Come on.'

A few minutes later, they were speeding along in Gordy's car, which was a plain-looking blue Ford Focus, one of numerous others used by the police up and down the country.

'So, what's happened?' Harry asked. 'And where exactly are we going?'

'Out past Widdale,' Gordy explained. 'You heard of the Ribblehead Viaduct? Big stone thing, lots of arches, looks good on postcards with a steam train going across it?'

Harry wasn't so sure but nodded anyway.

'Well, if you continue along here, that's where you'll end up. But we won't be going that far. We're stopping at a farm on the way. Like I said, boots would be a sensible choice. But you're no' so sensible, are you?'

They zipped past a derelict building on the left-hand side of the road, which stared out at them through two tall, arched windows. Whatever it was, whatever it had been, it looked lonely, Harry thought, and its state of decay almost made him feel sorry for it.

'Another farm accident?' Harry asked.

'Apparently so, aye,' Gordy said, dropping a gear and accelerating. 'Not suspicious at all considering what turned up yesterday.'

Harry finished off what was left of his toast and wiped his mouth. 'So, are you going to tell me what's happened, or is it a surprise?'

'Oh, this one can be left as a surprise I think,' Gordy said. 'Right then, here we are!'

The DI pulled the car over onto the right-hand side of the road and into the yard of a small farm. Compared with the one they'd been at yesterday, it was the polar opposite, Harry thought. The house looked cared for and even had some pretty little window boxes alive with colour. Not that Harry was into things like that, but he had to admit that it all looked rather picturesque. The farmyard and its buildings, which Harry noticed bridged both sides of the road, were all in good order. He could see other farm buildings set back behind the house as well. This was a place loved and cared for, he thought. So just what the hell had happened to bring them out here in the early morning?

'Come on, then,' Gordy said, opening the driver's door. 'Let's get out and see what's what, shall we?'

Outside the car, Harry was hit by the cool wind gusting down the road to bite at him gleefully. Around them stretched moorland and little else and Harry wondered what it took to not only live out here but work here, too. It was beautiful, yes, but lonely as well, with nothing for miles. Harry heard the low moan of cows coming from the buildings round the back of the farmhouse.

'You finished sightseeing?' Gordy called.

Harry hunched up inside his coat then made his way around the front of the car to stand with Gordy.

'I thought it was just sheep around here,' Harry said.

'They've a small herd of animals that they feed up and sell for beef,' Gordy explained. 'They're in the barn at the back and will be put out on pasture later.'

'So where's the body?' Harry asked.

Gordy nodded to the barns at the back of the house. 'Jim's already got the tape out, Matt's inside with the family, the poor beggars, and the rest of the party is on its way. Twice in two days, as well. Imagine how happy everyone's going to be about that!'

'What about Jenny and Liz?'

'Jenny got a call in to a domestic down in Aysgarth. Liz is with her.'

'Aysgarth?'

'Famous waterfalls,' Gordy said. 'Kevin Costner was all Hollywood in them when they filmed *Prince of Thieves*.'

As they walked past the house to where Gordy had directed, Harry spotted some children's toys in the garden by the house. It was just a little wooden swing and a tricycle, but the sight of them had Harry immediately thinking the worst.

'It's not one of the bairns, if that's what you're thinking,' Gordy said. 'I'd have given you fair warning of that, I can assure you.'

A bit further on was when the smell crept up Harry's nose. It was the kind of smell he'd heard people describe as the smell of the countryside, a healthy smell even, but to him, it was just cow shit, and he wasn't a fan.

The source of the smell was also the thing surrounded by Jim's cordoning tape. It was a concrete pit, sunk into the hill behind, the base of it sloping steeply downwards to disappear into a steaming, slick mass of brown slurry. Just a way off to its left side was the open-sided barn with the cattle. At the sight of Harry, the animals ran to the back of the barn.

Harry saw Jim and gave him a half-hearted salute, touching the side of his forehead with his left hand.

'I know I'm going to regret asking this,' Harry said, 'but what are we dealing with here? What happened? And how is it possible to collect that much cow shit from so few animals?'

Jim came over.

'I'll let him explain,' Gordy said, nodding at the PCSO.

'About the shit or the body?' Jim asked.

'I think you can do both, if that's okay with you?'

Harry, with another look at the slurry pit, wasn't so sure that he wanted him to.

'The slurry collects over winter,' Jim said. 'The animals are kept inside during the colder weather and the muck is cleaned out regularly. Keeps them clean and healthy, and you've then got some excellent stuff to throw on your land. Good fertiliser.'

'So why are they in the barn right now?' Harry asked.

'It's been a wee bit hot,' Gordy said. 'That right, Jim?'

Jim gave a nod. 'Hot weather you have to keep them indoors. Can't have your herd getting heatstroke.'

Harry went to laugh but realised Jim was serious. 'Heatstroke? Cows can get that? Seriously?'

'Badly,' Jim said. 'Anyway, you ready?'

'Not really, no,' Harry replied, pulling on some PPE. 'But let's get on with it and see what we have.'

Jim then led Harry and Gordy around the outside of the cordon tape and pointed over at the pit. 'Call came in just over an hour ago. The farmer spotted something floating in the pit and went for a closer look, thinking a sheep or a deer maybe had fallen in, something like that.'

'Only it wasn't a sheep,' Harry offered.

'No,' Jim said. 'Most definitely not a sheep.'

Harry strained his eyes to see if he could make anything out in the muck, but all he could see was a pool of brown and he had no real urge to get any closer to it. 'Any idea who it is?'

'Not a clue,' Jim said. 'The body is on its front and covered in cow muck. Won't be able to see until it's pulled out. And I'm happy to leave that to the CSI lot. Also, I'm a PCSO, and I'm pretty sure that fishing a corpse out of a lake of cow shit is above my pay grade. By which I mean, way above.'

'You sure about that?' Harry asked, then looked over to Gordy for a bit of mutual support. 'From what I've been told, PCSOs are the backbone of the police force, isn't that right?'

'Absolutely,' Gordy said. 'Because they're willing to go the extra mile, I think.'

'Where would we be without them?'

'It's something I don't want to even consider, so I don't think I will.'

Harry could see from the look on Jim's face that he was hearing their words but not exactly listening to them. He glanced back at the farmhouse. 'So it's definitely not one of the family, then?'

'Nope,' Jim said. 'They're all accounted for. The farmer's pretty shaken up by it, but that's fair enough. Reckon he thought it was one of his kids when he first saw it, even though it couldn't be, seeing as they were all still in bed.'

'And so should we all be,' Harry grumbled.

'Now that I'm here, I think I'll go and relieve the family of Matt,' Gordy said, sensing a momentary break in the conversation. 'It should be the other way around, but this is Matt we're talking about, after all. I doubt he's shut up since he got in there.'

Harry watched Gordy head off to the farmhouse. 'She's really not what I'm used to dealing with when it comes to Family Liaison Officers.'

'Why's that?' Jim asked.

'She's just a little bit more abrupt than you'd expect,' Harry said.

'Well, she's good at it,' Jim said. 'I hear you had fun with Nick last night? Matt was telling me about it.'

Harry wasn't so sure fun was the way he would have described it. 'Yeah, we didn't exactly learn much.'

A shout caught Harry's attention and he turned to see Matt striding out towards them.

'Fancy seeing you here,' he said.

'I know,' Harry replied. 'Shocker.'

'Bit of a rough one, this, isn't it? Drowning in shit! What a way to go.'

'I'm assuming that's you just guessing at what happened,'

Harry said. 'Unless you've got some kind of crystal ball in your pocket.'

Matt went to say something, but his voice was cut off by the sound of vehicles pulling off the road and in at the front of the farmhouse.

Harry looked over.

'She's not going to be happy about this, is she?' Jim said, seeing who'd just arrived.

'No, she's not,' Harry said, a hint of a smile cracking his face. 'Not in the slightest.'

CHAPTER EIGHTEEN

Harry stood with Jim and Matt as the photographer he had met yesterday worked his way around the crime scene taking photos from all angles, as well as a little video. The divisional surgeon had already been and gone, pronouncing death with the immortal words, 'Dead? Well, of course, they're bloody dead! It's a bloated body in a pond of cow shit! How could it be anything else?' She had then spoken briefly to her daughter, Rebecca Sowerby, the pathologist, before heading back off into the day.

'You'd think he'd have gone for something like wedding photography instead,' Harry mused, watching as the photographer leaned over the slurry pit, snapping more photos.

'I guess,' Jim said. 'Though can you imagine it? Weddings, day in, day out? The married couple ordering you about, the family getting pissed and falling out with each other?'

'Free food and booze, though,' Matt suggested. 'And I doubt it stinks like this does.'

The photographer, having finished his job, dipped his

head down and under the tape and walked over towards Harry and Jim.

'I'm done,' he said. 'Not a nice way to go, is it?'

'Don't think such a thing exists,' Harry said.

The photographer wandered off back to his car at the side of the road when Harry called after him.

'You sent the files through from yesterday yet?'

'Sure did,' the photographer said. 'They're with, oh, what's he called . . . Swift?'

Harry bristled at this.

'The hell have you sent them to him for? I'm the SIO!'

'He asked for them,' the photographer shrugged. 'Told me to send them to him first. I thought he was forwarding them on. I guess not.'

'You guessed right.'

'I'll send them as soon as I get back,' the photographer said. 'Sorry about that.'

'Hmm,' Harry grumbled. 'I bet he isn't, though.'

Harry turned his attention back to the slurry pit and the body floating in it. Walking towards it now was Rebecca Sowerby and a couple of others dressed head to toe in white paper PPE suits.

'Swift usually ask for stuff before the team sees it?' he asked Jim and Matt.

'Not that I know of,' Jim said, then gestured towards the white figures surrounding the pit. 'Rather them than me.'

One of the figures reached into the pit with a long, hooked metal pole. After a couple of attempts, they managed to snag the body and was able to start pulling it towards the side, before guiding it slowly towards the front of the pit, where it could be easily accessed.

Matt turned away from the pit to face Harry and Jim.

'Reckon we may as well leave them to it,' he said. 'Not much we can do here right now, is there? And it's not exactly grabbing my attention as a spectator sport.'

'Need to speak to the pathologist first,' Harry said. 'Then we can head back to the office.'

Once the body was at the front of the slurry pit, the three figures who had guided it over walked past Harry, Jim, and Matt to start wading into the oozing, brown, steaming pool, to gently drag it out. One of the figures peeled off and came back to stand in front of them.

'Grimm,' it said, from behind its white mask.

'You could say that,' Harry replied. 'You got the report on yesterday's find?'

The figure lifted the mask from off her face and Rebecca Sowerby stared up at Harry. 'It's with Swift,' she said. 'He was supposed to forward it to you.'

'Well, he hasn't,' Harry said.

'Take it up with him, then.'

'Oh, I will,' Harry muttered, then said, 'but if you can give me a quick summary, that would be really helpful.'

'As you can see, I'm a little busy.'

'Wading through shit, quite literally,' Harry said.

Not even the faintest hint of a smile cracked the pathologist's stern demeanour.

'Well, there's sod all to report,' Sowerby said. 'The body was in a pretty bad way, as you saw for yourself. Finding anything would've been a challenge anyway, with the trauma it had experienced. But after two days out in the elements?'

She shook her head.

'So what did you find, then?' Harry asked. 'DNA? Footprints at the scene? Fingerprints? Anything?'

'No DNA, no hair,' Sowerby said.

'What about the feather?' Matt asked, interjecting suddenly.

The pathologist, Harry was sure, pretty much growled at Matt's interruption.

'We found bruising on the deceased's neck,' Sowerby said.

'Strangled?' Harry asked.

Sowerby shook her head. 'Windpipe wasn't crushed. More like a sleeper hold, you know, arm around the neck, squeeze, cut off the blood supply, instant rag doll.'

Harry raised an eyebrow. 'Instant rag doll? That's a new one on me.'

'The deceased was probably grabbed from behind, choked, knocked out. Not easy to do.'

'You sure about that?' Jim asked. 'I've seen it often enough.'

'Yeah, you've seen it in the movies,' Harry said. 'Doing it for real is a little different. You need to know what you're doing and to be strong enough to do it. Pretty dangerous, too, seeing as you can easily kill someone doing it. And John was a big dude so not an easy task to get done by any means.'

'As for the feather,' Sowerby said, staring at Matt, 'all we know is that it's an eagle feather. What breed of eagle I don't know, but I'll get the results to you when we have them in. No DNA on it other than that of the deceased.'

Harry stuffed his hands deep into his pockets and hunched his shoulders. 'So, someone put a sleeper hold on him, took him out to the field, stuffed him under the trailer, then ran him over, and as a final touch shoved an eagle feather in his mouth. Well, it's certainly creative if nothing else, I'll give them that.'

'Seems that way, yes,' Sowerby said. 'And before you ask,

the time of death is pretty difficult to nail down at the best of times, so with that one? Almost impossible. Best I can say is that the body had been there for at least two days.'

'How do you know?' Jim asked, and Harry took note of it, happy to see that he was always trying to learn. There was a lot to be said for it, he thought, and a lot of detectives could learn from it as well, some of them being proper know-it-alls.

'It's not just the state of the body,' Sowerby explained, clearly sparking at Jim's show of interest. 'Nature's been having its wicked way with it, so the flies, the maggots and their size, that kind of thing, all gives us a good indication. His body was basically a massive sex fest for all the creepy crawlies.'

'And we know that he was alive on Friday anyway,' Harry added.

There was a groan from one of the two PPE-clad figures.

'How you going to approach this one, then?' he asked.

'With a hose,' Sowerby said. 'We'll have to search as best we can through whatever's on the body as we clean it off, then get it back to have a proper look.'

'Sounds like fun.'

'Doesn't it just?'

Harry realised then that the conversation with the pathologist hadn't just been informative but almost civil. Not friendly as such, but neither of them had taken a bite at the other. He was as relieved as he was confused.

'What about footprints?' Harry asked. 'If someone did drive John out there in his own tractor to crush him under the wheels of the trailer, then they had to walk out.'

'Footprints, yes,' Sowerby said, 'but no treads. Looks like whoever was there with him had bags strapped around their shoes.'

'Clever,' Harry said. 'And annoying.'

'We've taken moulds, measurements, the usual, see if we can get some idea of weight, a guess on height from the length of stride, that kind of thing. What use all that'll be, who knows?'

'Well, we'll leave you to it,' Harry said. 'If you can get that report to me that would be great.'

'I said I would, didn't I?' Sowerby said, her voice sharp again. 'Christ alive! You really do think the world revolves around you, don't you?'

'That's not what I meant . . .'

But the pathologist wasn't listening and had gone back to join her colleagues.

'Back to the office, then?' Matt asked.

Harry thought for a moment and then pointed towards the farmhouse. 'You said the farmer found the body, yes?'

'Yep,' Matt said. 'Just doing his morning check of his stock and there it was, bobbing about.'

'I'd like to speak to him now if that's possible? And we'll want him to come down to the station to give an official state-ment, but a chat now would be good, while it's all still fresh in his mind.'

Matt quickly walked off towards the house to get the farmer.

'You don't think this is connected to yesterday's thing, do you?' Jim asked. 'John's death and now this?'

'Do you?' Harry replied.

Jim was quiet for a moment before he said anything more.

'Accidents happen on farms all the time,' Jim said. 'They're dangerous places. I've not known two to happen so close together though. But yesterday's wasn't an accident, was it? And now this? Doesn't smell right.'

'No, it doesn't,' Harry said, and he didn't just mean the body being pulled out of the slurry either. There was something about it all that gave him the horrible feeling that things would only get worse before they got better.

CHAPTER NINETEEN

'THIS WON'T TAKE LONG,' HARRY SAID TO THE MAN NOW standing with him, Matt, and Jim. 'Sorry to take you away from your family. This must be hard for you all.'

'Hard? It's bloody horrible is what it is,' the man said. 'Not every day you wake up to find a body on your land, you know. You're not all going to ask me questions, are you? I don't do well with questions.'

Harry attempted a smile, despite the fact that he knew it generally made his face look worse. 'PCSO Metcalf will just take notes, won't you, Jim?'

Jim gave a nod, brandishing his notebook and pencil.

'And Detective Sergeant Dinsdale and I just want to get an idea of what you found, that's all. Then if you can pop down to the office in Hawes later on today and give a statement, that would be very much appreciated.'

'I'm not due to go to Hawes today, though,' the man said. 'Mart's not on, is it? And there's nowt I'm wanting from the supplies shop.'

'Supplies shop?' Harry asked.

'It's like a supermarket for farmers,' Matt explained. 'Imagine a place where you can buy anything from a chainsaw to chicken feed. Worth a look if you get a chance.'

'I don't have much need for either of those,' Harry said.

'Come on, everyone needs a chainsaw,' Matt said.

Harry looked back to the farmer. 'I didn't catch your name.'

'I didn't give it.'

'Come on, Pat,' Jim said. 'We're here to help, you know that.'

Harry caught a look between Jim and the farmer, who then seemed to relax a little.

'Sorry,' he said. 'It's just that it's set me off a bit, if you know what I mean? I'm Pat. Patrick Coates.'

Harry recognised the name. 'Isn't Liz a Coates?' he asked, looking at Matt and Jim.

'Probably a very, very, very distant relative,' Matt said. 'There's names around here that have been around for centuries—Dinsdale, Metcalf, Coates, to name a few.'

Harry pondered on this briefly, then was back to Pat. 'So, Pat,' he said, 'if you could just run through what happened, that would be really helpful. And don't worry if you think the details aren't important, that's for us to decide, okay?'

Pat took a deep breath then started to talk, his thick, Yorkshire accent dancing around his words like children around a maypole. 'Well, I was up at five,' he said. 'Bit early for me, to be honest, but there we are. Got up anyway and decided I may as well just head on out and do something with my time. No point lying around in bed, is there?'

Harry wasn't exactly of the same opinion and asked, 'Why were you up so early, then?'

Pat shrugged. 'I think it was a fox that woke me. Heard a

scrabbling sound outside. That's why I went out, really. They can't half-scare the animals. And little Gracie, she's my youngest, she's got these two rabbits you see, and that's a tasty meal for any fox for sure, and I can't be doing with seeing her all upset.'

'You didn't hear a car?'

'Oh, there's always cars,' Pat said. 'It's a busy road, that.'

Harry turned to look briefly at the road behind them. Busy wasn't a word that immediately sprang to mind, and particularly not in the middle of the night. 'So, you heard a car as well?'

'No, I said there's always cars,' Pat replied. 'But there were one or two I'm sure, yes.'

'And then you went outside?'

'Not immediately, no,' Pat said. 'I grabbed my gun and then I went out.'

'Gun?'

'For the fox,' Pat said. 'At least it would scare the bugger off, sending a couple of barrels off in the air. Can't shoot a fox with a shotgun. Well, you can, but I don't think it's right, myself. Need a rifle for that. So I don't.'

Harry was beginning to wonder just how many households in the dales held their own private little armouries.

'And what did you find?' Matt asked.

'Nowt much,' Pat shrugged. 'I mean, I wasn't expecting to find anything, was I? I was just wandering around outside, checking for a fox, and then decided to go and have a look in on the animals, wish them good morning, like. They spook easily, but they were fine. And that's when I saw it. The body. In the slurry, if you know what I mean? And I shouldn't have been able to see it, should I?'

Harry tried to imagine what it must have been like, up

early in the morning, surrounded by the countryside, to then find a body in your backyard. 'Why not?'

'Why not?' Pat asked, more than a little incredulously. 'I've got kids, that's why not! You think I'd have a slurry pit uncovered when I've got kids? Of course not! And there it is as plain as the nose on my face, a body, just floating in the shit, and the cover has been all pulled back! Doesn't make sense! It's never uncovered! Never!'

'How did you spot it?' asked Harry.

'With my own bloody eyes, that's how!' Pat said. 'What kind of question is that?'

Harry was used to people being bristly so he reworded his question. 'What I mean is, what drew your attention to it in the first place? It wouldn't have been easy to see.'

'It was a bloody great lump sticking out of the muck,' Pat explained. 'That, and the fact that the cover had been pulled back. Thought it might be a deer or a sheep, perhaps even a badger, and I knew I'd have to clear it out later, because you can't leave something like that just floating there, can you? So I went over to check, which was when I realised what it actually was. Bit of a shock, if I'm honest.'

'I'm sure it was,' Matt said. 'Any idea who it is?'

'You're having a laugh, aren't you? How the hell do you expect me to know that?'

Harry jumped in with, 'I think what DS Dinsdale is asking is if there was anything about the body, something it was wearing perhaps, that you recognised? Anything at all?'

'Not a thing,' Pat said. 'All I know is that I've got some poor bugger floating dead in an uncovered slurry pit, police traipsing all over my farm, and I've a business to run. Can't stop just because of this, you know. I'm a busy man.'

'And there's nothing else you can tell us?' Harry asked.

'Nothing else you saw which was strange or out of place? Nothing else you heard or noticed?'

Pat shook his head and shrugged. 'Just the uncovered pit. And the body. That's enough to be going on with, surely, isn't it? Because someone must've pulled the cover off, and either that poor sod threw themselves in, or someone pushed them in.'

Harry was hoping for more. 'Right, well, thanks, Mr Coates,' he said. 'You've been a tremendous help.'

He hadn't been of any real help at all, that Harry could see, but perhaps something would come out later, you never knew. Had that fox he heard been someone in the farmyard, perhaps? Possibly, but still, what did that tell them other than sod all?

'That it, then?' Pat asked. 'I can go?'

'Yes,' Harry said. 'But if you can pop into the office in Hawes later on, that would be very much appreciated.'

'I'll have to see,' Pat said.

'By which I mean, I will expect you to come into the office today, Mr Coates.'

'Right, well, if that's how it's going to be.'

'It is.'

And with that, Pat Coates turned back towards his house and strode off, his gait not that dissimilar to that of a cowboy, Harry thought.

'Learned a lot there, then,' Matt said as they all watched the farmer go back into his house.

A call cut the air and Harry, Jim, and Matt all turned at the same time to see someone waving at them from beside the slurry pit. The pathologist and her two colleagues had been joined by other officers now that the body was no longer in the pit and they were busy examining the rest of the site for possible evidence. It looked like a terrible job to be on with, Harry thought as he walked over. 'What is it?'

Rebecca Sowerby walked over to meet him, pulling her facemask down on the way.

'This,' she said, and held up an evidence bag.

'Ah, bollocks,' Harry said.

'Exactly what I said,' Sowerby agreed. 'Looks the same as the one we found on the body yesterday. Kind of links the two deaths, doesn't it?'

'Links?' Harry said. 'Links! Hell, this pretty much handcuffs them together and throws them into the same bloody cell!'

Harry turned then and stormed back towards Matt and Jim.

'Let me guess,' Matt said.

'No I won't,' replied Harry, then he added, 'But yes, it's another sodding feather. Another!'

'Seriously?' Jim said. 'What does that mean, then?'

Harry knew exactly what it meant and already his gut was twisting up at the implications of what they could potentially be dealing with. 'What it means, Jim,' he said, his voice quiet, low and rumbling, the sound of it the approach of thunder, 'is that whoever did this, to whoever that is down there, killed old John Capstick as well.'

CHAPTER TWENTY

BACK IN HAWES, AND SITTING AT A TABLE IN THE MAIN room the local police used at the Community Office, Harry was staring hard into an enormous mug of tea which Matt had just handed him. Jenny and Liz were on their way back from the domestic. Gordy, having done her bit with the family at the farm, had headed back down the dale, but had promised to be in touch later on, assuming, she said, 'that all those wee squaddies at Catterick aren't out on the piss'. On the table in front of him was an open laptop which he'd used to go through the files sent by the photographer and pathologist from the day before. He'd left a couple of terse messages on Swift's phone, enquiring about the files, but hadn't heard a thing yet.

'How big actually is this?' Harry asked, his hands clasping the mug, his fingertips only just meeting around the other side of it.

'Well, it's a pint mug,' Matt said, 'so I'm guessing it holds a pint. I figured you needed one.'

'A pint? Of tea? And where did you get it?'

'Café over in Ingleton,' Matt explained. 'I've been going there for years, you see. Loads of cavers and walkers and whatnot use it. That's one of the café's souvenirs. Well, what I mean is, it's actually their only souvenir. I was over there the weekend before last. Meant to bring it in before, but I forgot.'

Harry picked up the mug and stared at it, trying to take in the scale of the thing. 'It's nearly as big as my head.'

'Can't beat a pint of tea and a bacon butty,' Matt said. 'So . . .' He removed a paper bag from his jacket pocket and handed it to Harry, who took it from him and stared at the contents for a moment before removing the roll inside, which was generously filled with bacon. 'Stopped in at Cockett's on the way through,' Matt said, then gave another bag to Jim. 'After what we saw this morning, I figured we all needed a little pick-me-up. And there's cake for later.'

Harry bit into the butty waiting for Matt to announce that he'd also bought cheese for the cake. He didn't, so Harry was a little relieved because he still hadn't quite got used to that particular food combination, though he had no doubt there was some lurking in the fridge in the corner of the room. 'Nice,' he said, his voice muffled a little. 'You not eating?'

'Already did,' Matt said, patting his stomach. 'Pushed mine into my face on the way here. I think I inhaled it, to be honest.'

For the next couple of minutes, Harry and Jim quietly munched their way through the butties, and all the time Harry was thinking about what they were now in the middle of. One death, one murder, well that was something folk could handle, not in a way that meant it was any easier, because all investigations were different, but more in the way that it was communicated. The press would snap at it but lose interest pretty quickly unless it was a particularly horrific death or involved a celebrity. Things would quieten down, and then you would be able to just get on with the job in hand.

But two murders, and within days of each other? Harry was pretty sure he could hear journalists up and down the country already sniffing it out like pigs seeking out rare and expensive truffles. Particularly that local one, Richard Askew, who'd got right up his nose a few weeks ago. And there was a nagging thought as well, one that was telling him that where there were two murders, three soon followed. He certainly hoped there wouldn't be, and that this was as far as it all went, but he had an awful feeling that whatever was going on, wasn't finished. And that meant they needed to get ahead of this and fast. But with no suspects, and bugger all evidence, where were they supposed to start?

'Right then,' Harry said at last, the bacon butty demolished, and his pint mug of tea halfway gone, 'best we get something up on that board.'

He stood up, grabbed a drywipe pen and pulled the cap off, then pointed at the whiteboard which had the name 'John Capstick' written on it, a few other scant notes, and nothing else. It didn't exactly inspire confidence in him that this was going to be easy.

'Should we not wait for Jenny?' Jim asked.

'Why?'

'She was doing the board, wasn't she?'

'I'm pretty sure that the three of us can do it just as well,' Harry said. 'I've used a pen before and it may surprise you to hear, I know, but I've even been known to write on a board screwed to a wall. Multi-talented.'

'That's not what I meant.'

Harry knew he was being sharp, but sometimes he just couldn't be doing with people being precious about things, and more times than he cared to remember, he'd found the board to be one of those things. From the way some laid it out, to what colour pens others used, the whole area of The Board in many ways got right on his nerves. It was a useful thing, and he was a big fan of its simplicity, the fact that it wasn't computer-generated and all technical, but as far as Harry was concerned, no board in any investigation belonged to any one person.

The office door opened.

'Hi, Jenny,' Jim said, then glanced at Harry who saw the smile on his face. 'Look, it's Liz and Jenny. Fancy that!'

Jenny strode in and caught sight of where Harry was standing. Liz sat down between Matt and Jim.

'Seems I got here just in time,' Jenny said and before Harry was even aware of what was happening, the detective constable had plucked the pen from out of his hand and was standing at the other side of the board. 'So, what have we got, then?'

Harry caught Jim looking at him, laughter creasing the corners of his eyes, and he sat back down. 'Before all that,' he said, 'what happened with you two, then?'

'You missed a classic,' Matt said. 'Death by slurry!'

'Yeah, I'm not really convinced we missed out at all,' Liz said.

'Well, come on then,' Jim said. 'Anything exciting, or not?'

Liz pulled a sandwich packet from her pocket, tore it

open, and handed half to Jenny. 'Two kids skiving off school,' she said. 'They'd been down at the tip, bin diving. Got caught, we were called in, and we had to sort it out.'

'How's that a domestic?' Matt asked.

'Oh, that's easy,' Jenny said. 'Just throw in a husband in a white vest with a can of Special Brew in one hand, and a wife who had moved on from Special Brew to something stronger by the time we arrived, and you can let your imagination do the rest.'

'A wee bit shouty, then,' said Matt, in a pretty terrible Scottish accent. 'As Gordy would say.'

'A wee bit shouty indeed.' Liz nodded.

'Anyway,' Harry said, bringing everyone back to why they were actually all there to begin with. 'The board . . .'

'The feather from yesterday,' Jim offered first. 'The one found in John's mouth. It's an eagle feather.'

Jenny jotted that down on the board, and as the conversation continued, started to join points up with lines if she thought it necessary. 'Why do that, then?' she asked. 'Seems a bit weird.'

'What, stuff something in his mouth?' Matt asked.

'No, not just that,' Jenny said. 'Why an eagle feather? Seems a bit specific.'

'Yeah,' Liz said, her mouth a little too full of sandwich, 'why not just a pigeon feather, something easy to find? And just where the hell does anyone get an eagle feather from, anyway?'

'Maybe it's some kind of reference to being a predator,' Matt offered. 'Birds of prey, right? They're pretty amazing predators and maybe that's what our killer thinks he or she is.'

'There was another today as well,' Harry said. 'Found in the second victim's mouth. Don't know if it's an eagle feather, but I'd put money on it being the same.'

'And we know that John was incapacitated before he was crushed,' Matt said. 'Someone used a sleeper hold on him, knocked him out, then drove him up into the field before finishing him off.'

'Which to my mind rules out Nick,' Jim said. 'John's a big bloke. Nick isn't. Even if Nick managed to knock him out, there's no way he could get him up to the field. Doubt he could drag him even a foot or two.'

'Someone did though,' said Harry. 'Bill, that farmer I spoke to over in Oughtershaw, he saw them, Saturday morning. Two people in the tractor. He assumed it was Nick, but if it wasn't him, then . . .' Another thought bumped its way into Harry's mind. 'So where was John when he was attacked?'

Silence took a seat in the room.

'Back at the house, I suppose,' Jim said.

Harry's stomach twisted just enough. 'I need forensics to go over there ASAP,' he said. 'I know there's probably nothing, particularly as we've all been in there, but it's worth a look, just in case.'

Jim quickly made a call while everyone waited. 'Sorted,' he said.

'Good,' nodded Harry.

What about the fact that they're both farm accidents?' Matt asked.

'Well, for a start, they're neither of them accidents,' Harry said. 'That much I'm pretty sure we can all agree on, right?'

'No, but they've been made to look like them, haven't they? Capstick was run over by a trailer, now some poor sod's been drowned in slurry. And the first one is surely more common than the second.'

'We don't know that they drowned,' Harry corrected. 'And how do you know one's more common than the other?'

'He's got a point,' Jim said, agreeing with Matt.

'Has he now,' Harry said. 'And you can support that statement, can you?'

Jim gave a nod and explained further. 'The three most common causes of fatal accidents on a farm are falling from a height, being hit by a vehicle, and being hit by a moving object. Those three alone account for around sixty percent of deaths.'

Harry was impressed. 'But what about being shot, then?' he asked. 'I've met two farmers in two days, both with guns.'

'People are careful with shotguns and rifles,' Jim explained, 'because they know they're dangerous. Other stuff, well, they can get complacent, make a mistake, just forget what they're doing because it's so routine. That's usually what happens, which is why the common accidents are what I said they are.'

'You always read up on farming statistics?' Harry asked.

'There was an article on it in the Farmer's Guardian a while back,' Jim said. 'Can't recall a mention of death by slurry pit. They're usually covered up these days, like Pat said, remember? So how had his cover been pulled back?'

Harry did remember and at the time hadn't thought much of it, wondering if the farmer had forgotten to do it himself. But now, thinking about it, what if someone else had done it? Didn't that make more sense?

'So, we've got two farm deaths,' Matt said, 'and that's a bit weird, however you look at it. Why do it like this? Go to all that trouble? What's the point?'

'There's something else though,' Harry said. 'We've got two victims. The second one we don't have an ID for yet. When we do, we will need to establish a link. Because there has to be one, doesn't there? Unless it's just some mad bastard out killing at random for shits and giggles, which I doubt.'

'That's a delightful phrase,' Jenny said, then asked, 'But why? I've met a few mad bastards in my time. We all have, right? Isn't there a chance someone is just out doing this for the sheer hell of it?'

Harry wasn't convinced. 'None of this looks random. It looks planned. And planning takes effort. It also implies that there's more to it than just the sheer hellish joy of murder. And trust me, that's been given as the reason for a killing or two more often than any of us would care to imagine.'

'Anything else?' Jenny asked, pen poised. 'And I don't mean just from the crime scenes.'

'Yes, what about that Reedy bloke?' Harry asked. 'He's clearly a local dealer. What if John was tied up in something and it came back to bite him? And there's the text that Nick got, which reminds me, have we got any data from that phone, yet?'

Matt gave a shrug. 'Reedy is Nick's contact,' he said. 'Nick's world. John wasn't into anything like that. And Reedy's all flash for sure, but that's about all he is, to be honest.'

'And you're sure John isn't involved in whatever it is Reedy gets up to?'

'You saw his house, how he lived,' Matt said. 'The bloke was sailing close to bankruptcy his whole life, like basically every farmer in the country. If he had extra money, he'd have spent it, for sure. Any cash he had that the taxman didn't know about, well that went on drink, nowt else.'

'What about location?'

'Well, it wasn't over in Oughtershaw,' Jim said. 'Best they could give us was that it came from somewhere in or around Hawes.'

Harry let his head fall back while he took that information in. It didn't give them much except confirmation that this was all turning out to be worse by the hour. Harry raised his head and stared at the board beside Jenny.

'One more thing,' he said, 'I want all of this kept quiet. Now, I know that's impossible, what with Nick being involved, and this being the Dales and the fact that every single one of you seems to know every-sodding-one else, but we don't want anything leaking out, not without us being in control of it.'

'Can't help but think it's already a bit late for that,' Matt said.

'Doesn't matter,' Harry said. 'As soon as the media find out that we've got what looks like two killings in just a few days of each other, and only a few miles apart, they'll be all over it. And the only information that I want them getting is what we give them, when we want to give it. Nothing else. At all. Because once this goes public, it doesn't take too much imagination to see that folk will start to panic. And that's never good.'

'You mean you want a media blackout?'

Harry went to speak but was interrupted by his phone

buzzing in his pocket. 'Yes?' he snapped, slapping it against his ear.

When he put the phone back down, the rest of the team stared at him, waiting for him to speak.

'That was the pathologist,' Harry said. 'They've identified the second body.'

CHAPTER TWENTY-ONE

HARRY STOOD IN THE MORTUARY WITH THE pathologist. Jim was with him as well, having driven them both over in the police Land Rover after deciding that it was best to leave Matt and Jenny back in Hawes with Liz. Their rank would serve better should people come around asking questions. And if the press turned up, they had strict instructions on what to say and what to keep to themselves. Harry had put it as succinctly as he could, 'Give them sod all. And if they ask for more, give them even less.'

It was mid-afternoon and having spoken to Sowerby briefly on the phone, Harry had insisted on heading over to have a look at the two bodies for himself.

'But I've given you all the information you need.'

'I'd still prefer to speak to you face to face and to see the bodies.'

'Why?'

'I don't need to give you a reason. It's my job. And yours. I'll be there in an hour.'

'But I'm busy!'

'Yes, I know you are. With me.'

It wasn't ghoulish fascination. Instead, it was because sometimes seeing things for real helped him sort out his own thoughts. Also, Harry preferred to have a face rather than just a name. These were people who had suffered, usually terribly, and it was his job to find out who had done bad things to them and then put them away as quickly as possible and for as long as possible. In some ways, he almost felt like he owed it to the victims to introduce himself, to let them know that he was going to do everything within his power to give them the justice they deserved. Maybe it was a bit old fashioned, but what was wrong with that?

The room was like every other mortuary Harry had ever been in, all stainless steel and the disturbingly confused scent of death and disinfectant. The vapour rub which he had dabbed under his nose before handing it to Jim to do the same was only so effective and the reek still pushed through. It was a cloying sweet sourness and just when you thought it was gone, it would swing back and churn your stomach.

Bright lights gave the room a washed-out glow. It was a place devoid of colour, a silvery grey palette as lifeless as the bodies hiding silently in the freezer drawers in the wall.

Harry stared at the two body-shaped sheets in front of him. 'You don't have to be here for this,' he said, glancing over at Jim. 'You can just wait for me outside. This won't take long, I'm sure.'

'I want to be,' Jim replied. 'Well, I don't mean that I want to be, because there's plenty of other places I'd rather be, but I think I should be, if you know what I mean.'

'I do,' Harry said, once again impressed with Jim and his attitude to his job, then turned his attention to the piercing stare he was receiving from the pathologist.

'Thanks for seeing us,' he said, working hard to keep things civil between them. 'It's been a busy couple of days, hasn't it?'

'It's always busy,' Sowerby said. 'People die every day. Sometimes horribly. It's what happens.'

Harry stepped forward, bringing himself closer to the two bodies thankfully still hidden from sight. 'So, which one's which, then?'

'The one nearest you is John Capstick,' Sowerby said, with a quick point of a finger. 'This one is Mr Hutchison.'

'Hutchinson?' Harry said.

'No, Hutchison. Only one N. Don't ask me why. Can well imagine he spent far too much time correcting people on that one.'

Harry took a look at the as yet unrevealed body as it lay before them. Whoever this Mr Hutchison was, he was certainly tall. Not massive, just long, Harry thought. Probably six-four. The kind of height that, if you have it, you exaggerate a bit further, and suddenly everyone thinks you're six-six.

'What do we know about him, then?' Jim asked. 'I don't recognise the name.'

Sowerby grabbed a clipboard from behind her. 'Hutchison, Barry,' she said. 'Born 1970. He's from Richmond.'

'Then what the hell is he doing in a slurry pit in Widdale on the other side of Hawes?' Jim asked.

'What about witness statements?' Harry asked. 'Anyone see anything?'

'Not a thing,' Sowerby said, shaking her head. She stepped forward and reached out to pull back the sheet, revealing the man's face and torso. The body was grey and no longer covered in cow muck, which Harry was relieved about. However, with the removal of the sheet, he noticed the strangely sweet tang of dung in the air, the stench of it still clinging to the body. It mixed appallingly with the underlying scent of delayed decay and Harry found himself having to really focus to not let it get to him and turn his stomach too much.

'So, what do we know?' Harry asked.

'Same MO as yesterday,' said Sowerby and pointed at the body's neck. 'See here? Bruising. Not strangulation, because he didn't die like that. Just enough to knock him out. But there's more of it, like it was done twice. Then there's this . . .'

Harry looked to where the pathologist was pointing, which was at Hutchison's wrists. 'What exactly is it that you're showing me?'

All Harry could see was wrinkled flesh, like the skin on a joint of pork.

'There's bruising at the wrists,' explained Sowerby. 'It would suggest that he was tied up as well.'

'What, he was chucked in with his hands lashed together?'

Sowerby shook her head. 'This is how we found him. There was nothing on the wrists.'

Harry could feel his brain seizing up. 'So someone incapacitated him, tied him up, presumably to transport him from wherever he was to the farm, then put a chokehold on him again, before untying him and throwing him in the slurry pit? Why do that?'

Sowerby shrugged. 'Why do any of it? And it looks that way, yes. Oh, and he was gagged as well, and that was removed before he was thrown in. Really went for it this time, whoever it was.' She pointed at some marks on the dead man's face.

'And that wasn't found either?' Harry asked. 'The gag or whatever it was that was shoved in his mouth?'

'No. Just the feather.'

'So, how did he actually die, then?' Jim asked.

'He drowned,' Sowerby said. 'Lungs were full of cow shit.'

'Jesus . . .' Harry muttered.

'He didn't stand a chance,' Sowerby explained. 'At that end, the slurry is about ten feet deep. You can't swim in it. Once you're in, that's it. The poor bastard.'

'It's why they're usually covered,' Jim said. 'Slurry pits, I mean. They're dangerous things.'

'So why wasn't it covered?' Sowerby asked.

'The farmer seemed to be asking the same question,' Harry said, staring at the body. 'He's got kids so he said it was covered all the time and I got the impression that he was pretty hot on safety. The house, the whole place, it was immaculate. Can't see him being lax about covering up a slurry pit. So, someone else uncovered it before throwing old Barry here into it and to his death.'

There were terrible ways to die, Harry thought, but drowning in cow slurry, drinking the stuff down, sucking it into your lungs, well that was right up there with some of the worst he'd ever had to investigate.

'What about the feather?' Jim asked.

'Oh, that,' Sowerby said, checking her notes again. 'Eagle feather. Like the one found in that one there.' She pointed with her pen at the other body.

'Was it in his mouth?' Harry asked.

Sowerby gave a nod.

'So how did he drown and not spit it out?'

'Well, for a start, that's a pretty good sign he was unconscious,' Sowerby said. 'And second, it was jammed in there, stuck between his teeth, so that it wouldn't just float on out.'

Harry suddenly felt as though something very heavy had been placed on his back.

'You alright?' Jim asked.

Harry rubbed his eyes. 'Yes,' he said. 'It's just that, well, you know, these are linked now, aren't they? I knew they were when another feather was found. But the fact that it's the same kind of feather? Well, that's it for certain. Confirmation. Barry and John here, they were killed by the same person. And we need to find out why and who sharpish.'

'We also found this,' Sowerby said, and hoisted into view a plastic bag inside which was a mobile phone.

Harry immediately thought back to the text Nick had received. 'Is that Capstick's?'

'His are the only fingerprints we found on it, so yes, it must be,' she said. 'Other than that, we can't get anything from it. Lying in cow shit is clearly not very good for your average, everyday smartphone.'

'And it was on this body?'

'Stuffed in his pocket,' Sowerby said, covering up Hutchison's body, before moving onto the next. 'Look, I know you've seen this one before,' she began, 'but it's a real mess. That first one, well he still looks normal, because he's intact. But this one? Not so much.'

'Before you ask, I'm fine,' Jim said. 'I was the one who was at the scene first, remember?'

Harry nodded to the pathologist to get on with it and she quickly pulled the sheet back. 'Bloody hell . . .' he hissed.

Jim was silent, though Harry watched the colour drain from his face like sand in an egg timer.

'It's a bit of a mess isn't it?' Sowerby said. 'But you can

just make out the bruising on the neck. Other than that, there's nothing else to add. You know about the feather, and we know how long he was out there in the open.'

'And you found nothing else?'

'No,' Sowerby replied. 'For crime scenes that are so messy, they were both very clean.'

'How do you mean?' Jim asked.

'There's nothing other than the feather that tells us much about the person who did this,' Sowerby said. 'We've got no hairs, no trace DNA, nothing. Not even footprints. Whoever did this was really bloody careful. You'd swear they'd shaved themselves then hosed themselves down in bleach.'

'That's not what I need to hear.'

'It's all that I can tell you.'

Harry stepped back from Capstick's body. 'Thanks again,' he said, looking over at the pathologist.

'If I find anything or learn anything else, I'll let you know,' she replied. 'Now, if you don't mind? I've got lots of other things to be getting on with and this has already taken up time that I didn't have.'

Harry gestured for Jim to follow him and they were soon back outside breathing air which, though perhaps not as fresh as the stuff blown from off the hills in the dales, was still a hell of a lot more pleasant than what they'd just emerged from. 'You okay?' Harry asked.

'Yes and no,' Jim replied. 'I've never seen anything like this.'

'You and me both,' Harry said. 'So let's just hope that the others have something more to go on when we get back to the office.'

CHAPTER TWENTY-TWO

OF ALL THE THINGS HARRY WANTED TO FIND WAITING for him when he got back to Hawes, the absolute very bottom of the list were journalists. In fact, they were so far down the list that they weren't even on it. He never wanted to find journalists anywhere. He was pretty sure good ones, honest ones, existed, but as yet he hadn't met any of them. And the ones who swooped in at the first sniff of a murder were, he believed, the very worst of the bunch. Vultures after meat on the bones of the dead—the stories behind the stories, relevant or not, interviews with relatives, little tasty bits of history from the victim's lives so beloved by the tabloids—anything to feed the unthinking masses a news story that promised just enough darkness to have them wanting more.

Harry knew it was a cliché—a cop hating the press—but that was just the way it was. One day, perhaps, he'd meet one he could trust—a journalist who wasn't just in it for the blood money and the shock-horror headline—but until then, he'd just stick with showing them the same amount of love as he would a cockroach.

'Drive around again,' Harry said to Jim, as they came up to the end of the cobbles on The Hill and saw the crowd milling around in the marketplace. 'Need time to think.'

Without a word, Jim took a right and swung them back down The Holme and onto Penn Lane.

'Pull over.'

Jim did as instructed.

'You okay?'

'No, I'm not,' Harry said, leaning his head back. 'We need that lot cleared out otherwise we're going to get nothing at all done. Call Swift.'

'You sure about that?'

'Of course, I'm sure!' Harry roared, then caught himself. 'Sorry, Jim. Journalists. They bring out the worst in me, that's all. But call Swift. We need to get him down here to deal with it. Right now, I'd probably only make it worse.'

'He won't be happy.'

'That's what I'm hoping,' Harry said. 'A grumpy DSup is a very useful weapon against the press, trust me.'

Jim made the call.

'Sir? It's PCSO James Metcalf. Yes, that's the one. I was wondering if—'

Jim's voice was cut short by whatever was being said at the other end. He then looked at Harry and handed him the phone.

'He wants to talk to you.'

Harry took the phone.

'Sir, we need you over here in Hawes. Bit of a situation with the press.'

'I've been on the phone with your Detective Superinten-dent,' Swift said, ignoring Harry completely. 'She's a delight, isn't she?'

That she is, Harry thought.

'Have you now, sir? And what did she want?'

'You misunderstand,' Swift said. 'I called her. About you.'

'Go on . . .'

'You see, I'm not really sure that you quite fit in up here, and I was just voicing my concerns.'

'Were you now?'

'It's nothing personal,' Swift continued. 'It's just that I think perhaps your ways are different to how things are done around here. And that kind of friction is something we can do without.'

'Do you mean *we* or *I*?' Harry asked. 'Have you had any complaints from the team?'

Harry eyeballed Jim at this point and received a very clear shake of the head.

'Nothing overt, no,' Swift said. 'It's a feeling, that's all, Grimm. Born of years of experience. You can understand, yes?'

'What did she say?'

A pause in the conversation. The kind of silence behind which one can hear the sound of a mind thinking, chewing something over.

'She thinks very highly of you,' Swift said, and Harry could hear the pain in the man's voice as he said the words, and the surprise which leaned towards disbelief. 'She thinks you'll settle in just fine.'

Harry did his best to not let the smile on his face show in his voice.

'That "years of experience" you just mentioned, sir? I could do with its help right now, actually.'

'Really? Why? What's happening? Is something up?'

Harry couldn't have thrown a better hook and line.

'Yes, it's a situation that I really need your input on, actually, sir. Can you help?'

Harry knew exactly what he was doing, saying just enough to appeal to Swift's ego, and taking him away from his thoughts about Firbank.

'Oh, well, if you insist,' Swift replied.

'I think your seniority in this, your experience, would be hugely appreciated by the rest of the team, sir,' Harry said, doing his best to sound as convincing as possible. 'I hope that's okay?'

'Well, of course, it's okay!' Swift said, his voice biting impatiently at the heels of Grimm's. 'What exactly do you need from me?'

Harry paused just long enough.

'Well?'

'The press is here, sir, and I've given them your name as the point of contact. I know you're not SIO on this, but I thought it best that you be the one to front this.'

'The press? SIO on what? The incidents you've been investigating? They don't know about it all yet, surely? They can't!'

'They can and they do,' Harry said. 'Not everything I'm sure, but enough to be here and needing to be dealt with. And I can't be spending my time on it when, as SIO, and as I'm sure you will understand and support, I need all the time and staff hours I can get to find who's responsible as soon as possible.'

More silence, the sound of Swift clearing his throat.

'Right, I'm on my way. I'll be there within the hour.'

'Thank you, sir,' Harry said. 'I can't say how much I app—'

The line went dead.

Harry handed Jim his phone back.

'Sorted?' Jim asked.

'Looks that way,' Harry said. 'Right, best we go tell the press Swift is who they need to speak to, eh?'

A few minutes later, Jim pulled them up into the market-place and Harry climbed out to witness a sea of faces turn to stare at him. There were cameras, too, and microphones, and lots of people getting very shouty about things. And Harry wasn't in the mood for shouty unless, of course, it was him that was doing the shouting.

As the faces crowded in, Harry turned back to Jim's Land Rover and climbed up onto the bonnet. He then turned around and stared down at the crowd.

'Right then,' Harry bellowed. 'How's about you lot all shut it for a moment and listen up? You can do that, can't you? Listen?'

A tall man thin as a string pushed his way to the front of the crowd and looked up at Harry, notebook in one hand, pen in the other.

'DCI Grimm,' the man began, 'what can you tell us about the two murders that have occurred over the last few days?'

Harry glared at the man, willing his face to melt under the heat of his fury. He'd met this one before. It was Richard Askew, from the Westmorland Gazette. A big mouth in a small paper doing his best to shout the loudest.

'Come on, Grimm,' the man said, 'the people have a right to know! Are they safe? Is there a serial killer on the loose?'

'Was I talking to you?' Harry asked. 'Specifically, I mean?'

Askew shrugged.

'Is that a yes, a no, or an I don't give a shit?' Harry asked.

'Just so we're both sure. Because I, unlike you, prefer to be clear on things, before I act.'

'No, I guess,' Askew said.

'Exactly!' Harry replied. 'So, why don't you wind that thin neck of yours in and see if you can find a little bit of courtesy, while I chat to everyone else, and not just you?'

Askew's mouth fell open to say something then snapped shut.

'Anyway,' Harry said, now back on with the rest of the crowd, 'I've just been on the phone with Detective Superintendent Swift and he will be here within the hour to give a statement and answer your questions. Until then, can I ask that you give myself and my team the space we need to get on with our jobs? Thank you!'

Harry was about to climb down when Askew piped up again.

'Can you confirm that the victims went to school together, Detective? Right here in Hawes, as a matter of fact?'

The words cut into Harry like shrapnel and it was all he could do to not grab a hold of Askew and introduce him to the loud end of a really good slap.

'Were you not listening?' Harry asked. 'Or is it deliberate? I mean, do you act like an idiot and hope I'll take pity on you and answer your questions, is that it?'

'So they did,' Askew said.

Harry leaned in, making full use of his size, but more of his ruined face, to add to his menace.

'The DSup will be here soon enough to answer your questions. I suggest that you wait until then to ask any more.'

Then, without another word, Harry pushed on through

and over to the Community Centre, crashing through the doors and into the office to find the rest of the team.

'Bollocks!' Harry roared, as the door crashed shut behind him. 'Absolute bloody arse bollocks!'

Matt stood up and met Harry halfway. Liz and Jenny remained seated.

'They just turned up,' Matt said. 'Word's got around about what's happened. That's just the way it is around here. And with La'll Nick involved, it's got around even quicker. Everyone will be talking about it now. And by everyone, I mean literally everyone. Knock on any door right now, and it'll be the topic of conversation, for sure.'

'What's this about the victims being at school together?' Harry asked. 'And how is it I'm hearing it first from that streak of piss, Askew and not from you lot?'

Harry watched as Matt composed himself.

'They were at Hawes Primary School together,' Matt then explained. 'Names around here, they don't get forgotten. They just sort of keep on rolling. Again, that's not exactly going to help with keeping it all quiet.'

'But how did that information get out?' Harry asked.

'I don't think it did,' Matt said. 'It was just there. People hear the name, they remember stuff, and there we go.'

Harry slumped down into a chair as Jim entered the room.

'Don't think they've seen anything like that before,' Jim said, then turned to the others and explained what Harry had just done. 'And that Askew bloke, how is it that he knows so much? He's not even with one of the main papers, is he? He's just local!'

Harry took a deep breath, sucking in as much calm as he could.

'Swift's on his way,' he said. 'He can deal with them from now on. As for us, here and now? I want to know everything about the victims. And I mean everything. They went to school together, but so what? Something else connects them. School isn't enough. I want to know what they had for breakfast, their favourite magazine, who their friends are, if they're allergic to dogs, if they buy Lottery tickets, everything!'

'On it, Boss,' Matt said, then added, 'I'll put the kettle on.'

CHAPTER TWENTY-THREE

HARRY WAS SITTING IN A CHAIR, WHICH WAS FAR TOO small for him, in a tiny waiting room decorated with some very colourful and unique pieces of artwork by various artists he'd never heard of, including, Emma S, age 7, (A Dinosaur That Is Big), John G (My Mum Is Smiling), Tom S (Our New Puppy Called Sammy), and Nicola B (The Night Sky At Night).

He'd been sitting there for fifteen minutes, his backside becoming increasingly numb, waiting for the headteacher to come and speak with him. It was four-thirty in the afternoon, school was over, and Harry was having flashbacks to his own childhood. He'd spent rather too much time back then waiting for the headteacher to talk to him thanks to a habit of not just getting into fights, but of starting them.

The rest of the team were sifting through any and all information they could find on the two victims, with another round of door-knocking in Oughtershaw, and a number of uniformed officers doing the same in Richmond around the residence of Mr Hutchison. And Detective

Superintendent Swift was now dealing with the press, and growing increasingly sweaty and red in the face while doing so. Forensics was also at Hutchison's house, searching the place for anything that would give an idea as to how he had got from his home to a slurry pit in Widdale.

A door to Harry's left opened and out walked a woman wearing a genuine smile and the shiniest red shoes Harry had ever seen.

'Mr Grimm,' she said, and Harry rose to his feet, momentarily stuck in the chair and having to prise himself out of it. 'I'm Jennifer Alderson.'

'Yes, hello,' Harry said. 'Thank you for seeing me.'

'It's not a problem, especially under the circumstances,' the headteacher replied. 'Come in, won't you?'

Harry followed the woman back through the door, which she eased shut behind him, before inviting him to sit in a chair on the nearside of a large desk. She made her way to the other side and sat down.

'Would you like a coffee?'

Harry shook his head. He was already somewhat wired thanks to the amount of tea he'd drunk that day thanks in the main to the monstrous mug from Matt.

'Water will be just fine, thank you.'

The headteacher poured him a glass from a jug on her desk.

'So,' she said, relaxing back into her chair, 'how can I help?'

'I don't know if you can,' Harry said, 'and to be honest, this is a bit of a long shot, but you never know, right?'

The headteacher said nothing, waiting for Harry to continue.

'Does the school have records of pupils going back into the seventies and eighties?' Harry asked.

'Of course,' the headteacher replied. 'Goes back decades. What exactly is it that you need?'

'I have the names of two pupils,' Harry said. 'I know they both attended here at the same time. It might be useful to learn more about the school at that time, other pupils who were there with them, if there was anything that happened during the years they attended, that kind of thing.'

'Am I right to assume this is about, you know, the awful goings-on we've all heard about?'

'I'm afraid so, yes,' Harry nodded. 'People are talking, then?'

'Yes,' the headteacher said. 'You could say that.' She then fell quiet for a moment, resting her hands together on the desk in front of her. 'Our records are confidential,' she said eventually. 'As I'm sure you would understand. But under the circumstances . . .'

Harry said, 'This is entirely a police matter. Confidentiality is pretty much the order of the day.'

Rising then, the headteacher walked to a large metal cupboard and unlocked it. Opening the doors brought into view numerous, well-ordered files.

'These belong to the decades you mention,' she said, gesturing at a row of files on a shelf in the cupboard. 'Are you able to narrow it down a bit at all? We have photographs as well, you know. Not just the official class ones, but of activities, sports days, that kind of thing.'

Thinking about Capstick and Hutchison, Harry said, 'Maybe seventy-eight onwards?'

If they'd been at school together, then he figured seeing files and photos from after they'd been there at least a few years made a little more sense than trying to look at everything. It was somewhere to start, anyway, even if it came to nothing.

'Do you know what you're looking for specifically?' the headteacher asked, pulling some files out and placing them on her desk.

'No, not really,' Harry said.

'I'll leave you alone for a while, then,' the headteacher said, then slipped out of the room, pulling the door shut behind her.

Harry stared at the files. The two victims being childhood friends—if they had been friends that is—was intriguing enough to have him at least have a look, which was why he'd wandered up to the school, leaving the rest of the team with everything else.

But there was one other thing which had sent him to the school for a nosy, and that was what Little Nick had said, something about John not even being liked when they were at school, or something along those lines, anyway. For him to have brought that up at all had struck Harry as odd. To harbour that kind of resentment for so long took more than just getting your head flushed in the toilet a couple of times. He doubted there was anything to it, but it was worth a look, and anything that gave them a better understanding of the victims and their lives was never a bad thing.

With his little notebook open, ready to jot anything down of importance, Harry opened the files, which he discovered to be logbooks and diaries recording the daily goings-on at the school, including absences, illnesses, visitors, holidays, and any accidents or incidents that happened. There was even mention of a government information film, Harry noticed, which had been shown to the whole school each year. Seemed that at the time the then-headteacher hadn't entirely approved of it being shown at all, and there had been some resistance from a number of the parents, particularly by one who had voiced concerns about its impact on his daughter, but it had still gone ahead. Harry wondered for a moment what on earth could be so bad about a film designed to help kids stay safe for a headteacher to not want it shown. He jotted down the title, then further on found not just two, but three names he recognised: John Capstick, Barry Hutchison, and Nicholas Ellis. John was a year older than the other two, but due to the size of the school, they had all been in the same class—thirty-two children in total.

Harry backtracked through the files briefly, then followed the three names through the school. He cross-referenced these with a number of the other files, which contained within them the photographs that the headteacher had mentioned. And in those he found himself staring into the long-ago eyes of two men he only knew as corpses. Nick was there, too, and he seemed almost unchanged, thin and rat-like as a child, it seemed, not just as an adult.

John, it was clear to see to Harry, was not a happy boy. And he didn't just gather that from the photographs, which in their fading colours showed a boy whose clothes were threadbare, his hair unkempt, and an empty expression on his face. He read it as well in the daily logs written by the teachers, with John's name coming up all too often. They spoke of a boy who didn't so much struggle at school as fight against every part of it. He had behaviour problems, it seemed, he wouldn't concentrate, he had run away from school too many times to count. Then, as he'd grown older and hit age ten and a growth spurt all at once it seemed, bullying had risen to the top of the reasons why he was in trouble, with John throwing his weight about rather too often and with far too much enthusiasm.

Harry shuffled through more logs, more reports, more photographs. He found some notes and photographs from a sponsored walk along the Roman Road, which crossed the fells behind Hawes, and in those opened the briefest of windows onto John's group of friends at the time. There were six in total, Harry found, including John, Barry, and Nick. The other three, names and faces new to Harry, were Simon Swales, Jack Iveson, and Ian Snaith.

In the last year John spent at Hawes Primary School, before heading off on the bus down the dale to the comprehensive at Leyburn, those six names made frequent appearances in the logbooks, and never, it seemed, for any good reason. Numerous mentions of them were made, not just as individuals, but as a gang, and Harry found it almost laughable to think of the six boys staring back at him from those old photos being described as such. He'd dealt with gangs, bad ones, and not just adults either. Kids could be just as mean, just as violent. But he just couldn't see it in the pages in front of him. And yet, years later, two of them were now dead, murdered. Why? A bit of bullying, playing cowboys and Indians with a little too much enthusiasm, throwing a few stink bombs around?

Harry turned a page to continue reading, his eyes drawn to a substantial section just down the page where the boys' names were noted, and a date, but the notes relating to these details had been scribbled out, which struck him as odd. Why would that be? The rest of the records were all clear, but this bit had been all crossed out for some reason. But what was it? The notes surrounding this particular section were from the winter of nineteen seventy-eight and seventy-nine, which had clearly been a bit of a tough one to go through. The school had been closed for a while with frozen pipes, a particularly lethal ice slide—which had stretched the entire length of the playground and been the main cause of at least two broken wrists and a case of mild concussion—had to be salted, much to the pupils' disappointment, and a mass snowball fight, between years five and six, had resulted in two of the dinner staff going home with bruises, and detention for both year groups. An eventful winter. Harry smiled imagining the fun that the kids must have had.

Harry thought back over the last few days, remembered their little chat with Nick, and how he'd found himself wondering if something had happened back at school. Was that this crossed-out bit in the notes? It was a leap, not least because Nick hadn't exactly said very much, if anything at all. But then again, Harry mused, by not saying much, perhaps Nick had ended up saying quite a lot. So, was this it, then? The something that either did or didn't happen? It was hurting Harry's brain to think like this and he was pretty sure a headache was coming on when a cough from behind him caused him to glance over his shoulder and find the head-teacher standing in the door.

'I'm sorry,' Harry said, glancing at his watch. 'I didn't mean to be so long.'

'It's not a problem, honestly,' the headteacher replied. 'However, I do have a meeting to go to and I need to lock up. Unless of course, you want to spend the night in a draughty Victorian school, which rumour has it, may even have its own ghost!'

'Really?'

The headteacher laughed.

'No, I don't think so. At least I've not seen anything,

though this is an old building, so it makes lots of weird creaking sounds. The children do like to spook each other though, with stories of something hiding in the boiler room under the school!'

Harry started to pack away the folders. 'I don't suppose you know anything about this, do you?' he asked, pointing at the crossed-out text.

The headteacher stared over Harry's shoulder.

'No, can't say that I do. Winters were a lot worse back then by all accounts. Though they can still be pretty harsh up here if the wind blows in the right direction. And that snowball fight sounds like it was fun, doesn't it?'

Harry laughed. 'Yes, it does, rather.' He tapped a finger on the file. 'Is there a chance I could take these with me? Down to the police office, I mean? If I had a few sets of eyes on them, they could be helpful.'

The headteacher looked thoughtful for a moment.

'I don't have a problem with that,' she said eventually. 'If you think they can be of help.'

'Anything can be of help right now,' Harry said.

Outside the school, and now carrying a very heavy bag of files, Harry made his way down the hill and back into Hawes. The weather had turned nasty again, the world around him a crashing, thunderous mess of stair-rod rain and howling wind. It was gone six in the evening and the town was still busy, regardless of the weather. On the wet wind, the delicious scent of fish and chips wafted by and Harry's stomach grumbled. He resisted though, walking past the chippy and on towards the community office.

It seemed as though the weather was doing its level best to act as a portent to the investigation, Harry thought. The week was moving forward, and with every step they took, the journey seemed to get darker, murkier, more awful, and the weather was doing just the same, matching it all step for step.

Pushing through the door, Harry found himself in the presence of a somewhat depleted team, comprising of Liz, Gordy, and a completely new face in uniform. He felt his phone buzz in his pocket but ignored it.

'Well, the mighty wanderer returns!' Gordy said, standing up and stretching. 'And how goes it at the hallowed place of learning?'

Harry heaved the bag of files onto a nearby table.

'Well, I've got homework, so make of that what you will. Where's Swift?'

'Oh, he buggered off once he'd made it abundantly clear that all he was going to give to the press was an official statement and five minutes of his time for questions. And they quickly followed suit. The weather may have helped a little as well.' She turned to the new face. 'This is Police Constable Jadyn Okri,' she said, and Harry watched as the owner of the new face stood up and reached out a hand. 'A wee bit too keen if you ask me, demonstrated by the fact that he's volunteered to come over from Catterick and join in the fun. And that was even after I'd told him about you.'

Harry looked the lad up and down. He was tall, looked fit, and his eyes burned bright, despite being the darkest of blues.

'Pleased to meet you,' Harry said, taking Jadyn's hand, then handing him the bag from the table. 'Best you get started on these, then.'

Jadyn took the bag, and much to Harry's barely disguised irritation, carried it as though it weighed little more than a bag of sugar.

'What is it I'm looking for?' Jadyn asked.

'Anything unusual,' Harry said. 'I know that's not much to go on, but sometimes that's just how it is; you don't know what you're looking for until you find it. Oh, and here . . .' Harry handed Jadyn his notebook. 'There's some names I've jotted down in there. See if anything crops up involving them, any incidents, anything odd I guess. That unclear enough?'

Jadyn gave a nod and took the files over to a corner of the room. Liz wandered over to join him.

'An extra pair of hands makes a lot of sense,' Harry said, seeing that Gordy was on her way to leaving.

'Like I said, he's keen,' said Gordy. 'Grew up in Bradford, great with kids, fit as pins. I think he was competing nationally as a sprinter at one point. Don't break him, will you?'

Harry said, 'Just so long as he doesn't try running away, then, eh?'

'Aye, well, I'll be off, then,' Gordy said. 'I'm not around tomorrow, but keep me posted, okay?'

With Gordy gone, Harry went to wander over to join the newcomer and Liz. He pulled his phone out on the way and saw the missed call. It was Rebecca Sowerby.

'Balls . . .'

Liz and Jaydn looked around.

'Everything okay?' Liz asked.

Harry had the phone to his ear and was dialling. 'Pathologist,' he said, then a beat later, 'Hello, yes, just got your message. What's up?'

'Forensics found something,' Sowerby said on the other end of the call. 'At Hutchison's house, and on his clothes. Not much, but enough to be significant.'

'Enough of what to be significant?'

Harry wasn't a massive fan of people not getting to the

point and was working hard to not lose his rag in front of the fresh, new face of PC Okri.

'It's probably nothing, but . . .'

'But what? Just tell me, otherwise we're going to have to talk to each other for even longer, and neither of us wants that, now do we?'

'We found paint,' Sowerby said.

Harry's heart sank.

'Paint? You rang me about paint?'

'Yes.'

'Then I'm assuming that this amazing paint can be linked to the other crime scenes somehow?'

'No.'

'Then why the hell are you calling me?'

Harry knew he was shouting. He knew that Liz and Jadyn were doing their very best to not stare at him. He also knew that he just couldn't get excited about paint.

'We've done a quick analysis,' Sowerby explained. 'It's not normal paint, by which I mean, it's not paint you'd buy from a shop. That's why I'm calling you. And I didn't have to, you know? I could have left it till the morning. But for some reason, and one I'm clearly regretting already, I thought that you might appreciate being told. More fool me, eh?'

Harry breathed deep.

'So, this paint then,' he said, 'in what way is it not normal?'

'I've sent you the details,' Sowerby said. 'Why don't you have a look for yourself?'

Harry felt the beep of the line going dead as much as he heard it. Then he pulled open his emails and clicked on what Rebecca had sent through.

CHAPTER TWENTY-FOUR

'CLAY, BERRIES, PLANTS, VARIOUS MINERALS, TREE BARK,' Harry said. 'Now who the hell makes paint out of any of that? Actually, *how* does anyone make paint out of any of that? And why?'

Late evening had rolled into the room and Harry was still sitting with Liz and Jadyn doing his best to ignore the hunger chewing at his stomach.

'And that's all we've got?' Liz asked.

Harry flipped his phone around and showed her the message.

'I remember making paint at school,' Jadyn said. 'We had this mad teacher in art, Mr Neville, and he was always trying to get us to try new stuff, instead of just sketching a picture of a shoe or a crushed can of coke or whatever. It was pretty cool, you know?'

'I'm sure it was,' Harry said, not really sure why Jaydn was telling them this.

'Why were you making paint?' Liz asked. 'We never did

that. Mind, that's probably because our teacher spent most of his time asleep or reading the paper.'

Jadyn shrugged. 'I think it was a school project or something? Yeah, that was it. We did this thing on the Stone Age or the Bronze Age, one of the ages anyway, you know, they weren't living in caves and stuff, but were a bit more advanced, with tools and stuff.'

'This is fascinating stuff,' Harry said, with a sly wink at Liz, who did her best to not laugh.

Jaydn continued, 'They made their own paint, right? To decorate stuff, draw pictures on walls and bits of wood, even on each other.'

'You mean like woad?' Liz asked.

'Do I?' Jadyn said.

'War paint,' Liz explained. 'You've seen *Braveheart*, right? Mel Gibson in a skirt and running around a lot? We had a trip to the Jorvik museum place in York once. Vikings and whatnot. Right smelly place, too, and proud of it, like actually being able to smell what it was like to walk through a shit-covered street in the ninth century is a good thing!'

'And you learned about woad there, did you?' Harry asked.

'No idea,' Liz shrugged.

'Well, as interesting as all that is,' Harry said, 'and ignoring your skirt reference, which I'm sure Gordy would be more than a little aggrieved about, what exactly am I learning from any of this?'

'Woad was a blue body paint that they wore for battle,' Liz said. 'That's all I know. Probably thought it gave them protection or something.'

'Well, I'm probably going out on a limb here,' Harry said, 'but I'm going to state here and now, for the record, that I very much doubt we're dealing with either Mel Gibson or a Pictish warrior.'

'And definitely not a Viking,' Liz added.

'Could be a reenactor,' Jadyn suggested.

'A re-en what?' Harry asked.

'You know, people who dress up like they're from a different bit of history?'

'No, I don't know,' Harry said, wondering why he was encouraging Jadyn to keep speaking. 'Do people like that actually exist?'

'We had this school trip once,' Jaydn began, but Harry held up a hand.

'Just out of interest, and before you go any further, are all of your anecdotes going to be referencing your school life?'

'Er, no, I mean, at least I don't think so, no,' Jaydn said.

'Just checking,' said Harry. 'Please continue.'

Jaydn didn't look too sure.

'I mean it,' Harry said, doing his best to sound convincing. 'Maybe you're onto something. I doubt it, but what have we got to lose? So, this school trip, then?'

'We went to this castle,' Jaydn said, a little more hesitantly this time. 'It was a ruin, and there were all these people dressed up like they were from the time when it had been an actual castle. They would answer questions and stuff, you know?'

'So it was a good day out, then?' Harry asked.

Jadyn gave a nod.

'What about the files, then?' Harry asked. 'Anything interesting?'

'Not really, no,' Liz said, 'but then we've only started looking, haven't we? Though there's this bit here, which is odd.'

Harry looked at the section Liz was pointing at and recognised it.

'It's all been scribbled over,' Liz said. 'Don't really know why and we can't make out the words behind the scribble. From the notes above and below it, whatever it is or was, it happened in the winter.'

'Yeah, the date's still clear,' Harry said, pointing at the page. 'And the names.'

'Most of the names from the class are still local,' Liz said. 'I thought I might give them a call, see if someone remembers anything? It's a long shot, but you never know.'

Harry yawned and said, 'Well, you may as well. And I'm assuming you're on duty tonight, right?'

'Nightshift is always fun,' Liz said. 'The files will give me something to do between making sure people don't dick around too much when they head home at closing time and answering the numerous emergency calls that I won't be getting.'

'And you've some company, hey, Jadyn?' Harry said. 'Just out of interest, if you're from down dale, where are you staying?'

'I've a bed at one of the pubs,' Jadyn said. 'But I don't need much sleep, so I'll be fine.'

Harry walked over to the office door.

'I'll see you both tomorrow, then,' he said. 'Who knows? Perhaps by then, we might have some idea of what we're all actually doing . . .'

Outside, the cool evening swept in to grab at Harry's clothes, snapping them around him as he made his way through Hawes to his new digs. The rain had eased just enough to keep the numerous puddles topped up. It was another late one, and this time Harry was pretty sure that a pizza and beer was a bad idea. So instead, he just grabbed enough bits and bobs to put together some decent sandwiches, then continued on his way.

The night sky was clearing, the wind casting the thick clouds above into long black wisps, like the tails of giant horses, and beyond the buildings of the marketplace he could just make out the distant silhouettes of the hills beyond, their presence ominous over the town below. It was quiet, too, and the haunting bleats from far-off sheep drifted faintly through the air. And behind that, he noticed something else. It was a cold scent, if something could ever be described as such, a smell of damp, or perhaps waves on a stony shore. Rain's coming again, he thought, and he hoped to God that the change in the weather wasn't an omen of things to come. Because if a storm was coming, he wasn't sure that the dales was ready for it, in more ways than one. But then again, perhaps the storm was already here . . .

MORNING CRASHED into Harry's life with a thunderous crack, which sounded like the roof had just been ripped off by some ancient and very angry demigod. On taking a peek through the bedroom window, Harry stared out into a day barely beyond dawn and as dark as a derelict dockside warehouse. Rain was hammering down, wind grabbing it and throwing it in all directions, twisting it into great spinning sheets to whip against the world. The hills he had spied the evening before were now hidden, the sky nothing but an angry grey mass attacking the world below with torrents of rain and thick, bright shards of lightning. Another blast of thunder broke free, shaking the window in its frame.

Harry checked the time and wished that he hadn't done

seeing as it was only four-thirty in the morning. But he knew that there was little to no point trying to get back to sleep, not with the violent maelstrom outside doing its very best to level the world beneath it. So, making far too many old-man noises, he heaved himself out of the bedroom and headed off into the day.

Showered and breakfasted, Harry sat back in the small sofa in the lounge and closed his eyes. Thunder was still rolling around outside and he had no real urge to venture out into the rain, because with the amount of it coming down, he figured he'd be swimming to the Community Office, not walking.

In the darkness of his own mind, Harry tried to get his still-tired mind to sift through the past few days of crazy. The sound of the rain on the windows, the rumble of thunder, was almost meditative, and Harry drifted for a while, not exactly asleep, but not entirely awake either.

Two local men had been killed. They'd been to school together and in the same gang. Whether they'd kept in touch in later life, Harry didn't yet know. The phone belonging to one had been found in the pocket of the other, the text sent to Nick that Monday morning coming from somewhere in the vicinity of Hawes. Eagle feathers had been stuffed into each of their mouths. And now some weird, primitive-style paint had been found.

Just how the hell was he supposed to make any sense of it? How could anyone? None of this was random, of that he was damned sure. It was planned, meticulously so, and by someone who was very, very careful. But as yet they had no suspects, no real leads at all, just two grisly deaths and a random selection of unconnected bits of evidence, which all pointed to bugger all.

Or did they . . .

Harry snapped his eyes open, something jabbing at his thoughts, though what it was exactly he wasn't quite sure.

The school reports, the logbooks he'd been reading, there was something in them, wasn't there? But just what was it? What had he seen? He couldn't remember now exactly, and perhaps it had taken his mind all night to just sift through it all for something important to float to the top, but something was there, in those pages, he was sure of it.

Harry sat forward, squeezed his eyes shut, focused on everything rolling around in his head, everything he'd seen, everything he'd read. What was it? Just what the hell was it?

Damn it . . .

Harry stood up, grabbed his coat, shoved his feet into his shoes, then strode out of his door and into the rain. It hit him like grit, stinging his skin, and the wind came at him like an invisible boxer, dancing around him and punching him and shoving him from all directions. Forcing himself onwards, Harry kept moving, his feet drenched in seconds, his trousers following soon after, so by the time he had reached the Community Office, he figured he was probably wetter than if he'd just thrown himself into a puddle and got it all over and done with.

Inside the Community Office, Harry almost broke through the door into the room he and the rest of the team were using, his clothes steaming in the warmth.

'Been for a swim?' Liz asked, looking up at Harry, eyebrow raised in amusement.

'That'd be funny if it wasn't so very nearly the truth,' Harry grumbled. 'The files, where are they?'

Liz pointed across the room.

'We didn't get far. Had to deal with a group of tourists

who'd had just a few too many, which wasn't fun. Then I got called out for a car accident involving a cow.'

'Over the limit?'

'No,' Liz said. 'The cow hadn't had a drop. The fact that it could drive, though? Now that was a surprise.'

Harry laughed. 'Where's Jaydn?'

'I sent him off,' Liz said. 'He looked knackered. And I figured he'd be more use to us later on if he was actually awake.'

'When is Jim swapping with you?' Harry asked, then added, 'And did you get anywhere with finding out anything about that scribbled out bit in the logbook? Anyone remember anything?'

'Yes and no,' Liz said.

'How do you mean?'

'Yes, I got somewhere, and no I haven't found anything out yet, well I have, but I haven't.'

'Well that makes no sense.' Harry sighed. 'How come?'

Liz shrugged. 'I asked around, people remember being at school pretty well, and John's little gang, who no one spoke highly of, then when I asked about that date, if there was anything that happened, they talk a lot about the winter, how it was the best ever, but that's about it. Someone mentioned something about an accident, but that could be anything, couldn't it? The logbooks mention a few broken wrists thanks to that ice slide, for a start. And Jim's here in half an hour.'

Harry thought for a moment, rubbing his head in an attempt to get his brain into gear.

'And that's it? Nothing else?'

'That's all that I could get,' Liz said. 'I reckon it's just too long ago for anyone to really remember, which is fair enough, like, isn't it? I mean, can you remember all that much about your time at school, a particular winter, anything that really happened?'

Harry shook his head. 'A mate split his lip open, I remember that. Bounced his face off the back of someone else's head running down a corridor. But yeah, I see your point.'

'Why not give the school a buzz at eight, ask the head?' Liz suggested. 'She might know.'

'That's a bit weird though, isn't it?' Harry said. 'Good idea, but what if that's the only information the school has on it? And she wasn't head back then, so there's a good chance she won't know anything more than we do.'

Liz yawned, rather too obviously. 'Oh, sorry about that.'

'No, it's fine,' Harry said. 'You get off home. I'll call you if I need you.'

'I'll head off in a minute,' Liz said. 'We could try the churches? Might have records or something. Local papers. Maybe the surgery?'

Harry remembered the doctor from the day they'd found John. 'I was supposed to go and see the doctor anyway,' he said. 'I'll try him first in a bit, see if there's anything there. If it was an accident, then they'd have a note of it somewhere, wouldn't they? Perhaps? That's not something the churches would record. They're only really interested in births, marriages, and deaths.' He strode over to the files from the school, sat down, and pulled the first one towards him, flipping it open. He wasn't exactly sure what he was looking for, but he knew it was in there somewhere.

Harry sensed Liz standing behind him but didn't take his eyes from the files. 'Something's nagging at me, you know? Like I've an itch I need to scratch, but I just can't find it.'

Liz sat down to Harry's left. 'They were in a gang, that's

for sure,' she said. 'John and that Barry bloke, and Nick. With three others.'

'Yeah, I saw that,' Harry said, scanning the pages of one logbook before closing it and quickly moving onto the next.

'Right little buggers the lot of them,' Liz said. 'Can you imagine teaching kids like that? Always running off or causing trouble or whatever? And we think our job's hard!'

Harry wasn't listening. He'd found something. It was there, staring back at him, and a few dots were starting to join up. Not enough to take him all the way to the person responsible, but they had to be followed.

'Liz,' he said, 'remember what Jaydn was saying about those reenactors? Well, I think he might just have been onto something . . .'

CHAPTER TWENTY-FIVE

Harry had the rest of the team in front of him, and at his side on top of a table, sat a laptop. It had just gone nine in the morning but looked darker than nine at night. Outside, the day's weather had eased off just enough to downgrade itself from apocalyptic to your everyday torrential downpour, guaranteed to chill you to your bones and make you feel that everything was, in fact, a bit rubbish. The thunder had rolled on to pester another area of the country, but the sky was still as grey as the sea. Clouds tumbled into each other as waves, tossing hapless birds around like shipwrecked sailors.

To make sure that everyone was absolutely up to speed with what was happening, the team had gone through the case file and read through witness statements, as well as any other additional evidence or information that had come in, such as the paint found at the house of the third victim. And now it was time to be getting on with the day ahead.

The only one not there was Liz, but she'd promised to be back for midday once she'd had a chance to get her head down for a while. Harry had been on the phone to the head-teacher as well, but she'd been unable to offer anything more on what Harry had found in the files, in the main, because she had only been at the school herself for three years, but also because there were no other files. What Harry had in front of him, well, that was it.

'Right, then,' he said, clapping his hands together in an attempt to get their attention. 'We're going to watch a movie!'

'What about popcorn?' Matt asked. 'I can go and get some if you want? Can't have a movie without popcorn.'

'Don't worry, I've already sorted that,' Harry said, then gave a nod to Jim. 'You mind handing it out?'

Jim stood up and, from a bag at Harry's feet, pulled out some bags of Spar's own brand sweet and salted.

Harry was a little bit unsure as to why he'd gone to the trouble, as it wasn't a behavioural trait most people would have immediately associated with him. But he was strangely pleased he had, as he watched everyone grab a bag and tuck in. He also hoped that if they were relaxed it would help them all think a little clearer.

'First though,' Harry said, 'has everyone been introduced to our surprise new addition, PC Okri?'

Harry watched as Jaydn stood up, casting a rather large and imposing shadow over everyone, gave a small and embar-rassed wave, then sat down again, clearly wishing that he'd just stayed in his chair in the first place.

'From what I understand, he's volunteered to come over from Catterick to join us. Not sure how long for, exactly, but I'm sure he'll be very useful.'

'At last,' Jim said, 'someone else to make the tea.'

'And do the cake run,' Matt added.

Gordy was first with the questions about what it was

they were actually going to watch. 'So, what have we got, then? Dodgy home movies? Snuff?'

'Well, no to the former,' Harry said, 'and it's been pretty much proven that the latter is little more than an urban myth.'

'Or so you say,' Matt chipped in.

Harry folded his arms. 'What we do have is something I had to find on the internet,' he said. 'And before any of you start whispering or rumour-mongering, the reason I had to, is because that's the only place I could find it. What we're about to watch isn't something you can buy anywhere. It's simply not available. Also, I'm pretty surprised that I found it at all, because I wasn't actually expecting to find it, seeing as I wasn't looking for it. If you know what I mean.'

Jim raised a hand and received a nod from Harry, who was already pretty sure, from the looks on everyone's faces, that no, they didn't know what he meant at all.

'So, how does this relate to the case?' Jim asked.

'Right, yes,' Harry said. 'I was looking through the files from the school and I came across a mention of a government information film.'

Harry could see only blank expressions facing him now, which was understandable, he thought, because he knew he wasn't really making that much sense as yet.

'It wasn't the fact that it was a government information film that caught my attention,' Harry said, 'but its title.' And at this, he looked over to Jaydn. 'PC Okri, can you tell everyone your thoughts on the paint found at Hutchison's house, please?'

Jaydn, clearly none too happy about being the centre of attention again, and so soon after the previous embarrassing experience, made to stand.

'It's alright,' Harry said, raising a hand to stop Jaydn from standing up again. 'You can just tell us from where you are. You don't have to get up and deliver it like a speech. Well, not every time, anyway.'

Clearly relieved, Jaydn sat back down, and then quickly told everyone what he had said the day before to Harry, Liz, and Gordy about the paint found at the house of the second victim.

'So we're watching *Braveheart* then?' Matt asked. 'I've seen it, but I don't mind seeing it again.'

'No, we're not watching *Braveheart*,' Harry said, wondering why that film suddenly seemed so popular. 'So, about the paint, and what Jaydn just told us about his clearly very exciting, life-changing school trip . . .'

Harry pressed play on the laptop.

For a moment, the screen was blank, and the only sound in the room was that of popcorn being munched. Then words appeared on the screen, explaining little more than the fact that what they were about to watch was a Central Office of Information Film for the Health and Safety Executive.

'It's not exactly the *Star Wars* intro, is it?' Matt said, his words muffled by the amount of popcorn he was shovelling in.

On the screen, the words faded to be replaced by a cloudy sky beneath which sat the black slab of a rough horizon, onto which then ran the silhouettes of six children. Then, above them, one word appeared in yellow: APACHE.

Harry paused the film.

'Right,' he said, 'any thoughts so far?'

Silence. The kind of silence, Harry thought, that just sits there, staring at you, almost like it's daring you to challenge it. Which he was more than happy to do.

'I've done an extra little bit of digging,' Harry said, 'and there's two things I've found out.' He raised his left hand, index finger standing tall. 'One, Apaches wore eagle feathers in their headdresses.' He then raised his middle finger as well. 'And two, the body paint they used was made up of the ingredients our friendly pathologist found in the paint at Hutchison's house.'

'You think someone's dressing up as an Apache to commit murder?' Jim asked. 'Really? But that's crazy!'

'Eagle feathers and war paint,' Harry said. 'I know, it seems far-fetched, but . . .'

'It seems crackers,' Matt said. 'Who'd do that? And why?'

'I'm not sure I can answer that,' Harry said. 'But I think this film is important. I promise you, it'll become very clear as it plays out. At least, I hope it will.'

Blank faces still stared back at him and Harry took a very, very deep breath, half-convinced he should just explain everything, but he wanted the film to have the same impact on the team as it had on himself just over an hour ago.

'And,' said Harry, 'I want you to remember as you watch this that it was shown to primary school children in the late seventies and early eighties. Primary school children, would you believe? You'll soon understand, I think, why it's got a pretty notorious reputation. Ready?'

Everyone nodded, Matt somewhat more enthusiastic than the others.

Harry unclicked pause and allowed *Apache* to play on.

At first, the movie played out through scenes of a group of primary-school-age children dressed up as Apache warriors and running around a farm. It was very much of its time, the clothes and the overall colour palette screaming, 'This Is The Seventies' almost too loudly. There was a rough, rugged nature to the film, but it was clear that this was on purpose, and Harry wondered if it had been done to unsettle the viewer from the off. The children in the movie looked like they were having quite the time of it, running around, pretending to shoot at each other. But then, at just over five minutes in, the first death happened. Harry turned his eyes from the screen to the team to watch their reaction as, in the film, one of the children, a blonde girl, jumped up onto the trailer being towed by a tractor they were all chasing. Just as the girl cheered victory for slaying their foe, the trailer bounced over a bump and she tumbled forwards, sending her to fall head-first under the wheels of the trailer, the camera hovering just long enough over her broken, blood-covered toy rifle.

'Dear God, no!' Gordy gasped. 'And they showed this to kids? What kind of messed up government thinks that's a good idea?'

Harry saw just a flicker of shock ripple through the others.

The film continued. Coming up to eleven minutes in, the second death occurred, a boy drowning in a pit of slurry, his body disappearing into the filth as he screamed out for his dad.

Harry figured he could stop the film there, but it was important that it played out. They all needed to see it, to understand what it could mean, why he believed it was important.

The film eventually drew itself to a close twenty-six minutes later, a funeral party described to the viewers by the voice of one of the dead children wishing he was there with his family. Then, to add an extra touch of ghoulish awful-ness, a roll call of child deaths on farms spooled down the righthand side of the screen, all of which happened in the year before the film itself was made.

Harry closed the laptop then turned to face his team, sitting himself down on the table.

'They don't make them like they used to, do they?' Matt said.

'And thank God for that,' Gordy chipped in. 'Who in their right mind thinks it's okay to show that to children? Why would you? What the hell were they thinking? Parents must have been up in arms!'

Harry waited for the team to quieten before he spoke.

'So far,' he said, 'we have two deaths. Capstick was crushed to death by a tractor and trailer. That's child number one. Hutchison drowned in a slurry. That's child number two. Those are the first two deaths in the film. In total five children die, if you don't count the quite frankly horrendous roll call of death at the end.'

Jenny said, 'So you think someone is killing off John's gang like the kids in the film?'

'We've got six lads in John's gang,' Harry said. 'Two are already dead, killed in the same fashion and order as the kids in *Apache*. That gives us four others to find before anyone else gets hurt. And if the film is anything to go by, with only one survivor, we can't rule out that we also now have four suspects. Though to be honest, I think it's three, as Nick's movements don't fit with any of it. But we can't be completely certain, not yet.'

'But why wait till now?' Jim asked. 'What's the point? And why do it like this?'

Harry looked to Matt. 'Can you remember what Nick said about what it was like at school?'

'Only that it was rough,' Matt said. 'And their little gang used to play games a lot.'

'Any specific games?'

Matt thought for a moment. 'Kick the Can? Oh, and Cowboys and Indians, a little politically incorrect now, really, isn't it? And something kids these days wouldn't even know about. I used to have a great little cowboy outfit myself.'

'Now there's an image we could've all done without.' Jim laughed.

'Nick also said that they were always the Indians because they were John's favourite,' Matt said. 'Maybe that's because of this film, seeing as they watched it, right?'

'Right, so I have the start of a theory,' Harry began. 'Looking through the school files, we found a few things, mentions of John's gang, bullying, that kind of thing. And there was something in there, an event, with John and his pals all mentioned, but then the incident, whatever it was, was all crossed out.'

'So what was it?' Jim asked. 'What happened?'

'Liz tried to find out,' Harry said. 'It's a long time ago, folk can't remember much, or are just refusing to tell us, but we think there might have been an accident of some kind, but that's a wild guess. Like I said, Liz asked some of the people from that class if they could remember anything but didn't get any details.'

'So what now?' Jaydn asked.

'What if John and his gang were influenced by the movie you all just watched?' Harry asked. 'What if they played Cowboys and Indians a lot because of it? They're farming kids, right? So they'd have identified with the kids in the film. Maybe even saw themselves as the Apaches. And what if their games got a bit rough and someone from way back then ended up in a bad way and is now after some payback?'

'There's a hell of a lot of what-ifs in that.' Gordy sighed. 'And the idea that someone could resent a bit of bullying that much, and from all those years ago? I don't know . . .'

'Neither do I,' Harry said, 'but it's all I can come up with when I put everything together.'

'So it's someone local, then,' Jim said. 'Someone from the school back then?'

'I guess so,' Harry said. 'Possibly. Maybe. I don't know. It's just a theory. Whatever, we need to get on this, and now.' He rose to his feet. 'I want everyone from the class that John was in contacted again, properly this time. I'm not sure how many Liz managed to speak to. We need to know where they are, who they are, their movements, what they can remember from school. And I want Nicholas Ellis, Simon Swales, Jack Iveson, and Ian Smith found. Jim?'

Jim was on his feet in a beat.

'You and me, we're off to see what we can find out about this mysterious incident. Matt?'

Matt glanced up. 'Boss?'

'Keys!'

CHAPTER TWENTY-SIX

Outside, Harry raced over to the police Land Rover, Jim on his heels. He jumped into the vehicle and kicked the engine into life as Jim clambered up and in beside him.

'Where are we going?' Jim asked.

'Open that file,' Harry said. 'Skip through until you find the section I mentioned, the one that's all scribbled out.'

Harry slipped the gear lever into first then wheelspun out of the parking space and onto the road.

'Didn't think it could do that,' Harry muttered to himself as the steering wheel spun in his hands and he accelerated down The Holme and onto Penn Lane.

'Found it,' Jim said. 'Now what am I looking at?'

'The date,' Harry said, a few seconds later indicating left and pulling off the road into the car park for the local surgery. 'Something happened on that day. No idea what it was and like I said, Liz has asked around a bit, but got nowhere.'

'Can't say I know anything about it either,' Jim said. 'And I've lived here all my life. Everyone talks about what winters were like way back, but that's about it.'

'Exactly,' Harry said. 'So what's that crossed out bit? All a bit too mysterious if you ask me. Come on. And bring that file with you.'

Harry was out of the Land Rover and striding across the car park to the main reception. Inside, he walked up to the main desk, pushing himself ahead of the not insubstantial queue, immediately aware that a cloud of muttered curses was now snapping at his heels.

'I'm DCI Grimm,' Harry said to the man at the reception desk, flashing his ID. 'I need to see Doctor Smith, urgently.'

'Then you'll wait patiently like everyone else,' said the receptionist, a man whose ginger hair was edging towards bright orange, his face a picture of forced, practised politeness.

'I'm not here to make an appointment,' Harry replied. 'This is police business.'

'And this is a doctor's surgery and as you can see there are plenty of people here already who are ill and need to see a doctor. Are you ill?'

'No,' Harry said, then quickly changed his mind. 'Actually, yes, I am. Terribly so, in fact.'

'You don't look ill. Sweaty, yes, but not ill.'

'Oh, I am,' Harry said. 'Horribly. Violently even.'

'He is,' Jim said, leaning in around Harry. 'This is pretty urgent.'

'You'll have to wait,' the receptionist said.

Harry gagged, then coughed, then fell forwards just enough to slap his hands loudly on the reception desk. 'I can't wait,' he groaned. 'If I don't see Doctor Smith right now, then I won't be responsible for the mess.'

The receptionist, for the first time, looked unsure.

'I'll paint the place,' Harry said, groaning even louder than before, waving his hands at the walls rather expressively. 'It'll be everywhere! From both ends. The mess will be something to remember for generations! Hurry, man!'

The receptionist was on the phone immediately.

Harry groaned, gagged, groaned some more.

'I'd hurry if I were you,' Jim suggested.

'Through the doors, follow the signs,' the receptionist said, dropping the phone down and sliding his chair away from Harry and Jim. 'That way!'

Harry offered a polite thank you and, with the rest of the surgery behind them rising in indignation, disappeared through the doors and on to find Doctor Smith.

'Here,' Jim said, pointing at a sign on the wall.

Harry followed and they came to a door partially open with the doctor's name on it. He didn't knock. 'Doctor Smith?'

Inside the room, Doctor Smith, his shiny head reflecting in the cold, white light from the bulbs in the ceiling, was in the middle of getting his things together to leave.

'I was told this was an emergency?' the doctor said, and Harry caught the irritation in his voice. 'That you're very ill? I have another call to attend to I'm afraid. I can spare you a minute or two at best.'

Harry sat down and smiled. 'Well, I'm not ill,' he said. 'But I'm a very good actor.'

The doctor didn't look exactly impressed. 'Look, I can't just have you barge in! I'm not being rude, I promise, it's just that police or not, it's not fair on everyone else, is it? Can you come back later? I should be able to find some time at the end of the day. I'm assuming this is about the thing on Monday?' He checked his watch. 'Look, I really need to get going.'

Harry sat forward, folded his hands together, and stared across at the doctor. 'This is urgent,' he said. 'And we really need your help. It can't wait. I'm sorry. Two minutes, that's all we need.'

Doctor Smith leaned across his desk. 'I'm not sure what else I can help you with or about,' he said. 'You got the files I sent through, yes?'

'PCSO Metcalf here shared them with me,' Harry said, 'but it's not about that.'

'Then what is it about?'

Harry quickly explained as much as he could, then took the file from Jim and opened it at the page with the section that had been scribbled out.

'What am I looking at exactly?' the doctor asked, peering at the page in front of him.

'These are school files,' Harry said. 'Logbooks, from the primary school at the end of town. And we have reason to believe that something happened on this date and I need to know what it is.'

'Why?'

'Because I do,' Harry said. 'Can you help?'

'I'm not sure how.'

'We think an accident might have happened,' Jim said. 'Thought here would be the best place to start.'

'But that's over forty years ago!' the doctor exclaimed, glancing at his watch once again. 'I mean, yes, we have records, but that's asking an awful lot. Surely the school is the best place to find out rather than here?'

'Already tried that,' Jim said. 'You're looking at all the information the headteacher had available.'

Doctor Smith stood up and grabbed his coat from the back of his door. 'Look, I have to go. Have a word with reception. Someone there will be able to help you, I'm sure.'

'Emergency call out, is it?' Harry asked.

Doctor Smith shook his head. 'No, but it doesn't do to be late. One of my regulars, you see. They can't get down to the surgery, and sometimes, if there's no one available to collect them and bring them in, I pop out to see them myself.'

'That's very good of you,' Harry said, impressed.

'I'm a doctor,' the doctor said. 'It's my job.'

Harry and Jim followed Doctor Smith out of his room and through to reception.

'Ah, Greg,' the doctor said, leaning over to speak with the receptionist. 'Can you help these two gentlemen, please?'

The receptionist looked over at Harry and Jim, barely able to conceal his irritation.

'Yes, of course. If they would be so kind as to wait?'

'No,' Harry said, 'we wouldn't.'

The doctor then said, 'And could you just grab me that prescription, please? Iveson.'

Harry snapped around to look at the doctor. 'Who's that you're seeing again?'

'Jack Iveson,' the doctor replied. 'Why?'

Harry looked across at Jim, then eyeballed the doctor. 'He around the same age as John Capstick?'

'Year younger I believe,' the doctor said. 'Why?'

'I'm coming with you,' Harry said, then looked at the receptionist. 'Greg, you're going to help PCSO Metcalf, okay? Jim, as soon as you find anything out, you call me, understand?'

Jim gave a short nod. Greg managed to make his already furious face look even angrier. Then, before the doctor could argue, Harry was hurrying him towards the surgery door.

CHAPTER TWENTY-SEVEN

'You can't just come with me!' Doctor Smith said, staring at Harry through the open window of the Land Rover's driver's door. 'A patient needs privacy. I can't allow it!'

'Look,' Harry said, slipping the key into the slot and starting the engine, 'I only want to speak to him, okay? So, you do your doctor thing, then I'll do my police thing, simple as that. He will probably have been contacted by one of the team anyway, so he won't be too surprised.'

'He's rather ill,' the doctor said, somewhat abruptly. 'I'm not sure he'll be able to cope.'

'Hey, I know my face is pretty bad,' Harry said, 'but I don't think I've managed to kill anyone just by looking at them so far. I mean, I've tried to, yes, and I've wanted to be able to on a number of occasions, but it's never actually happened. Yet.'

Harry could tell that the doctor wasn't convinced. And in Harry's mind, that at least showed that he was someone who took his job seriously and who cared about his patients.

'It'll be fine,' Harry said. 'There's nothing to worry about, I promise.'

'Fine,' the doctor replied. 'Follow me, then. It's not far. I'll go in, complete my visit, then let Jack know that you're there, too, and invite you in. How's that sound?'

'Just peachy,' Harry said.

With the doctor heading over to his car, Harry punched in a quick call to Matt.

'Yes, Boss?'

'I've found Jack Iveson,' Harry said. 'Anyone spoken to him yet?'

'Let me just check . . . Yes, and he's happy to speak to someone. Jenny was going to head out there in a minute or two.'

'She doesn't need to,' Harry said. 'I'm on my way there now. He's a patient of the good doctor, but then I suppose everyone around here is, right?'

'Jim going with you?'

'No, he's staying at the surgery, trying to dig a bit to see if he can find anything about that date. Any news on the others?'

'Yes, actually,' Matt said. 'Gordy and Jaydn are heading out to bring them in for a chat.'

'Even Nick?'

'Amazingly, yes,' Matt said. 'Though he didn't exactly sound too happy about it. We've commandeered a couple of extra rooms here so we should be fine to see folk without it getting too busy, you know, maintain privacy as well.'

'Right, I'll be in touch,' Harry said, but Matt interrupted.

'We've got a bit of a problem, though, Boss.'

'What? What problem?'

Harry didn't need more problems. Two murders were plenty enough to be getting on with.

'We've had a few people knocking on the door, asking what's going on. And by *a few people*, I pretty much mean *angry hordes*.'

'Well, tell them to bugger off!' Harry said. 'By which I mean, inform them that the police are working hard, blah blah blah, okay?'

'I'm not sure that's going to work,' Matt said. 'Word spreads quickly round here. I don't think Swift's statement to the press yesterday did much good.'

'What's the problem?' Harry asked. 'Is it just a few concerned citizens or what?'

'Or what,' Matt said, and Harry heard the sigh in the man's voice, a mix of annoyance and despair. 'They want to know how we're keeping them safe. Some are saying that they're too scared to leave their own house. I've even had one or two tell me they're going to sleep with their shotguns under their beds. Others are just a little bit too keen to get out there and see if they can find the person responsible themselves.'

'Brilliant.' Harry moaned, his mind suddenly filled with images of gangs of locals driving around the lanes in their four-wheel drives, all armed with shotguns. 'That's all we need. A nice bit of panic.'

'What should I do?'

'Right now, nothing,' Harry instructed. 'Just keep an eye on things. Calm people down. Reassure them. Smile. Actually, don't smile. Won't look good to have the police smiling in the middle of a murder investigation.'

'Will do, boss,' Matt agreed.

Harry hung up, as just ahead of him, he watched the

doctor pull out in his smart-looking vehicle and head off out of the car park.

Harry rolled the Land Rover out onto the road and up behind the doctor, following him left out of the surgery and up out of Hawes, passing the auction mart on his right. A mile or so out of Hawes, the doctor turned right and Harry recognised where he was, as he followed on up a hill into the small village of Burtersett. The weather had eased, Harry was pleased to see, but the Land Rover still felt skittish on the slick, wet roads, drifting just a little too much around corners, and forcing him to swear as they continued onwards, and to grip the steering wheel more than a little tightly.

Out of Burtersett, the doctor sped on. Harry followed him up onto the fells, across the junction with the old Roman Road, then on and down towards Semerwater. Seeing the lake come into view, Harry was swept back a few weeks to his first investigation in the dale, which had started as a missing persons and then tragically turned into a murder, the body found on its shore. But the lake brought another memory, too, one of being the coldest he had ever been in, in his entire life, having for some mad reason persuaded himself to have a go at wild swimming, after talking to a couple of the witnesses, who'd been in the lake at the time. Looking at it now, though, he wasn't so sure he fancied going back in any time soon.

The lake was a black hole under a brooding sky, and it didn't exactly look welcoming. It was an unnerving thing to see from on high, Harry thought, as he followed the doctor down the road towards the lake, almost giving him vertigo, the odd feeling that at any point he could be sucked down into it and into oblivion.

Ahead, instead of going to the lake, the doctor turned

right and onto Marsett Lane, which clung to the side of the hill, Semerwater visible down to Harry's left. The road was narrow and in places puddles had worked together to turn into localised floods blocking the way ahead. Harry was pleased that he wasn't in his own car as he was pretty sure it wouldn't have made it through some of them. But for the doctor's Discovery and Harry's police Land Rover, a bit of water wasn't a problem.

A few minutes later, and with Semerwater now having disappeared behind them, Harry followed the doctor into the village of Marsett. To Harry, though, the place looked nothing like a village at all, but more like a sprawling farm. On the village green, if it could be called such, were parked three tractors, all pulling different types of machinery, and Harry hadn't the faintest idea what any of them were for and a red telephone box next to a noticeboard. Farm buildings and large barns seemed to be as much a part of the village as the few stone houses Harry could see. In front of him the road split, leading left and right. The doctor took the right-hand lane and eventually pulled up next to a small house with a blue door. Harry eased in behind.

'I'll come and get you when I'm done,' the doctor called over to Harry. 'Shouldn't be too long.'

'What's wrong with him?' Harry asked.

'Diabetes,' the doctor replied. 'It's one of the worst cases I've ever seen. He's not been best at looking after himself and it's progressed to neuropathic damage, so he can't walk, though I think there's a part of him that won't walk as well. So he's been getting sores, from not moving enough.'

'Sounds lovely,' Harry said. 'Just come and get me when you're done.'

With the doctor gone, Harry had a few moments to

himself. The Land Rover was warm from the journey, the rattling heater having done its best to bake him alive and deafen him at the same time. Outside, there was a hint of rain in the air, so Harry decided against going for a walk.

Leaning forward onto the steering wheel to rest his chin on his folded arms, Harry thought back over everything that had happened since Monday, the murders, the scant evidence. The thought that someone was out there hunting down a group of adults who used to be in a gang at school struck him as beyond bizarre. Something had triggered it, of that he was certain, and his gut was telling him that once that trigger was found, then the identity of the killer would be revealed.

Did it have something to do with that scribbled out incident in the school logbook? If it did, what kind of incident could be so bad as to cause what was happening now? Revenge was one thing, but revenge lasting all the way back to the school playground? That was something Harry had never come across before. But there was a first time for everything, wasn't there?

A sound trilled into Harry's thoughts and it took him a second or two to realise it was his phone, which had somehow slipped from his pocket and was in the passenger footwell. He reached over, grabbed it, and answered.

'Grimm.'

'It's Detective Superintendent Firbank,' came the reply. 'This won't take long because I haven't got long. Can you talk?'

Harry stared out of the windscreen to where the doctor had walked but there was no sign of him coming out yet. 'Yes, I can speak. I'm assuming this is about Ben.'

'It is, yes,' the DSup replied. 'First, Ben is safe. I want

you to know that, and it's why I'm calling you myself. He is safe, Harry. Is that clear? Do you understand those words? You need to.'

'Crystal,' Harry replied, already wondering why the DSup was laying it on so thick.

'Good, because it needs to be as what I'm about to tell you is confidential.'

Harry didn't like the sound of that at all. 'Confidential? But I'm his brother! His only blood relative other than our dad, and that bastard doesn't count, does he?'

'Ben has been moved,' the DSup said, ignoring Harry's protestations. 'Based on the information you gave me, a threat was identified. Because of this, and also because of who you are and what your father is known to be involved with, Ben has now been taken to an undisclosed location.'

'What the hell does that mean?'

'It means, Grimm, that you are not to know where your brother is, for now, anyway. It's too dangerous, for him, for you.'

'What?' Harry couldn't believe what he was hearing. How the hell was he supposed to be a big brother, to look after his little brother, if he didn't even know where Ben was? It made no sense! 'You can't do that!' he shouted. 'I need to know. I have to!'

'It's not actually my decision,' the DSup said. 'Ben doesn't even know where he is. And, not only that, we've given him a new identity. Nothing too difficult to remember, so he should be fine. But right now, where he is, his identity, everything, is classified.'

Harry laughed, the sound cold and hard. 'Classified? This is starting to sound a little James Bond if you ask me. What the hell's going on? What aren't you telling me?'

'I'm not telling you what I can't tell you, Grimm,' the DSup said. 'Ben is safe. And right now, that should be your only consideration. Now, if you'll excuse me, I have other things to be getting on with, as I'm sure you do, too.'

'He's my brother!' Harry yelled. 'You don't get to keep anything to do with him a secret from me! You can't!'

'I can, Harry,' the DSup said. 'I'm sorry, but I can, and I have to. Goodbye.'

The line went dead.

Harry threw his phone down hard hoping that it would smash into a thousand pieces. It didn't. Instead, it sort of just landed with a dull metallic thump and then started playing some annoying music. As he went to reach down to pick it up, movement caught Harry's eye. Sitting back up, Harry found himself staring at the shambling figure of the doctor, stumbling towards him, blood streaming down his face and soaking into his jacket.

CHAPTER TWENTY-EIGHT

HARRY GRABBED HIS PHONE AND WAS OUT OF THE LAND Rover bullet-quick. He raced over to the doctor who fell to his knees and into a dirty puddle just as Harry got to him.

'Shitting hell!' Harry hissed. 'What's happened to you? I'm calling an ambulance!'

The doctor pushed him away. 'I'm fine, honest, and there's not much an ambulance can do that I can't do myself, is there? But someone was in the house! They attacked me, hit me over the head with something. Knocked me flat out.'

'What about Jack?' Harry asked, undecided as to whether to make chase or stay with the doctor. 'Where is he? Is he okay?'

The doctor stared up at Harry, his eyes dead. 'No,' he said. 'He's ... he's dead, but whoever it was, I saw them leave! You have to get after them! There's a back door. They left through it! You might still get to them! Go!'

Harry was on his feet. 'You're sure you're okay?'

'Yes! Go!' the doctor hissed painfully. 'Go!'

Harry turned to the house and sprinted. The shock of the

222 DAVID J. GATWARD

sudden movement sent stabs of pain through his body, but he ignored them. He crashed through the front door of Jack's house and found himself in a quaint little cottage.

The room was a lounge and dining room all in one, with a low ceiling and stairs in front of him on which sat a chair lift. Around a fire burning in the hearth, sat a two-seater sofa and an armchair, as though in conversation. On the floor, Harry spotted a blood-splattered log, the weapon used on the doctor, he assumed. Considering the size of the thing, he was surprised the doctor wasn't still inside with his head little more than a smashed coconut. And sitting in the armchair was a frail man with the palest skin and who was terribly, terribly still. Harry went to the body, checked for a pulse. Nothing. Backing away, he took in the blood that was splattered about the place, probably from where the doctor had managed to walk out of the house after being attacked, he thought. The flowery wallpaper, which had seen better days, was the backdrop to numerous family photos.

Pulling himself away from the eerily quiet scene before him, Harry raced through the room and out of a door opposite, which led into a small kitchen. Here, pots and pans had been knocked to the floor, no doubt by the house invader as they'd made their escape. A door stood open on the other side of the room and Harry was out and through it in a few steps and standing in a small, neat yard. A lean-to was to his left, filled with chopped wood for the fire. A gate at the far end of the yard stood open and Harry ran through it, coughing with the exertion, ordering himself to work harder at getting into shape.

Out back of the house, he ran along a small path that backed onto the yards of other houses. At the other end, the path spilled out onto a road and Harry stopped, partly to get his breath back, but also to listen. All he could hear, however, was the everyday sounds of the dales, living and breathing above, beneath, and around him. Sheep in the distance, wind scooting between buildings and around trees, birds calling. And in all of it, there was no hint of anything that would suggest someone was racing away from a crime scene. He dropped to the ground, attempting to see if there were any signs on the ground that would give him an indication of where the assailant had gone, but there was nothing, not even the faintest hint of a heel print.

Standing up, Harry looked left, looked right, decided that left felt more obvious as an escape route, and started running again, trying to put himself in the mind of the kind of person who would commit murder and then scarper. But it didn't take long for Harry to realise that what he was doing was hopeless. Whoever it was, they were gone. Bastards . . .

Harry pulled out his phone, saw there was a missed call from Jim, but ignored it, and rang Matt once again.

'Yes, Boss?'

'There's been another murder,' Harry said. 'Jack Iveson. And Doctor Smith has been attacked. We're up in Marsett. I think the suspect has done a runner. What are the odds on us getting a helicopter out?'

Harry heard Matt's laugh, but it wasn't one brought to life by humour.

'Non-existent,' Matt said. 'There is one, but it's based miles away. Wouldn't get to you quick enough. I'll get Gordy, just a mo.'

Gordy jumped on the line.

'Grimm?'

Harry quickly explained everything to the DI.

'Right, I'll call it in,' Gordy said. 'I'll see if we can get a dog handler out as well, might get a scent on something. Worth a try. You alright?'

'I'm fine, yes,' Harry said. 'The doctor's in a bit of a poor way, though. I'd best go check on him. Oh, and we need to know where Nick Ellis, Simon Swales, and Ian Smith are right now.'

'Oh, well that's easy,' Gordy said. 'They're here. With us. And they've all been very helpful so far. Even nice Mr Ellis. Liz is here, too.'

'What?' Harry said. 'They're there? All of them?'

'Well, I'd know if they weren't,' Gordy said.

Harry rubbed his head, more than a little confused. If it wasn't any of the remaining three from Capstick's gang, then who was it? What the hell was going on?

'They need a police presence with them at all times,' Harry said. 'I don't care what you have to do, but you get Uniform over and have them watching over the three of them. I don't want anyone or anything getting near them without our knowing, you hear?'

'Already on it,' Gordy said, and Harry hung up.

Making his way back down the road, along the alleyway, and through the house, Harry paused briefly to look at the dead man in the armchair. There was no point going in for a closer look. It was obvious that he was gone. The how of it, well that was best left to the cheerful world of Rebecca Sowerby and her team, Harry thought, and strode back outside and over to doctor. He found him leaning up against the right wing of his vehicle. His face was cleaned up and he was holding a white pad against his head, which was growing slowly more crimson from the wound it covered.

'You find anything?' the doctor asked.

Harry shook his head. 'No, not really. Someone obviously left in a hurry. I could see that from the stuff knocked onto the floor in the kitchen. Not a trace of them outside though. How are you doing?'

The doctor winced. 'I'm okay, honestly. It's just a knock.'

'A knock?' Harry exclaimed. 'You were twatted on the bonce with a log! You're lucky that your skull isn't cracked!'

'Yes, I suppose so,' the doctor agreed. 'Sorry I didn't get out here quicker. I can't believe someone would do . . . what they did. Poor Jack.'

Harry moved to stand beside the doctor. 'Can you remember what happened?' he asked, taking out his little notebook.

'My head's a little fuzzy,' the doctor said.

'I'm sure it is,' Harry replied, 'but if we can get the details down now, that stops you from forgetting anything.'

'Right, yes,' the doctor said. 'So, what happened . . .'

Harry watched as the doctor stood up and moved away from the vehicle. When he turned to face Harry, there was more than a hint of determination in his eyes. 'In your own time.'

'I was talking with Jack,' the doctor explained. 'Just going through his drugs, asking how he'd been keeping, if he'd been doing as I'd requested and moved more, that kind of thing. Then he sort of just fell silent, I looked up to see him staring over my head, and then I think that was when I must have been struck, but the next thing I remember is coming to, blood everywhere, seeing Jack, checking him, realising he was gone, then running out here to get you.'

'Where were you in the room?' Harry asked.

'On the sofa,' the doctor answered.

Harry closed his eyes for a moment, picturing the lounge. He could see the sofa, that it was pushed up close to the wall.

'But you just said that Jack stared over your head. The sofa is up against the wall.'

The doctor rubbed his eyes and let out a moan.

'Ah, yes, sorry, memory is fuzzy. I was on the sofa to begin with, then I was down on the floor, to check Jack's legs.'

'That makes sense,' Harry said. 'And you saw nothing of the person who hit you?'

'Not a thing,' the doctor replied. 'And whatever they hit me with, it certainly put me down quick.'

Harry thought about what he'd seen, what he'd just been told. If he was looking for the case to get any easier, then what had just happened was only going to do the opposite.

'Something bothering you?' the doctor asked.

'Yes, I mean, I don't know,' Harry said. 'It's just that I can't see why the suspect would sneak up and hit you on the head? Why risk being seen at all? Why not wait until you'd left?'

'Don't ask me,' the doctor said. 'Maybe I disturbed them or something. All I know is that my head hurts like hell and this shirt will need to be dry cleaned.'

'You're not wrong there,' Harry said, slipping his notebook back into his pocket. 'Now, are you sure you're alright?'

The doctor nodded. 'I'm fine, honestly.'

'You don't look fine.'

'The head always bleeds a lot,' the doctor said. 'You must remember splitting your head open as a kid, then just carrying on with the day as though nothing had happened, the only evidence of it being a plaster on your forehead?'

Harry laughed. He had many such memories, and not just from being a kid.

'So what now?' the doctor asked.

'The circus comes to town,' Harry said. 'Only it's not as

much fun and the ring keeper is a very serious pathologist who would probably take the easy way out and eat the lions rather than tame them.'

'Oh dear,' said the doctor.

'Exactly,' agreed Harry.

CHAPTER TWENTY-NINE

HARRY WAS BACK AT THE COMMUNITY OFFICE, HIS hands clasped around the pint mug of tea Matt had brought for him. The day had rolled on with no consideration for lunchtime, and having seen the Scene of Crime team turn up, and heard the grumbles about being called out for the third time in three days to the arse end of nowhere, Harry had watched the comings and goings just long enough to be polite, before heading back to Hawes. Doctor Smith had made the sensible choice of leaving before any of them arrived, having given his statement to Harry. And in front of him now was a plate of sliced cake from Cockett's and another plate with some crumbly Wensleydale cheese, and standing in front of him was a dapperly dressed man with the build of an ex-rugby player and a smile on him as warm and welcome as a fire on a winter's day.

'You didn't have to, Dave,' Harry said, reaching for a piece of the cake. 'But it's very much appreciated.'

And Harry meant it, about the cake at any rate. The

cheese he still wasn't so sure about, particularly the eating of it with cake.

Harry had met Dave Calvert on his first day in Hawes. He'd been good enough to give him a lift through town and up to meet Jim at the auction mart. And over the past few weeks, he'd often popped in to see how things were going and how Harry was getting on. He usually brought food with him as well.

'Oh, it's no bother,' Dave said. 'From what I've been hearing, it's pretty tough for you lot right now. And I'm heading off tomorrow, so thought I'd just pop in and wish you well.'

'Very kind,' Harry said. 'So you're on the rigs, then?'

'Aye, back in a few weeks, mind.'

Harry sipped his tea. The only other person in the room with them was Jenny, who was taking a statement from someone who had been at the school at the same time as John Capstick and the others. They'd managed to take dozens of statements over the course of the day, not just from those who were in the same class as the deceased, but from other years as well.

The rest of the team were out and about. Matt was still up in Marsett, having headed up to be Scene Guard with Jim. Gordy was at the scene as well. She'd managed to get a dog team in, and with Jaydn and a number of other uniformed officers that she had called in, was doing a search of the surrounding area to try and find something, anything, that would help. Harry didn't exactly rate their chances, but it was worth a go. Jim and Liz were doing their level best to show a bit of police presence in town, doing a walk around, and a nice bit of face-to-face chit chat with the locals, trying to ensure that everyone felt safe and that they could go

about their everyday lives without worrying about being the
next victim of whoever was out there gradually killing their
way through the members of a late-seventies gang of
children.

'Folk are getting jumpy,' Dave said, grabbing a seat.
'Can't blame them, either. All sounds pretty terrible, like.
What makes you want to do a job like this, then?'

'It's a long story,' Harry said, as a hard knock hammered
at the door and in walked two men with gun bags hung from
their shoulders.

'Right, who's in charge, then?'

The question was from the one on the left, the older of
the two at around sixty, Harry guessed. He was wearing
green boots and a blue boiler suit covered in oil stains. And
on his head was a flat cap defying all physical laws by
managing to somehow cling on at an impossible angle.

'I am,' Harry said, his eyes on the gun bags. 'Can I help?'

'It's the other way round,' the old man said. 'We've come
to ask you the same thing.'

The younger of the two stepped forward then. He was
dressed in exactly the same clothes as the older man, except
that his boots were black and instead of a flat cap he was
wearing a bright red woolly hat.

'Me and my dad,' he said, 'we've been talking with folk
down at the pub, like. Reckon we can help. There's a few
others who are keen as well, you know, to do the right thing.'

'Help?' Harry said. 'With what?'

'The murderer!' the old man said. 'We reckon you need a
hand and people need to feel safe, like, in their own homes,
don't they? So we thought we might just drive around a bit,
see if we spot anything, that kind of thing.'

Harry's eyes were still on the gun cases. 'That's a very

kind offer,' he said, 'but this is a police matter. The best thing you can do is to leave us to do what we're paid to do.'

'But there's not many of you, now, is there?' the younger man stated. 'A few of us can be out patrolling, like. It's no bother.'

Harry remembered then what Matt had told him about people panicking. For some, it had clearly upped a gear into getting a posse together.

'I understand that,' Harry said, doing his best to sound calm, 'but we can't have people taking the law into their own hands. I hope you can understand that.'

'All I can understand is that we've got a psycho out there,' the old man said, raising his voice, 'and you buggers haven't caught him yet!'

Harry went to speak, but another voice joined in.

'Come on now, Eric,' Dave said, rising to his feet to stand beside Harry. 'You need to be sensible. I don't think we need you or anyone else driving around looking to take a pot shot at someone with that, do you?'

Dave pointed at the gun bag on the older man's shoulder.

'This is just for show,' the older man replied.

'Doesn't matter,' Dave said. 'Police work is best left to the police.' He then looked at the younger man. 'Reckon you should take your dad home, Danny, before he does himself or anyone else a mischief.'

The younger man bristled a little at Dave's words.

'Who are you to be telling us what to do, eh?'

Dave, Harry noticed then, seemed to grow in size, as he stepped forward just enough to force the other two men to take a step back.

'A friend,' Dave said. 'As you well know, isn't that right, Eric?'

Harry watched Eric give the faintest of nods.

'Good, now be on your way, then,' Dave said. 'And leave the nice policeman here to do his job.'

The two men paused for a moment then turned back to the door. As they reached it, Dave called out, 'Best you let everyone else know that the police don't need any help, okay?'

The two men nodded, then were gone.

Harry sucked in a deep breath and let out a long, thankful sigh.

'Can't say I was expecting that,' he said.

'Their hearts are in the right place,' Dave said.

'I don't doubt it,' Harry agreed.

'Now then,' Dave said, 'about this long story you mentioned. Just how long is it, then?'

Harry laughed. 'You don't want to know.'

'I measure time in pints,' Dave said. 'Are we talking just one or two, or six-plus?'

'Oh, definitely six-plus,' Harry said. 'Possibly even ten.'

'Right, well then, when I'm back, we'll go out and have a good old chinwag, how's that sound?'

'It sounds great,' Harry said, as Jenny finished off her interview. 'Just out of interest, how local are you, Dave?'

'Local enough, but not too much,' Dave replied. 'I was born over in Middleham. You been over that way yet? You should pop down if you've not. It's a smashing place. Even has its own castle, if you like that sort of thing. And horses. Lots and lots of horses. Why do you ask?'

'Something happened at the school in Hawes,' Harry explained. 'Years ago now, late seventies. I'm trying to find out what it was.'

Dave looked thoughtful. 'Late seventies? It was a hell of a winter in seventy-nine, that I do remember.'

'So I keep hearing.'

'Bloody freezing it was. River was iced over and folk were skating on it. Villages were cut off. It was pretty harsh. That any help?'

'Haven't the faintest idea,' Harry replied. 'But I'll let you know if that helps me crack the case.'

Dave laughed. 'Right, I'll be off, then. See you when I get back. And we'll go for those pints, okay?'

And with that, the big man was gone.

'So, just you and me then,' Jenny called over, and gave a brief wave to Harry. 'How you doing?'

'Rubbish, if I'm honest,' Harry said.

'And the running?'

'Don't ask.'

Jenny walked over to sit with Harry.

'A little bird tells me you have, in many ways, been eating a right load of old shite this week, am I right?'

Harry groaned. It was all well and good being in a place where everyone knew everyone else, because it felt friendly and welcoming. It also meant that you couldn't keep many secrets.

'Who told?' Harry asked.

'Doesn't matter,' Jenny said. 'But you can't exercise and expect to get into shape if you're not eating properly.'

'I am eating properly,' Harry said, and took a huge bite from a slice of cake. 'See?' he said, when it was finished, 'I didn't drop a single crumb. Amazing!'

'Yeah, pure talent,' Jenny said. 'But I'm serious.'

'I know you are,' Harry said. 'And I appreciate your concern. But I've other things on my mind right now.'

'Well, exercise is good for stress,' Jenny said. 'You have to make time for it.'

She had a point, Harry knew, but time was one thing he really didn't have.

A knock butted into the moment and Harry looked up to see a shadow on the other side of the door. 'Who's that?' he asked. 'We expecting anyone?'

'No, we're not,' Jenny said, and rose to her feet to walk over to the door.

When she opened it the shadow on the other side stood there for a moment before entering the room. At which point, Harry's phone buzzed.

'Grimm,' Harry barked.

'Sowerby,' came the sharp reply. 'And I just need to check if this is going to be a full week of crime scenes or if I am actually able to make other plans?'

Harry hoped there was more to her call than a mere insult. Though he couldn't really blame her. 'Well, if you've any further evidence that you think will help us identify who's responsible, that would be a great help,' he said.

'And do you always make a mess of a crime scene?' the pathologist asked.

'There's nothing wrong with the crime scene!' Harry said. 'In fact, I didn't touch anything. Not a thing!'

'You walked through it, though, didn't you?' Sowerby replied. 'Oh, and your PCSO has already left. He's actually rather nice, you know. Polite. You could learn a thing or two there. And I've updated him on everything as well. I know that's not the normal way of doing things, but I was hoping it would avoid my having to talk to you so soon. Clearly, I misjudged.'

'I checked on the victim,' Harry said, 'and then chased after a suspect.'

'Who mysteriously vanished.'

Harry composed himself. He was going to have to learn how to work with Rebecca Sowerby because so far he wasn't doing so well at it. 'So, have you got anything?' he asked. 'You know, from the crime scene. Anything at all? How he was killed, anything like that? Or is this just a social call?'

Harry heard the sharp intake of breath from the other end of the phone.

'There's a lot of blood and none of it is his,' the pathologist said.

'Whose?' Harry asked.

'The victim's,' came the reply.

'I know, it's the doctor's,' Harry agreed.

'He was smashed over the head with a log by all accounts,' Sowerby said. 'And with the size of that thing coming down on him, he won't just have a cut or two. There would be bruising and a possible fracture as well, I should guess. Though how it happened at all is anyone's guess.'

'What?' Harry asked. 'How do you mean it's anyone's guess?'

'It's quite simple,' Sowerby explained. 'You smash someone over the head hard enough to create that amount of blood, then you have blood spatter, correct?'

'Yes, correct,' Harry agreed. Everyone knew that, so why was she asking him?

'Well, there wasn't or isn't any. Like none.'

'But the blood,' Harry said, 'I saw it.'

'Yes, you did. And there's a lot of it. But the spray pattern doesn't match what's supposed to have happened, you know, with someone battering the doctor over the head.'

'I don't understand,' Harry said. 'What are you saying? That he wasn't hit over the head? Because I was there! I saw what I saw!'

'All I'm saying,' said the pathologist, 'is that it's not what you'd expect. Perhaps he was clobbered and then the blood got thrown everywhere as he stumbled out. That might work.'

Harry's brain had stalled, and his voice.

'You still there?'

'Yes,' Harry said. 'But he was attacked! Maybe you've missed something?'

The laugh down the line was a mix of anger and disgust that Harry could suggest such a thing.

'Where is he now? The doctor? Hospital?'

'He headed off,' Harry said. 'I took his statement.'

'What, he drove? And you just let him? Are you mad? He can't have been in any fit state to drive! At all!'

Harry thought back to the doctor, the blood that had covered him when he'd stumbled out of Jack Iveson's front door, then how he'd found him after chasing through the house. 'Well, he seemed fine,' he said. 'And he was in a better position to judge than me, don't you think? Being a doctor and all.'

The line was quiet for a second or two.

'He was poisoned,' Sowerby said. 'And by the looks of things the MO was the same: incapacitated with a choke-hold, then whatever it was that killed him was poured down his throat.'

Harry remembered the *Apache* film and poison fitted in as the third death. 'Anything else?'

'No, of course, there isn't anything else!' the pathologist snapped. 'Except for another sodding eagle feather, as with the others. I have the autopsy to perform, and the place is being combed for evidence. As for the dog? It found nothing. So whoever it was that was here and attacked your doctor friend, well they pretty much upped and flew away.'

'Well, thanks for that,' Harry said. 'I'm now more confused than ever.'

'I think everyone would prefer it if you weren't,' came the reply and then the line fell quiet.

Harry dropped his phone into his pocket, baffled now, more than ever. So what had exactly happened at the house? He'd seen the doctor, the injury, the blood. But the blood splatter--or lack of it—didn't lie. He needed coffee. And lots of it.

'Harry?'

Jenny's voice dragged Harry back into the moment.

'Yes? What is it?'

Harry glanced over to the detective constable to see that she was standing with a man of around eighty years old, judging by the usual giveaway signs, such as the receding grey hair, stooped walk, all beige clothing, and a walking stick. But whereas the ravages of time were more than apparent on his body, the man's eyes still burned with a ferocious youth, and they swept around to stare not just at Harry, but through him, seeking him out like the piercing beam of a searchlight.

'Who's in charge here?' the old man asked.

'I am,' Harry said, a little stunned by the tone of the old man's voice. 'DCI Grimm.'

'Oh, so that is actually your real name,' the old man said with the faintest hint of a chuckle creasing up the corners of his mouth. 'I thought someone was having me on.'

'No, sadly not,' Harry said. 'Real name, and the face to go

with it. Would you like to sit down and then DC Blades here will take your details?'

The man slipped further into the room, his steps careful and measured, and sat down in front of Jenny. 'My name's Allan,' he said. 'Allan Rawson. I'm eighty-one years old. And I've come to hand myself in.'

'For what?' Harry asked, his mind to grinding to a halt, like he was trying to crunch a gearstick into the wrong gear. 'What possible crime could you have committed?'

Harry wanted to laugh, regardless of how unprofessional it would seem.

'What do you think?' Allan said. 'The murders of course!'

For Harry, time stalled, spluttered, then stopped completely. Had he really just heard correctly? This old man, who clearly had trouble walking, had honestly, truly, come in to confess to murder? It didn't make sense. And there was a good reason for that, mainly the fact that it was total bollocks. It had to be. But they still had to hear him out, regardless. He'd dealt with time wasters before, people who were just a bit mad, or who wanted to make themselves sound notorious, usually a mix of both. Old Mr Allan Rawson wasn't exactly ticking either of those boxes. Not yet, anyway.

'So, you're saying you're here to confess,' Harry said. 'To murder. Are you sure about that?'

'Of course, I'm sure,' Mr Rawson said. 'Do you think I just came in here to waste your time and mine? It's not like I've got much of the stuff left to waste, now, is it? Trust me, the older you get, the more valuable time is. So, shall we just get on with it?'

Harry looked over to Jenny, his left eyebrow well and truly raised.

'We can't really take a confession here,' Harry explained. 'This needs to be done properly, in Harrogate. It needs to be recorded, that kind of thing, I'm sure you understand.'

Mr Rawson bristled at this, pulling himself up nice and straight in his chair. 'There's been enough killing,' he said. 'I've decided it has to stop. And I'm going to confess here and now whether you like it or not!'

Harry held up a hand in an attempt to calm the old man down. 'I'll record it on my phone,' he said, pulling it from a pocket to show Mr Rawson. Then, after a minute or two of fumbling with the thing to try and navigate the numerous screens and menus, so that he could actually do what he'd said, he gave up and looked over to Jenny.

'Here,' Jenny said, pulling out her own phone and quickly flipping through to the right screen to record what Mr Rawson wanted to say. 'Just speak when you're ready.'

Mr Rawson edged forward on his seat, shuffled a bit to get comfortable, then started to tell them all about what had happened in the winter of nineteen seventy-nine.

CHAPTER THIRTY

'WE MOVED HERE, YOU SEE, IN SEVENTY-EIGHT. IT wasn't for the work, a promotion, anything like that. Back then, the dales, well it wasn't exactly a rich seam of employment begging to be mined, if you know what I mean. There was a bit of tourism, but really, it didn't offer that much to anyone moving in. You either had to have a job you could do at home, or have a job that you were happy to travel miles to do. And I had the former, you see. I was a salesman, and a bloody good one, too. Paper of all things, if you can believe that. Made me more than enough to move us here and justify my time away on the road. But like I said, it's not because of any of that. No, it was because of Sally.'

'Sally?' Harry asked. 'And she was your wife?'

Mr Rawson shook his head and Harry saw the sadness in the movement, as though a weight was slowing it down. 'My daughter,' he sighed, 'she was a wonderful little girl, you know? The brightest eyes, and a laugh that could bring you back from a coma. God, she was . . .'

Harry heard the break in the man's voice, the words crumbling as he tried to force them out.

'Anyway,' Mr Rawson said, shuffling himself in his chair and pulling himself upright, 'it was because of Sally that we moved here. We had lived in the city, you see? Down south, Cambridge. Properly busy it was. Obviously, nothing like it is now, but even then, it was a bustling place. Beautiful, yes, but busy.'

'And that's why you moved?' Jenny asked, and it was at this point Harry noticed that she was taking notes.

Mr Rawson nodded. 'It was too much for Sally, you see? The sound, the crowds, all of it. It was just too much for her and her needs. Of course, back then, we didn't really know what they were, no one did. And that bloody school!'

Rage tore into the old man's words and Harry saw a glimpse of what he must have been like as a younger man. He was more than a little pleased that he hadn't been around to deal with him back then.

'What about the school?' Harry asked.

'They thought she was a problem child,' Mr Rawson sneered. 'Kept telling us that she was causing trouble, doing things wrong on purpose, even fighting! Our Sally? Fighting? If you'd have met her you'd have seen she could never fight. She was built like a sparrow! But no, she was a problem, an issue, and would you believe it, other parents were starting to complain!'

'So that's why you moved then, yes?' Jenny said, repeating herself. 'To take Sally out of the school?'

'And it was a private bloody school, too!' Mr Rawson's voice was quiet, but anger burned in it. 'Happy to take my money so long as my children weren't a problem, but oh no, as soon as Sally turned out not to be like all the others, that was it, wasn't it? And the other parents! How dare they! Them and their precious little offspring! All of them, bastards! And they said they were our friends, too, you know? What kind of friend asks for your child to be taken out of school? I'll tell you: no friend of mine!'

Harry wasn't really sure where the story was going, but he couldn't help but be drawn in. Whatever he was telling them, he had no doubt that, so far, it was all true, that much was clear from the passion with which it was being told, the little details that if someone was making it up would probably forget to include.

'We took her to a specialist,' Mr Rawson said, his voice calm again. 'Ran lots of tests on little Sally, told us she was autistic. Said that the best thing for her was to get to someplace quiet.'

'I didn't know that was a thing,' Harry said. 'With autism, I mean. I thought it was just a learning disability.'

'Learning *need*,' Mr Rawson corrected. 'And it is very much a thing it turns out. Everyday noises that you and I take for granted? Well, for Sally, they were very painful. They'd intrude into her life and she'd be overwhelmed. That was why she played up at school, because it all sort of just built up, and then she'd lose it, I suppose.'

'Sensory overload, then,' Jenny said.

'Exactly that, yes,' Mr Rawson said. 'Hugely stressful for her, and for all of us. So we moved. Sold up, told that school where to stick its fees, and came here, to Wensleydale.'

'Why did you pick here, then?' Harry asked. 'It's a hell of a long way from Cambridge.'

'Well, that's one reason,' Mr Rawson answered. 'Another was because we'd had a holiday up this way. It was the happiest we'd ever seen Sally. So it seemed to make sense. And it did, for a while.'

Harry saw the opening in what Mr Rawson was saying, the hint at what was to come, the reason for him having come to speak to them in the first place. 'So what happened?' he asked.

'We bought a lovely little place up in Gayle,' Mr Rawson said. 'Far enough away from the main roads, but close enough to be a part of the community, because we thought that was important too, you see? We didn't want Sally to be overprotected. No, she needed, we all did, to be a part of the place we'd moved to, so we could call it home.'

'And was it?' Jenny asked. 'Home, that is?'

Mr Rawson smiled then and Harry saw that it was born of memories still very much at the surface of his mind.

'Very much so, yes,' he said. 'It's a wonderful place, isn't it? You can't come here and not forever have a piece of it with you. And Sally was so much happier! It was quieter, so much more space, none of the hustle and bustle. It was all fresh air, fields, countryside. We were so happy.'

'Were,' Harry said. 'Something changed that, then?'

Harry watched as the old man sunk back into his chair, as though pushed down by something, and a shadow fell across him, and for a moment he stared off into the distance, a storm gathering behind his eyes. It was a look Harry had seen before, the thousand-yard stare they'd called it back in the Paras, the look a soldier has when they've been in the thick of a firefight, rounds zipping past, people shouting, people screaming, people dying. It was a stare he'd used himself too many times, far too many times.

'Sally was very happy at her new school, here in Hawes,' Mr Rawson said. 'The teachers were lovely, really supportive, and so were the children. They sort of just took her in and looked after her, you know? It was wonderful. We'd never seen her like that before. And when we would go to pick her up she would be smiling. Can you imagine it? Smiling after a day of school! I can still see her now, every day, that smile. God, I miss it.'

Mr Rawson paused again, leant forward, his hands clasped together and resting on the table. A shudder ran through him and the faintest sound of a muffled cry slipped from his mouth.

Jenny reached out, placing a hand onto his. 'It's okay,' she said. 'In your own time.'

Harry stared at this little action. It wasn't the kind of thing he'd ever seen happen in a police interview before and wasn't really sure it should be encouraged. But there was something in it which demonstrated to him the kind of police officer Jenny was, and it wasn't just down to being professional. No. She was more than that. She actually damn well cared. And what more could you ask for?

'I'm sorry,' Mr Rawson said. 'It's years ago now, I know, but it may as well be yesterday.'

The room fell silent for a moment until Mr Rawson spoke again.

'They showed this film,' he explained. 'At school. To the whole school, would you believe? Some new initiative by the government to warn children of the dangers of being on a farm.'

At this, Harry snapped a look around to Jenny whose eyes were wide.

'This wouldn't happen to be *Apache,* now would it?' Harry asked.

'I've no idea what it was called,' Mr Rawson said. 'All I

know is that they had everyone in that hall together to watch what amounted to little more than a horror film, with children being killed off one by one. It was horrific! And to think that just a few years later there was all that stuff going on about banning films because of their violence!'

'So it was you, then,' Harry said, remembering the school logbooks.

'What was?'

'In the school records,' Harry explained. 'I found mention of the film. That some parents hadn't been too happy about it, one in particular because of concerns for his daughter. And that was you.'

'Yes, it was me,' Mr Rawson said. 'Bugger all the good it did!'

'But why were you so worried?' Jenny asked. 'Couldn't you just have kept Sally at home?'

'Yes, we could,' Mr Rawson said, 'but we didn't want her to be singled out. Can you imagine it? Being the only kid kept home because your parents didn't want you to see a film that everyone else was watching? No, we couldn't do that. It wasn't fair. We were there to give Sally the best chance, and part of that had to be about making her life as normal as possible.'

'But something went wrong,' Harry said. 'At least, I'm assuming it did.'

'Sally didn't react well to it,' Mr Rawson explained, and again Harry could hear the sadness in his voice. 'In fact, at some point, she ran out of the hall screaming, or so I was told. It was too much for her, what was being shown on the screen. She was sensitive to things, so much more than anyone else. There was an innocence to her, and that film? Well, you may as well have just given her a puppy and then shot it in front of her, that's how badly affected she was. Nightmares for weeks! It was horrendous! Horrendous!'

'What happened afterwards?' Jenny asked. 'Did the school apologise?'

Mr Rawson shook his head. 'It wasn't the school's fault really,' he said. 'They were told to show it by the powers that be, so that's what they did. I demanded to see it for myself and I was shocked. I'm not a prude, you understand, but really, at what point is a film like that ever appropriate to show kids?'

Harry didn't want the conversation to drift off into the realms of censorship, but he could see that from Mr Rawson's perspective, there was certainly an argument to be made. 'So, afterwards, then, what happened with Sally?' he asked. 'I'm assuming she got over it eventually.'

Mr Rawson turned his head slowly and the face which came to bear on Harry sent a shudder down his spine. There was a heat behind it, a fierce burning of decades-old rage, and he had a sense that he was about to get a taste of what that was actually like.

'Oh, she would have, I'm sure,' Mr Rawson said, his voice a quiet, rumbling threat. 'Yes, she would have, if it hadn't been for those bastard kids . . .'

CHAPTER THIRTY-ONE

HARRY HAD AN IDEA AS TO WHO EXACTLY MR RAWSON was referring, but he wasn't about to put words into the old man's mouth. 'Which kids?' he asked. 'What happened?'

'You know which kids!' Mr Rawson growled. 'I don't need to give you the names, I'm sure.'

'Actually, you do,' Jenny said. 'We're here to record what you're saying, to ask questions. We're not here to provide information.'

Her reply was harder than Harry had expected it to be, but he was pleased by that. Whatever had happened to Mr Rawson's daughter, they still had to maintain distance, to be objective, and to not be pulled in to being a part of whatever it was that was spooling out before them.

'Capstick,' Mr Rawson said. 'John Bastard Capstick, and his little gang of Apaches! Yes, that was it, I remember now! They called themselves that after that godawful film, didn't they?'

'Go on,' Harry said, encouraging the old man to keep talking, because even if Mr Rawson's confession was a wonderful piece of fiction, he was pretty sure that the back-ground to it wasn't, and he'd already learned a few things, so perhaps more was to come, which would help.

'He was a bully,' Mr Rawson said. 'Sally was never on his radar because she was so looked after by the staff, by everyone at the school. And he obviously had other people he preferred to pick on. But when it happened, when she ran out of that hall? He must have seen her as an easy target.'

'So he bullied her?' Jenny asked.

'Bullied is such a tame word to describe the abject torment that boy and his friends put our daughter though,' Mr Rawson snarled, the words spitting out through the spaces between his teeth. 'She'd been at the school a year, and they showed the film in the autumn of seventy-nine. She was never the same.'

'How so?' Harry asked.

'She would wake in the night screaming,' Mr Rawson said. 'She started to wet her bed, and that was something she'd never done before. Every night, too. It was awful for her. She would be sick before going to school, and when we did get her there, she would hide from the teachers, hide from everyone. You wouldn't believe how many places there are for a small girl to hide in a school like that!'

'And Capstick?' Harry asked.

'He singled her out,' Mr Rawson said. 'Picked on her at every opportunity. Made fun of her. Encouraged all the other children to do the same, and they did, because they were scared of him, scared of being victims themselves, I shouldn't wonder. Then winter came, and the cold. It was like nothing we had ever experienced.'

'Did the bullying stop?' Jenny asked.

Mr Rawson shook his head.

'Sally loved the snow. I think it was because it made the world so quiet, you know? And it is magical, isn't it? The way a blanket of snow can just quieten everything, silence the world, make everything pure for just a while. Like Sally, really. She was pure, in her own way. And for such a short time.'

Harry couldn't remember the last time he'd seen a decent snowfall. 'If the bullying didn't stop, what happened?' he asked. 'What did you do?'

'In the end, we pulled her out of the school,' Mr Rawson said. 'Didn't have any choice. It got that bad. But we made sure the school kept it as quiet as possible. I forced the headteacher to let me look at the records myself, just to make sure there was nothing in there that would follow her, you see? I didn't want anything to haunt her, to turn up at her next school and be used as a rod to beat her with.'

'You read the logbooks?'

Mr Rawson nodded. 'Of course, I did! Obviously, it wasn't allowed but I wasn't having any of it! There wasn't much in there to worry about anyway. Except for one bit which was all about how we'd taken her out of the school because of her reaction to the film a couple of months previous. I had that scrubbed from the records. Did it myself actually. And rather enjoyed it, too.'

Harry thought of the crossed-out section in the logbook.

'That Capstick lad was suspended a few times,' Mr Rawson said. 'Never expelled though. Don't ask me why. I guess it was because there was never anything physical as such. He never beat her up. Nothing like that. But the verbal abuse, the way he had others rally against her, pick on her, make fun of her, ridicule her. It was awful. And his father?

God, now if there was anyone to blame for anything, it was him!'

'You had words then, I'm assuming?' Harry suggested.

'Words? Ha! I went round there and threatened to burn his house to the ground!' Mr Rawson said. 'I stormed in, wading through all that shit and muck in his yard, kicked his door open, and I had him! I had him with my hands around his throat, the bastard!'

Harry watched as the old man reached out with his hands and squeezed them around an invisible neck, the fire in his eyes terrifying, despite his age.

'He would've deserved it, too, for what his son had done to my girl! I wanted to kill him! Just choke the absolute bloody life out of him!'

'What stopped you?'

'He did,' Mr Rawson sighed, slumping back into his chair. 'Look at me; I'm not a big man! Never have been. Anger only got me so far, and the element of surprise. He was drunk, but it didn't matter. He was strong. Threw me out on my arse. Chased me across the yard with a stick. Threw a few rocks at me. But I wanted to go back, I tell you. And you know why? Not because of what his son did to my daughter. No. But for what he said about her, to my face.'

'When was this?' Jenny asked.

'The school arranged for a sort of parlay, I suppose,' Mr Rawson said. 'Tried to get the parents together, to discuss what could be done. He turned up in his tractor, waltzed in, three sheets to the wind, and just started going on at me, at my wife, at the headteacher, about how some kids just weren't worth the effort, how some shouldn't even be allowed to live. And he didn't just mean our Sally either, but his own son! Can you imagine it? Evil, he was. The worst.'

Harry had been wondering for a while just where all this was going. It was quite the story, for sure, and it was very clear that it had all been terrible for Mr Rawson's family. But he still wasn't any clearer about what it was that had led them to where they were now, years later, and with three dead men lying in freezer drawers in the mortuary down dale.

'You've got that look,' Mr Rawson said, glancing at Harry.

'What look?'

'You don't believe me, do you?'

Harry breathed deeply, folding his arms across his chest. 'Whether I believe you or not is irrelevant right now,' he said. 'I'm just not sure how all of what you've said so far brings you to us, now, to confess to three murders. It's a tragic tale, yes, but three murders, Mr Rawson? That's a whole world away from a kid being bullied and you having a scuffle with a drunk farmer.'

Mr Rawson nodded thoughtfully. 'You're right,' he said. 'But the story isn't finished, is it?'

'Only you know that,' Harry replied.

'Like I said, Sally loved the snow,' Rawson continued. 'She loved to go sledging, to go exploring with her brother.'

Harry sat up. 'Brother? What brother? You never mentioned a brother!'

Mr Rawson raised a hand to calm Harry. 'Her older brother, by only a year,' he said, 'but he acted older, really looked after her. Really cared for her. And they were out together in the snow, you see? They'd been sledging in the morning, then that afternoon they headed off along the path down from Gayle to Hawes, you know the one.'

'I do,' Harry said, recalling his little run-in with the local teenagers and their attempts at trying to be cool while smoking cannabis.

'Sally was fascinated by the way the beck had cut its way through the snow. She loved to just stand and watch it, and her brother, James, well, he would just stay with her, look out for her, make sure she didn't get too cold.'

'So what happened?' Jenny asked.

'Capstick's what happened,' Mr Rawson said. 'Him and his little gang, they came along the path, sledging down all the steep bits to the beck, then I suppose they saw Sally and just couldn't resist.'

'You were there?' Harry asked.

Mr Rawson shook his head. 'No, but James, he remembered everything. Every detail. Could never forget it either, which I suppose was why he did what he did.'

Harry noticed a change in Mr Rawson's intonation, the last few words coming out slightly different to the rest, almost as though he was referring not only to what his son James had done that day, but to something he did later. It confused him, but he wasn't given a chance to ask, as Mr Rawson was still talking and clearly didn't want to be interrupted.

'All six of them were there, Capstick and his little band of followers. They started with snowballs, and that set Sally off. She started to scream and panic, so James retaliated, only that made it worse. So, he decided to bring Sally home, because that was the most sensible thing to do, but the thing was, Capstick, you see, well they blocked the way. No matter what James did, Capstick and his gang would run and stop them, throw a snowball, call Sally names. And James? Well, James got angry, didn't he? And I don't blame him for that. How could I?

'He went for Capstick, and I mean he properly went for

him. Lamped him one hard on the side of his face. Nearly broke his wrist doing it, but he knocked that Capstick kid to the ground. The trouble was, he didn't make sure that he stayed down, did he? And that was where it all went wrong. The rest of the gang grabbed him, Capstick was on him then, and they gave him a bit of a pasting. And all the time, Sally was standing there watching and screaming. So they went for her next.'

'How do you mean?' Jenny asked, her pen poised above the copious notes she'd taken. 'What did they do?'

'They chased her,' Mr Rawson said. 'Chased her right down to the beck, tripping her up on the way, yelling at her, forcing her on, herding her I suppose. And James couldn't do anything about it, because three of them sat on him in the snow, forcing snow into his mouth, his nose, slapping him, laughing, and he could hear her screaming, not just in fear, but for him, screaming his name. Can you imagine what that must have been like?'

Yes, Harry thought, I can.

'Then the screaming stopped,' Mr Rawson said. 'Just stopped, like it had just been switched off. And then Capstick and the others, they just ran off. And after what they'd done, I'm not surprised, the little shits! The evil little bastards! They deserve to die, you know? For what they did! They deserve it!'

'What did they do?' Harry asked.

'She was on the edge of the beck,' Mr Rawson explained, his voice quieter now, slower, sorrow and memory and shock and anger all twisting his voice into a distant thing, something lost to time and horror. 'And she fell. They frightened her so much, kept pushing closer and closer, until she just fell. Into the water. In winter. James ran up to where she had fallen in. The river was running fast as well, under the snow, fed by the meltwater from the fells, and he jumped in, went after her. It could have killed him, too, but he got snagged on a rock, then someone spotted him, from the bridge over the beck, you know, the one in town? And they rushed around, got some help, grabbed him. If they hadn't I would've lost both children that day. In many ways, I think I probably did.'

'What about Sally?' Harry asked, not really wanting to know, knowing that he had to.

'She wasn't found for two days,' Mr Rawson said. 'She made it over the falls, disappeared under the ice, and just got swept downstream. Can you imagine the terror of it? The cold? The helplessness? Knowing she was going to die? Can you imagine that at all?'

'So,' Harry began, keeping his voice level and calm, 'are you saying that all this has led to what's been happening these past few days?'

'My wife, Jean, she was the next casualty,' Mr Rawson said, his eyes on Harry. 'Burying your own child, it's the worst thing, Mr Grimm, I promise you that. Nothing is worse. Nothing! And Jean, she broke apart that day and I just couldn't put her back together again. Drink took her in the end, two years later. Sometimes I think it was probably for the best. She was never the same. None of us were. God, I miss her.'

Harry left Mr Rawson to continue in his own time, the memories now washing through him relentlessly, tears starting to fall.

'Next was James.'

'Your son?' Jenny asked. 'Oh, dear God, I'm so sorry . . .'

'He did well, to keep going at all,' Mr Rawson said. 'After what he saw, what happened, he blamed himself. Nothing we said made a dent in the guilt he carried. He was a shell from that moment on, kept saying how he wished it had been him who had died. He changed. Drew into himself. Put on so much weight, just eating because it made him feel better, sort of a comfort thing, I guess. He got into fights at school, usually ended up on the wrong end of it all. But he was bright, and he managed to pass his exams, and head off to university. And that was the last I ever saw of the boy I called my son.'

'Do you mean he just never came home?' Harry asked.

'He called me one night,' Mr Rawson said. 'He was the most lucid that I'd heard him in years. He sounded calm. Happy almost. Said that he knew what it was that he had to do and that I wasn't to worry. Said he was sorry that he hadn't been able to protect Sally and that he hoped what he was going to do would make up for it.'

Harry suddenly felt sick, his stomach knotting itself up, his own experience on the job, the hell and anguish he'd witnessed over the years more than enough to guess where the story ended.

'The police came the next day,' Mr Rawson said. 'A letter was found in his room in the halls of residence. They found his clothes by the river, which was only a walk away from where he was staying.'

'Suicide,' Harry muttered.

'I'm afraid so, yes,' Mr Rawson said, the sadness in his eyes so deep, Harry could tell the man had spent years drowning in it. 'The note was what he'd said to me the night before on the phone, almost as though he had read it to me before heading off to do what he did. So, in the end? I lost my whole family. Because of that boy. Because of that gang. Because of what they did.'

Harry leaned back in his chair, the weight of what he and Jenny had heard seeming to almost push him back, and his breath felt suddenly short, taken away by the sadness that now sat with them in the room, the cloaked figure of death leaning on them all.

'So it all comes down to revenge,' Harry said. 'All of this. Everything that's happened. It's revenge for everything you've told us.'

Mr Rawson sat up straight, as if to display pride in what he'd come to confess. 'It was Sally's birthday on Saturday,' he said. 'Or would have been. Every year it comes around I think about what happened. This year, though, it's a little different. You see, I have cancer, Detective. Stage four. I won't see her next birthday. I needed to do something, to see some sense of justice.'

'They were kids,' Harry said. 'And if what you said is true, as tragic as it was, it was never intended, Sally's death, I mean. They didn't set out that day to see her die.'

Mr Rawson visibly bristled at this.

'How can you sit there and say that? They chased her! They scared her! She fell into the river because of them! They killed her! I lost my wife, my son!'

'And you decided, seeing as you were running out of time, to go after them.'

'Exactly that!' Mr Rawson snapped. 'So, are you going to arrest me or not?'

Harry was thoughtful for a moment. 'You've not told me how you killed them,' he said. 'And you've not explained why you've stopped now. I mean, there were six in the gang, weren't there? Why stop if you blame them all for what they did?'

'I don't have to explain anything to anyone!' Mr Rawson

said, anger in his eyes. 'We all died the day Sally fell into the river! Those boys, they got away with it! It was called an accident, a tragic event, and life just moved on for everyone else. But not for us! No, not for me! It couldn't! I bloody well wouldn't let it!'

'But it's still a leap,' Harry said. 'From all that, all those years ago, to murder, now. I'm just not buying it. Because they're not just murders, are they? What you did, I mean, there's a lot more to it.'

Harry saw Jenny swing round to stare at him.

'Oh, don't worry,' Harry said, looking to Jenny, 'we have to arrest him. We can't not arrest him, not after what he's said. But there's just one thing I don't get . . .' He turned his attention back to Mr Rawson. 'Your third victim, Jack Iveson. Why did you risk it?'

'Risk what?'

'Ignoring the fact that I doubt you're strong enough to twist open a barley sugar, never mind put a chokehold on a grown man, the first two victims were alone when murdered. Not only that, their deaths were clearly planned down to the last detail. Jack though? There was someone else there, wasn't there? The doctor, attending to Jack? And you still went for it. Took him out first before you could have a go at Jack. Why? Why not just wait until he'd gone?'

'Jack had it coming,' Mr Rawson said. 'I was there. I had to get it done!'

'But a rolling pin, though,' Harry said. 'You could've stoved his skull in!'

Mr Rawson paused, his eyes flickering just enough for Harry to notice.

'It was the first thing that came to hand!' Mr Rawson said. 'I wasn't really thinking.'

'And that's the problem,' Harry said. 'Right there. Because this, whoever's doing it, they do a lot of thinking. In fact, I reckon they've been thinking about it for years and years. Just like you. And now it's all come to a head, the fantasy spilling out into reality, perhaps.'

Harry stood up. 'Jenny, you can do the official arresting business, and that means you're going to have to take him up to Harrogate. You okay with that?'

'Of course,' Jenny replied.

'What about the others? Where are they?'

'Jadyn and Matt have eyes on Swales, Ellis, and Smith.'

'All at once?'

'They decided it was safer to stick together,' Jenny said.

'And Jim and Liz are still out in town?'

Jenny nodded.

'Give them a call,' Harry said. 'I want Jim to meet me in the station car park, behind the Ropemaker. And I want Liz here with you.'

'Aren't you coming to Harrogate? You heard the confession.'

'No, I'm not,' Harry said. 'And I want you to hang fire on that for a while. You mind doing that? Babysit Mr Rawson with Liz until I give you a call?'

'Why?'

Harry turned and made for the door. 'I'm going to catch me a killer.'

CHAPTER THIRTY-TWO

HARRY SAW THE WELCOME SIGHT OF JIM SWINGING HIS vehicle into the car park and flashing his headlights. As Jim pulled in beside him, Harry jumped out of his vehicle and jogged around to speak to the PCSO.

'First,' Harry said, 'what did you find at the surgery? Anything?'

'Nothing,' Jim said. 'But one of the women there, she asked what it was I was looking for, and I told her about what you'd found in the school logbooks.'

'And?'

'And she said she remembered her mum saying something about a girl who drowned years ago. Said she was pretty sure that her mum had made it up just to scare her into not messing around in the beck. Didn't happen at the school though.'

'Well,' Harry said, 'she wasn't making it up.'

At this, Jim's eyebrows scrunched together. 'Seriously? And you're saying it's got something to do with all of this?'

'Very much so,' Harry said. 'Now, how do you fancy

coming along to help me check on our good friend, the doctor? He had a little accident earlier, as you know. Thought we should see how he is. Show the caring side of the police, that kind of thing.'

Harry watched as Jim's face moved from serious contemplation to abject confusion.

'Er, yeah, I guess so,' Jim said. 'And that's why you called me down here?'

'Absolutely!' Harry said. 'Is there a problem?'

Jim quickly shook his head. 'No, not at all. It's just that, you know, that's the crime scene, and, well, I'm sure the doctor is alright.'

'Exactly!' Harry said. 'Come on then, out you get!'

Harry strode off, not waiting, and heard Jim scramble out of his Land Rover, slam the door, and jog over to catch him up.

'You okay?' Jim asked.

'Never better,' Harry said, staring ahead. 'You?'

'Er, yes, I'm fine,' Jim said.

'Well, that's good,' said Harry. 'We're both just peachy then, aren't we?'

At the top of the road, with the Ropemaker's on their left, Harry swung right, crossed Brunt Acres Road, and then made his way over to the surgery. Inside, he saw the receptionist glance up and roll his eyes.

'Hello!' Harry said. 'We're back! And you'll be pleased to know that I'm much, much better now.'

'I'm afraid that Doctor Smith is with a patient,' the receptionist said.

'And how is the doctor?' Harry asked. 'You know, after what happened?'

'Fine, I'm sure,' the receptionist replied. 'If you would be good enough to take a seat?'

'So he's not dizzy or anything?' Harry asked. 'He's been alright to get straight back to work?'

'Of course,' the receptionist said. 'It was just a little bump from what I gather. That was all. Nothing serious. Now, if you could . . .?' He gestured to some empty seats against the wall.

'Over there?' Harry said.

'Yes.'

'Those chairs?'

'Yes.'

'And you'll tell him we're here? It's police business after all. We just have to check up on him, as I'm sure you understand.'

'He'll be with you as soon as he can, I'm sure,' the receptionist said, then picked up the phone and, Harry was pretty sure, proceeded to dial a number that didn't actually exist. And as he did so, Harry turned to the doors leading through to the consultation rooms beyond, and marched on through, with Jim right behind him.

'Hey! You can't do that!' shouted the receptionist. 'You can't! I'll . . . I'll call the police!'

'We're already here!' Harry shouted back, and a few strides later was outside Doctor Smith's door.

Harry knocked.

'I have a patient!' the doctor replied sharply, clearly irritated by the interruption.

'My apologies,' Harry called through the closed door. 'We're just here to check up on you, that's all. It's a procedural thing, what with what happened. And I've a few questions I need to ask.'

Harry listened at the door to the sounds of scuffling and a muffled apology to whoever the doctor was with.

'Look, I'm really sorry about this,' Harry said through the door. 'This won't take long. You're a busy man, I know. Very busy indeed.'

The door opened and out bustled an old lady wearing far too much makeup and enough layers to keep her dry and warm at the North Pole. She tutted as she shuffled away.

'Grimm,' the doctor smiled. 'Come in, come in. Sit down, please.'

Harry walked past the doctor and into the room, Jim behind him. He noticed that the doctor now had a small plaster on his forehead, the edge of it coming away just enough to grab a hold of. He'd changed, too, which was fair enough. There had been an awful lot of blood, remembered Harry. But where was that bruising the pathologist had seemed pretty adamant should be there, too?

'Please, sit down,' the doctor said. 'Now, how can I help?'

Harry sat down and really made a point of getting himself comfortable. He shuffled to the left, to the right, really hunkered down into the chair, like he was settling in for what was left of the day. 'Just thought we'd come and check up on you,' Harry began. 'It was quite a time of it, wasn't it, up in the village?'

'What? Marsett? Oh, yes, it was indeed,' the doctor said, then a pained look scratched across his face and he rubbed his head. 'Can't say I was expecting to be hit on the head.'

'No, I dare say you weren't,' Harry said, and leaned forward a little. 'And that's where you were hit, was it? On your forehead there?'

The doctor glanced up, as though by doing so he could see the injury himself. 'It's nothing, honestly,' he said.

'And you've felt alright ever since?'

'I've been fine,' the doctor replied. 'But it's exceedingly kind of you to ask.'

Harry turned to Jim and said, 'You were up at the crime scene, am I right, PCSO Metcalf?'

'I was,' Jim said.

'And I understand that the pathologist gave you a good overview of what she found?'

'Yes, she did, actually,' Jim said, sitting up straight now.

'Did she say anything about the intruder? The person who clobbered the doctor, here, before getting to work on poor old Jack Iveson?'

Jim turned thoughtful for just long enough, which made Harry smile inside, because the lad had obviously caught on to what it was they were doing. 'She did,' he said at last. 'Told me that you were hit with a log. Is that right?'

The doctor nodded and Jim looked back at Harry.

'To be honest, I was expecting worse,' Jim said. 'The pathologist said she would expect whoever had been hit by the log to be in a pretty bad way. Bruises, perhaps even a fractured skull.'

'I must've been lucky, then,' the doctor said. 'I'm fine, I really am. Now, is there anything else?'

'Can you remember how you were hit?' Harry asked.

'Pardon?'

'You know, when whoever it was smashed you over the head with a chunk of tree? Was it hard? Did it crash into you and feel like your neck was going to snap? Did it knock you across the floor? What?'

The doctor's face shifted from bemusement to irritation to forced thoughtfulness. 'It, well, it was hard enough to knock me out,' he said.

'Exactly!' Harry said, raising a finger. 'So it must have come in very hard indeed, the kind of attack that would take you off your feet for sure, and send you sprawling. Right?'

'Yes, right,' the doctor agreed. 'That's what happened. I mean, I don't really remember, because I was knocked out by it, but that seems to make sense, doesn't it?'

'You tell me, doctor,' Harry said. 'Does it make sense that being thwacked over the head with a massive log left you with nothing but a wound small enough for a plaster no bigger than a stick of gum?'

The doctor shrugged. 'That's medicine for you,' he said. 'It's not an exact science. Is there anything else?'

Harry leaned back and folded his hands together on his lap. 'Yes, there is, actually,' he said. 'And I thought, seeing as you had been on the receiving end of that nasty bit of the old violence there, that it was only right that you were told.'

'Told what?'

Harry pulled out his phone, flicked through his contacts, and punched in a call. 'Jenny? Yeah, it's Grimm. Could you do me a favour, please? Would you and Liz mind bringing our guest down to the surgery? Yes, that's what I said. Just park up outside if you will. That would be great.'

'We caught him,' Harry said, slipping his phone away and looking back at the doctor. 'The person responsible, I mean. Well, I say caught, what I actually mean is that he just turned up out of the blue and handed himself in! Gave a full confession. Quite surprised me, if I'm honest. Doesn't usually happen.'

'A confession?' the doctor asked. 'Someone's admitted to the murders? Who? Why?'

'You see,' Harry said, ignoring the doctor's questions, and leaning forward, 'a confession is a very serious thing. An admission of guilt isn't something most people are up to providing. Well, not the kind who have gone to the length of planning what we've seen this week, anyway. Wouldn't you agree, PCSO Metcalf?'

Jim gave a firm nod and said, 'Actually, most suspects are usually found close to the scene and pretty quickly, too. But then, most murders are spur of the moment things, acts of passion, the heat of the moment. That's right, isn't it, Boss?'

Harry nodded in agreement. 'And this isn't that, is it?' he said.

'No,' Jim replied. 'It isn't. Not by a long shot.'

'And you think they did it, do you?' the doctor asked. 'This person who's confessed. You think that they're really guilty?'

'We've no reason to suspect otherwise,' Harry said. 'Though obviously, we need to cross-reference a lot of things, look at the evidence in detail, check the confession. There's a lot to do. A great deal to do, in fact, isn't there, PCSO Metcalf?'

'Oh yes,' said Jim. 'A lot.'

'For a start,' Harry said, 'we need to be absolutely sure that the suspect is actually capable of the murders. Physically, I mean. Motive is one thing, for sure, but I think you'll agree, if you remember what happened to poor old John Capstick, well, there was a lot of effort involved, wasn't there? Moving him can't have been easy. You'd need to be strong to do that, wouldn't you?'

Harry stared at the doctor, eyes narrowed, jaw clenched.

'Well, I don't want to keep you from it,' the doctor said. 'I really do appreciate you stopping by.'

'And that's where the problem is, you see,' Harry continued, talking over the doctor now. 'The suspect, he's eighty-one years old. And I'm not convinced. What do you think, PCSO Metcalf?'

'I can't see it, myself,' Jim said, shaking his head. 'But, you know, a confession is a confession. Got to be taken seriously.'

'Indeed it has,' Harry nodded. 'Interrogation. Hours and hours in those horrible little cells. And they can be royally cold, too. I once heard that someone went to use the toilet and it was so cold that their arse froze to the pan. Imagine that!'

'Not a place I'd want to be,' Jim said. 'Not at all.'

Harry rose to his feet, Jim beside him doing the same. 'Anyway, Doctor, thanks for your help,' he said, and held out his left hand. 'It was very much appreciated.'

'It's not a problem,' Doctor Smith smiled, reaching out with his left hand as well to shake Harry's. 'Not a problem at all, I'm sure.'

'Well, that's good to hear,' Harry said and gripped the doctor's hand good and hard, giving it a nice little extra squeeze for good measure. 'Now, how's about you tell us how you injured that other wrist of yours, eh?'

CHAPTER THIRTY-THREE

TIME SLOWED.

Harry was suddenly very, very aware of the sound of his own blood pumping through his head, his own breath, the squeak of his shoes. He had the doctor's hand in his, and they were staring at each other, watching, waiting.

'I'm sorry, what?' the doctor said.

'Your wrist,' Harry asked. 'Your right wrist. You said it was an old injury. How did you get it?'

'I don't really remember,' the doctor said. 'It was a long time ago.'

'A very long time indeed, I should say,' Harry said, pulling the doctor a little closer, feeling the resistance there. He looked down at the doctor's hand, sensing the strength in it, and noticed something.

'Look, I'm busy . . .'

'Are you naturally bald?' Harry asked.

The doctor's eyes grew wide. 'I beg your pardon?'

'Your massive, shiny pate,' Harry said, nodding towards

the other man's head. 'Is it natural, or do you shave? What do you think, PCSO Metcalf?'

'Hard to tell,' Jim replied. 'I'm sure there's a test we could run.'

'You're being awfully personal now,' the doctor complained, and Harry felt the man try to pull his hand back.

'I only ask,' Harry continued, 'because your hands, your wrists, well, they look strangely hairless as well, wouldn't you agree, PCSO Metcalf?'

Jim leaned in for a closer look. 'They do that, like,' he said. 'Smooth, I'd say.'

'Bet you don't leave hairs anywhere, do you?' Harry said. 'Except in your own shower, obviously. But elsewhere, out and about? Probably not.'

'I've had enough of this,' the doctor snapped. 'If there's anything further you need to discuss, you'll have to come back tomorrow.'

Harry didn't let go of the man's hand. 'There's something you need to know about me,' he said. 'And it's this, I don't take kindly to being taken for a fool.'

'I'll second that,' Jim added.

'I never said you were,' the doctor replied.

'No, but you implied it,' Harry said, then he quickly reached out and snatched the little plaster from the doctor's forehead.

'What the hell . . .?' the doctor yelped.

'PCSO Metcalf,' Harry called over his shoulder. 'That cut on the doctor's forehead there. That look to you like it was the result of someone twatting him with a log?'

Jim leaned in. 'No, Boss,' he said. 'No, it doesn't.'

'No, it doesn't, does it?' Harry said. 'I'd say it looks more like a cut. A knife cut perhaps, or a scalpel.'

Harry watched the doctor raise his right hand to cover the cut.

'I have no idea what it is you're implying, but–'

Harry'd had enough, and his next words fired from his mouth with rage as hot as a furnace. 'You killed Iveson and made me your alibi,' he said. 'Well, it looks like that's all just gone to shit for you, doesn't it, Doctor? Or should I call you James?'

Without warning, the doctor yanked Harry hard across his desk, heaving the detective off his feet, then pulling his own hand free as Harry slid across the surface and over to the other side, onto the floor.

'Bastard!' Harry hissed, as the floor came up to meet his head, and he only just managed to bring his arms up in time to stop his skull from slamming into it. 'Jim! Stop him!'

Harry heard the sound of a scuffle, Jim shouting for the doctor to stop, and when he pushed himself back up to his feet, he saw why.

'You let him down now,' Harry said. 'You let him down, James, and come quietly, you hear? It's over.'

The doctor had Jim by the neck, his thick, strong arm latched under the younger man's chin, Jim's feet barely touching the floor. 'It's not over,' he hissed. 'Not until they've all paid for what they did!'

'Oh, it's over alright,' Harry said. 'And this isn't going to change anything.'

Jim croaked out the faintest of gasps and Harry could see that his face was turning a terrible shade of purple.

'I've three left,' the doctor said. 'That's all. And I'll get them. I will! But you wouldn't understand. You can't!'

'Oh, I can,' Harry said. 'I understand very well. Because I know all about it, James. Every little bit of it.'

The doctor's face twisted with confusion. 'What? No, you can't! You're just talking to stop me from taking this officer as a hostage! And I will! That's what I'll do.'

'I know all about Sally,' Harry explained. 'I know what happened in the snow, James. And how you faked your suicide. I'm guessing because you wanted to just forget every-thing and start again, am I right? A clean slate? I mean, if you're a completely different person, then that's what you've got, isn't it? A fresh start at things?'

Another choking sound came from Jim and Harry knew he had to do something sharpish.

'And you're wondering how I know, aren't you, James? It's bugging you now, because no one knows, do they? And I can't have guessed all of this, can I?'

The doctor lifted Jim off his feet.

'Your dad, James,' Harry said. 'It's your dad who confessed. He told us everything.'

A roar burst from the doctor, a primaeval sound of pain and anger and desperation, and before Harry even had a chance to respond, he swung Jim at him, then crashed out through the door.

The PCSO slammed into Harry, taking them both back down onto the floor of the consultation room.

'Get off me!' Harry roared, but Jim was in no fit state to respond, landing unconscious on top of Harry.

'Jim? Jim! Damn it!'

Harry checked the PCSO's vitals and found that he had a pulse and was still breathing. Relief flooded through him, but was scorched away in a flash by the rage now firing through his veins.

Harry was on his feet in the next instant and charging out through the now-open door of the doctor's consulting room and into the hallway beyond. Doors flew open along the corridor as he raced along, worried faces of patients and doctors wondering just what the hell was happening in their quiet little surgery.

'Stop!' Harry bellowed, as he worked to push himself forward on legs simply not interested in running. 'Just stop, man! Give up!' But he knew that the doctor wasn't about to stop, not yet anyway. People had two responses to threat: fight or flight. The doctor, clearly, was in flight mode. And he could shift, too, Harry thought.

Ahead, Harry saw the doctor smash through the doors into reception, trip over his own feet, and tumble down onto his knees. But he was up again in the same moment and racing on.

When Harry reached the doors, they swung back to crack him in the skull, and he swore loudly, before kicking them open and charging through like a bull with a sore head.

The reception room, which had been a scene of sombre quiet and contemplation just a few minutes ago, was now alive with panic, shouting, and just enough screaming to cause even more panic. There were even a few children running around like headless chickens, their parents chasing after them.

Harry saw the doctor bound towards the main entrance. He'd almost made it outside and into the car park. But no way was Harry letting him get away and he pushed himself on, hammering through the main doors.

Outside, Harry saw the doctor pause for just a moment, a deer caught in headlights. A car was in front of him, having just pulled into the car park. In the driver's seat, Harry saw

Jenny, and next to her was old Mr Rawson. The old man was staring at the doctor. Behind him, one of the rear passenger doors was starting to open.

CHAPTER THIRTY-FOUR

'DON'T . . .' HARRY SAID, WALKING SLOWLY TOWARDS THE doctor. 'You're done, James. It's over.'

The doctor snatched a look back at Harry then shook his head and launched himself off to the left. Harry made to race after him when he saw the rear passenger door of Jenny's car fly open and out of it came Liz. Then, as the doctor went to head off across the road, and despite the fact that cars were already screeching at the sight of the man sprinting towards them, Harry witnessed the other PCSO throw caution to the wind in a way that he would probably remember for the rest of his life.

With a desperate yell, PCSO Liz Coates launched herself at the doctor, throwing herself up and into the air with wild abandon. For a moment, the scene seemed to play out in slow motion, with Liz flying through the air, the doctor turning around to see what it was that was making such a dreadful sound, the young PCSO coming towards him and then crashing into him, her arms clasping around the man's chest, before the rest of her caught up, and they both tumbled to the ground, a mess of limbs and moans and swearing.

Harry was over to them in a beat as the doctor kicked Liz away and jumped to his feet. At the same time, he saw Mr Rawson and Jenny climb out of her car.

'Don't do anything stupid!' Harry shouted.

The doctor stared at Mr Rawson then turned his eyes slowly to face Harry.

'How did you know?'

'Know what?'

'That he's . . . that he's my dad.'

'To be honest, I've only just met him myself,' Harry said. 'But what happened at Jack's place, that just didn't add up, and it got me thinking that there was more to what you were about. He kind of just filled in the gaps for me.'

Harry watched as the doctor turned his attention back to the old man in the car. For a split second, he thought he was going to try running again, saw him tense up, ready to bolt, but then the man's shoulders sagged, and he just stood there, his eyes wide with disbelief.

'Don't,' Harry said, walking over to the doctor as Liz pulled herself to her feet, a pair of handcuffs already in her hands. 'Whatever it is that you're thinking of doing, just don't, okay? There's nothing more. You've done more than enough damage already. It's over.'

Liz cinched the handcuffs onto the doctor's wrists.

'You okay?' Harry asked, looking over at the PCSO.

'Never better,' Liz replied. 'I grew up with ponies. Once you've chased one of those flighty bastards, then a middle-aged man isn't that much of a challenge.'

'Still,' Harry said. 'That was quite something, what you did. Very dramatic.'

'That wasn't really on purpose, you know.'

'Let's pretend that it was, shall we?' Harry said. 'It'll sound a lot more impressive when we tell Swift.'

Harry turned at the sound of the surgery doors banging open and saw Jim stumble out, rubbing his neck.

'You okay, Jim?'

'Just about,' Jim said, 'but I don't think I'll be wearing any scarves for a while.'

'A shame that,' Liz said. 'I was going to get you one for your birthday.'

Old Mr Rawson shuffled away from Jenny's car then over towards Liz to stand in front of the doctor. Behind him, Jenny jogged over to check on Jim.

'James?' Mr Rawson said. 'It's you, isn't it?' Then he reached out his arms and took hold of his son, bringing him close. 'It is . . .'

The doctor leaned in, rested his head on his father's shoulder, and sobbed, his arms locked behind his back by the handcuffs on his wrists.

Jenny walked over to stand with Harry, Jim still a little unsteady at her side. 'You mind telling me exactly what the hell's going on?'

'Don't look at me,' Jim said.

Harry, having given the doctor and his father just a moment of privacy, closed the distance between them.

'Doctor James Rawson,' he said, gently reaching out to hold the man's left arm with his hands, just in case he had any last-minute thoughts about doing a runner, 'I'm arresting you for the murder of John Capstick, Barry Hutchison, and Jack Iveson. You do not have to say anything, but it may harm your defence if you do not mention when questioned something which you later rely on in court. Anything you do say may be given in evidence.'

'I know,' the doctor said. 'I know, okay?' Then he turned to his dad. 'I don't understand! Why confess? They would have all paid for what they did, dad! All of them! For what they did to Sally! To all of us! To mum! It's what you wanted, isn't it? It's what they deserved! How did you know it was me? How?'

Harry watched as the old man reached up to hold his son's face in his hands.

'How could it be anyone else?' Mr Rawson said.

'But you thought I was dead,' the doctor said.

'We all died, that day,' the old man replied. 'When Sally was found. Each of us, in our own way. But I don't understand; why didn't you tell me that it was you?'

'You didn't recognise me,' the doctor said. 'You came into my surgery, into my room, and you just saw the doctor I'd become, not the son that I had been.'

Harry saw tears start to slip down the old man's cheeks.

'Why didn't you say?' Mr Rawson asked. 'Why didn't you just come home?'

The doctor straightened then, stepping away from his father. 'I wanted to,' he said. 'But what happened to Sally, it just got in the way. You didn't know me.'

'If only you'd told me!' Mr Rawson said, desperation cracking his voice. 'We could have worked it out! Together!'

Harry heard anger and hurt in the old man's words.

'I couldn't, Dad! I just couldn't!' The doctor's voice was a wet rasp now, years of pain flowing out. 'Not until . . . for Sally! They had to pay! I owed it to her! To you! It had to be done! And . . . I couldn't come home, until I'd finally done it. It just, well it just took so long.'

'So why now, James?' Harry asked. 'After all this time? Why?

James seemed to shrink a little at his question, Harry thought, as though the weight not just of what he'd done, but the years now gone, were pressing down on him.

'The cancer, Dad,' the doctor said, answering Harry's question, but keeping his eyes on his father. 'I knew I had to do it, do something, do anything. For you. Before it was too late. I couldn't let you die without them paying for what they did. I couldn't!' Then he whispered, 'I'm sorry,' and looked over at Harry and said, 'Can we go now, please?'

Harry gave a nod and led the doctor to the police car, but Mr Rawson reached out and held onto his son's arm. Then he leaned in and kissed him gently on the cheek.

As Harry eased the doctor into the back seat of Jenny's car, closing the door gently once he was sat down and strapped in, Mr Rawson came and stood beside him.

'I would've gone to prison for him, you know,' he said. 'I'm old, I'm dying, he's still got years.'

'I don't doubt it,' Harry replied. 'But what you were saying, it just wasn't hanging together. It couldn't, not with the evidence.'

Mr Rawson let out a long, slow breath. 'How did you know?'

'Know what?'

'That it was the doctor, that it was James?'

'A few things,' Harry said. 'Not much though. We got lucky, but that's often the way. And what you said about his wrist,' Harry explained. 'When I first met him, I remembered that I went to shake hands, but he reached out with his left, instead of his right. Said he had an old injury.'

'And that's it? Nothing else?'

'It was enough to make me suspicious,' Harry said. 'Then when I questioned you about what happened to Jack Iveson, and I said that you'd hit the doctor with a rolling pin, you just agreed.'

'Caught me out, then?'

Harry shrugged. 'I did. It was a log, except that it wasn't. I think your son just nicked his forehead with a scalpel. Plenty of blood, you see. Nice and dramatic. Nearly worked, too. And he would've had me as an alibi. Clever. I doubt it was planned that way. He was probably going to off old Jack Iveson like the others, leave no evidence. But he changed his plans. Never a good idea.'

'He was a good doctor, though.'

Harry said nothing, keeping his own thoughts on the matter to himself. Then, as Jenny made to head off to Harrogate, he raised a hand to stop her.

'What?' she asked, lowering her window.

Harry called Liz over. 'I want you to go with Jenny,' he said.

'Me?' Liz asked. 'Why?'

'You're the arresting officer,' Harry explained. 'You caught him. You cuffed him. You get to take him in.'

Harry could see from her expression, Liz was a little taken aback.

'But, I mean, I'm a PCSO and well . . .'

'And well nothing,' Harry said. 'Now get your arse into Jenny's car and I'll be along in a while. And well done, PCSO Coates. Bloody well done, indeed.'

Harry stepped back as Liz jumped in beside Jenny and then they were on their way.

Mr Rawson turned then to face Harry and despite the

man's age, Harry felt himself shrink just a little under the man's piercing gaze.

'Remember the cancer?'

Harry nodded. 'Yes. I'm sorry about that. Awful, I'm sure. And with all this, too.'

'Who do you think it was that gave me the news?' Mr Rawson asked. 'Who do you think looked me in the eye and told me I had months left to live?'

Harry knew. And he didn't need to say, so he kept quiet.

'Imagine that,' Mr Rawson said. 'Imagine having to tell your own father that he was going to die and yet not being able to tell him that you're his son.'

'Revenge does funny things to people,' Harry said. 'It eats them up inside. Trust me, I know.'

'Yes, that's true,' Mr Rawson said. 'But it wasn't revenge that made him do it. Surely you can see that? Revenge could never drive someone to go to such lengths, to keep their identity a secret from their own family. It's just not a strong enough emotion.'

'Then what is?' Harry asked.

'Love,' said the old man, then he turned on his heels and shuffled off back into town.

CHAPTER THIRTY-FIVE

'LOVE? HE REALLY SAID THAT? WELL, THAT'S A RIGHT load of total bollocks, isn't it?'

'Bit cynical of you,' Harry said, staring at Matt as he continued to shake his head in disbelief.

It was early evening and Harry was standing in Hawes marketplace with the rest of the team. Well, the rest of the team bar Jenny and Liz, who were still busy transporting Doctor James Rawson to Harrogate to begin the process of booking him in, taking statements, questioning, and all the rest. Harry would follow on soon. PCSO Coates had done well, he thought. They all had.

'I'm not being cynical,' Matt said. 'It's just that, well, you know, to say it at all, like that, I mean? Well, it's nonsense, like, isn't it?'

Harry saw Jim wandering over towards them, his hands full with cardboard trays carrying disposable coffee cups. He handed them out then pulled out a bag of doughnuts. Harry went to grab one, but a hand slapped his away.

'What would Jenny say, now?' Gordy said with a wink.

'Any news from her and Liz?' Jim asked.

'Not yet,' Harry said, looking at his watch. 'They'll be there by now for sure, though.'

'I still can't believe it,' Matt said. 'Mike Smith? Everyone's known him for years!'

'Doctor James Rawson,' Harry corrected. 'Ah, he was a pretty good actor. Even his dad didn't know until the killing started. But even then, he had no idea who his son actually was, just that it was him that was doing it. Madness, really.'

Harry took a sip of coffee, which stung his lips and burned his mouth. He didn't care. Although the rain had eased, it was still a cold day, and the warmth was welcome.

'Can you imagine it, though?' Gordy asked, shivering as she sipped her own coffee. 'Planning it for all those years?'

'I'm not sure he was,' Harry said. 'I'd like to believe that he really did come home to be with his dad, to show him that he'd made something of himself, explain why he'd disappeared, faked his own death. Then, when he got here, and his dad didn't even recognise him? Well, I think that was just the start of it all eating him up from the inside again. Until, eventually, he just snapped.'

'Well, I think that's very generous of you,' Gordy sighed. 'Which surprises me rather, I have to say.'

'Perhaps, perhaps not,' said Harry. 'It's never just a simple matter of who killed who and throwing away the key. There's always more to it, more history. And none of it's ever good.'

'Aye, you're right there.'

Harry took another hit of the coffee. The earthy smell of it mingled with the damp, cool air of Wensleydale, and he wondered when the weather would change again, and bring back the promised summer.

'So what now?' Jim asked.

'What now?' Harry repeated. 'Well, I don't know about anyone else, but I'm already looking forward to the huge pile of paperwork we're going to have to go through. And then there will be all the stuff to do with the courts, solicitors to put up with, the press. It's going to be busy.'

'Is it always like this?' Jadyn asked.

'What, murder, bad weather, and the occasional doughnut?' Harry asked.

'No, I mean . . .' Jadyn spluttered.

'I know what you mean,' Harry said, smiling. 'And to be honest, I hope not. In fact, I hope with the very essence of my soul that from now on everything is very boring, very dull, and that the most any of us has to deal with are a couple of angry pensioners arguing over a bag of penny chews.'

'Wow, that's specific,' Jadyn said.

'It is,' Harry said. 'It's also happening right over there . . .'

The team turned to find themselves staring at exactly what Harry had described.

'Looks like a job for Uniform to me,' Matt said.

'But what about you?' Jadyn said, looking at Jim. 'You're a PCSO!'

Jim shook his head. 'No, that's definitely more your area I think,' he said.

'Oh, yes,' Matt agreed. 'Those two can get quite violent as well, so you'll need to be careful.'

Jadyn slipped his hat onto his head and started off, but by the time he'd crossed the road, whatever the argument had been about had been forgotten, and the two in question had shuffled off and away into the evening.

Harry raised his face to the sky. 'It's coming in again, isn't it?' he said. 'The rain? Does the weather ever make any sense up here? At all?'

'You get used to it,' Jim said.

'And you make sure you've got the right gear,' added Gordy.

Harry knew exactly what the DI was getting at and looked across the marketplace to the outdoor shop on the other side. He chucked what was left of his coffee down his throat.

'So you're going to finally do it, then, are you?' Jim asked.

Matt reached out and rested a concerned hand on Harry's shoulder. 'You sure about this, Boss? I mean, if you buy what I think you're going to buy, then this is serious.'

'Oh, it's serious alright,' Harry said, and with that, he headed off through the first drops of rain, quietly wondering if buying a pair of Wellington boots was a sign that perhaps, and after so little time, the dales were starting to get under his skin. And if so, would he ever be able to get them out again.

READ MORE grisly goings-on in Wensleydale for Harry and the team in Corpse Road

JOIN THE VIP CLUB!

INTRIGUED by how it's going to go for Harry as he heads off to buy Wellington Boots? Just sign up for my newsletter today get your exclusive copy of the short origin story, 'New Boots', and join the DCI Harry Grimm VIP Club. You'll receive regular updates on the series, plus VIP access to a photo gallery of locations from the books, and the chance to win amazing free stuff in some fantastic competitions.

You can also connect with other fans of DCI Grimm and his team by joining The Official DCI Harry Grimm Reader Group.

Enjoyed this book? Then please tell others!

The best thing about reviews is they help people like you: other readers. So, if you can spare a few seconds and leave a review, that would be fantastic. I love hearing what readers think about my books, so you can also email me the link to your review at dave@davidjgatward.com.

AUTHOR'S NOTE

I think I saw *Apaches* for the first time in 1982. I was nine years old. Looking back, I'm not sure it was the film that terrified me so much as the playground grapevine! Tales of what it contained ran around us like frightened hares, the older kids doing their best to terrify the rest of us with the gory details. And you know what? It did terrify me. It was supposed to.

Apaches wasn't filmed as entertainment but as a warning about the dangers of playing on a farm. I've remembered the death scenes my whole life, although one stuck with me the most: the boy drowning in slurry. Pretty nasty, that one.

Watching the film again, so many decades later, it really hadn't lost any of its edge. Yes, it's hugely contrived, with the children dying off one by one and yet still continuing to play on the farm as their numbers dwindled, but it still works. It is a stark movie. The soundtrack is non-existent, which only adds to the bleakness of the piece. The laughter and excitement of the children grates loudly against the darkness that unfolds in front of you, not just the deaths, but the scenes of items being taken away from a school desk, an empty cloakroom peg, a bedroom.

It would be easy to think, much like Gordy really, that perhaps showing a film like this to children isn't very sensible. It may scare them, after all, even scar them for life. (It's certainly stuck with me!) Yet that was its point, to scare children, to get the message across that bad things happen, and you need to be careful.

Other films like *Apache* were around at the same time, such as *The Finishing Line* and *Building Sites Bite*. I remember that we were shown the latter, which was even gorier than *Apaches* (boy crushed by earthmover and leaves behind a blood-filled shoe, anyone?). And, of course, everyone remembers what happened to the kid whose Frisbee ended up in the power station, right?

Stories are powerful. They affect us all in so many different ways and if they don't then they're doing something wrong. They entertain, they terrify, they teach. In them, we meet new friends, visit strange worlds, disappear down rabbit holes.

I love writing. I love reading. And I consider myself blessed to able to do both. More so, I count myself astonishingly lucky to be writing this little note at the end of a book that you've just read. Why? Because writing a book is one thing, but to be able to release it, to have others, like you, read it? Well, that's something quite different. It's exciting, it's terrifying, it's life-affirming. It's something I've created and that I hope you have enjoyed.

I will never claim to be a literary master; I'm simply someone who enjoys spinning a yarn in the hope that you, the reader, will have been entertained. If you have, wonderful! And I really hope you stick with Grimm as he continues to explore his new life in beautiful Wensleydale (and perhaps even write a review!) If not, well I would still like to thank you for at least giving it a go. We can't all like the same things, and I reckon that's all for the better! I mean, think how dull the world would be if we did . . .

Dave

ABOUT DAVID J. GATWARD

David had his first book published when he was 18 and has written extensively for children and young adults. *Best Served Cold* is his second crime novel.

Visit David's website to find out more about him and the DCI Harry Grimm books.

 facebook.com/davidjgatwardauthor

ALSO BY DAVID J. GATWARD

THE DCI HARRY GRIMM SERIES

Welcome to Yorkshire. Where the beer is warm, the scenery beautiful, and the locals have murder on their minds.

Milton Keynes UK
Ingram Content Group UK Ltd.
UKHW031043120324
439302UK00001B/14